IF TRIANGLES EXIST WHY NOT HENRY?

KEVIN JOHNSON

DEDICATION

FOR ROSEMARY

ACKNOWLEDGMENTS

Huge thanks to my wife who is always positive about my artistic activities no matter how futile they might be.

Thanks to the staff at the Royal Green Jackets Museum in Winchester for their help in my research of my grandfather's war record.

Thanks to my Grandfather Harry Hosker who did not father a child while on leave in 1915 but inspired the story of Henry.

Thanks to my parents Arthur and Iris Johnson who provided me with a great childhood in Padiham.

Thanks to Alicia Fernandez Gomez who translated a one - sided telephone conversation into Spanish.

Thanks to Rachel Wright for proof reading the final text and improving syntax and grammar as well as spotting several typographical errors.

THE PERSONAL EXPERIENCES OF THE CHARACTERS IN THIS STORY ARE PURE FICTION.

Chapter 1.

A workman putting tools back into a shed at the base of a quarry, saw a boy walking to the edge of the rock face. He watched him sit on the very edge of the precipice. "Look up there," the workman said to his friend, "there was a suicide here two years ago." They watched, straining to see. The boy was silhouetted against the skyline and it was difficult to see from the base of the cliff just how close he was to the edge. Eventually the boy sat down, and they thought they could see his legs dangling over the precipice.
"I'm going to call 999," the workman said. "I don't like the look of that" He looked to his friend for confirmation.
"I think you might be right."
He called the emergency services and reported, what he thought, was a 'jumper'. The boy sitting on the edge of the cliff face was 19 years old, and his name was David Watson.

David Watson was a very happy child until he started Primary School. Things started to go wrong for him on his very first day. He lived in a terraced house in the poorer part of town, with his mother and brother and two sisters. He had no memory of his father who had died in a car accident when

David was six months old. David was small for his five years and had dark unruly hair. He was the baby of the family. His brother and sisters were in their late teens. He was spoiled and fussed over by his sisters and his mother as an infant. They taught him to read before he even started school, encouraged by his extraordinary abilities. Although he was a chaotic and a disorganised child, he was able to read and write and pick out tunes on his sister's keyboard and carry on very mature conversations before he reached the age of five. He wouldn't just read books, he would talk to them. He also talked to an imaginary friend. His friend was called Henry. His mother accepted this fantasy. She thought it was a good way for a small child to compensate for the loss of a father. David told her that he didn't miss his father, because he had never known him. He could make very bold statements sometimes, that she found hurtful. However, David always insisted that his friend Henry was real, rather than imagined. David's friend didn't cause him any problems until he started school. The problems started on his first day. It hadn't occurred to David that talking to Henry at home might be perfectly acceptable, whereas talking to him at school could lead to difficulties. His teacher was a Miss Warburton. She took an instant dislike to David because he kept on talking to himself and she also thought he was very cheeky. On their first day Miss Warburton had given

3

each of her pupils a small cardboard box. On the lid was printed "TIDY BOX" in bold black print.

"Don't open it yet," she said.

"What do you think's in it, Henry? Probably books." He shook it. "Too light for books. Probably pencils. It's rattling. Pencils and scientific instruments."

"David Watson! Are we talking?"

"We are," he said.

That wasn't the reply she was expecting.

"We don't talk when I'm talking David. Do we?"

He looked at Henry for an explanation but nothing was forthcoming. He hadn't come across the word contradiction yet but he knew by instinct that there was something very wrong with Miss Warburton's question. David gave her a quizzical look. It was a face that expressed confusion, which she interpreted as cheek. More trouble came when David opened his box. He was disappointed to find a few wax crayons, a pencil sharpener with no blade, a plastic pig and some scruffy looking paper. Some of the pages already had drawings on them. He shared his disappointment over the contents with Henry and Miss Warburton had to tell him to be quiet again. One of the pages had a drawing of a penis and testicles on it. He knew it was a penis and testicles because he'd seen a similar illustration on the wall of a subway in town. He'd asked his sister if it was a rocket ship but she'd told him it was a penis and testicles. Because his two sisters and his brother were much older than David, in their late teens, he knew from an early age that he had been a mistake.

Miss Warburton wanted the class to do a drawing. David, who really liked drawing, didn't think that he could do a good drawing with two wax crayons and a plastic pig. He walked to the front, to ask Miss Warburton for a pencil.

"We don't walk to the front David. Do we?" David looked puzzled.

"What do we do when we want something David?" David didn't know.

"We put our hand up. Don't we?" David put his hand up.

"That's right David. Now, go back to your seat."

He went back to his seat, but he didn't put his hand up again. He'd only been in school a couple of hours but it was long enough to know that he didn't like it. He didn't like Miss Warburton either, and he could do a much better drawing at home. He sat there, exchanging the occasional word with Henry while Miss Warburton became almost catatonic with anger. She bustled down the aisle of desks to where David was sitting and said, "Let's see what you've done David." He hadn't done anything, but that's when she found the penis and testicles. "What's this?" she said.

He looked up at Henry again and wondered why a woman of her age and experience couldn't recognise a penis and testicles.

It wasn't long before the bullying started. David shared a desk with three other children. There was Sharon, who everyone called Poor Sharon. She wasn't any poorer than David or half a dozen other children in the class but everyone seemed to feel sorry for her. She was different and provoked pity and attempts at understanding, whereas David was unique and provoked envy, sarcasm and aggression. The bullies in the class queued up to torment him. Wayne, who sat across from David, was his biggest tormentor. David soon became quite terrified of Wayne- he had never come across unprovoked violence before. Sharon, who sat beside him, was a kind hearted soul but simple, quiet and other worldly. She would sometimes put Lego up her nose and be taken to the clinic to have it removed. The fourth child on David's table was Raymond, who was the mirror image of Sharon. Whereas Sharon was almost comatose most of the day, Raymond never stopped moving. His legs were pedalling up and down under the desk even when the rest of him was sitting still. His head was on the move constantly, swivelling from left to right, his attention never settling on anything for more than two seconds. He never listened to the teacher's instructions and had to ask his neighbours: "What she say eh? Whadder we ave to do eh? Drawin? Is it a drawin? You gotta pencil? Had it a minute since. Lost it." Sharon ignored him, Big Wayne was too stupid to understand the questions and so it was

David who normally answered his questions and got into trouble for talking. David looked at the 'top' table with some envy and thought he should be sitting with Amanda, Ian and Jenny. Amanda was the most beautiful thing David had ever seen. She had the face of an angel and quite a superior manner, as if she knew that she was everyone's favourite child. Ian and Jenny interested him - they seemed a lot brighter than Wayne and Sharon. He noticed that Ian didn't kick anyone under the table and that Jenny had lively conversations with her neighbours without being told to be quiet by Miss Warburton. Ian and Jenny lived at the opposite end of town from David. They lived on the 'posh' estate where houses were detached and surrounded by neat gardens and large German vehicles. David lived at the other end of town where the houses were terraced and the streets littered with detritus and M.O.T. failures. Living at the poor end of town wasn't a reason for not being on the top table, although it didn't help. He was on the unofficial remedial table because he was chaotic, noisy and was constantly talking to himself, ignoring the teacher and writing stories in a spidery script that nobody but David could decipher.

After a few months the staff had a meeting to discuss David's issues. Miss Warburton thought he ought to be sectioned. "I think he hears voices," she told the Head. Many of the staff thought that he had issues too, a syndrome, or a psychosis. The

Headmaster, who had taken on-line counselling courses and was a qualified core practitioner, thought they should take a more 'organic' approach. As none of the other members of staff knew what that meant, there was a long silence followed by a suggestion from Miss Warburton that 'his mother should be visited.'

Irene, David's mother, wasn't a tall woman, she had small neat features, short blonde hair and a short temper. As a mother, she was a loving tyrant. Her children followed strict guidelines of behaviour but the house was always full of fun and laughter and a certain happy chaos. They all knew where the boundaries were. David, being the baby of the house, was the one who stretched the boundaries further than his older siblings had ever been allowed. On the evening of Miss Warburton's visit however, the house was in lockdown. There was no running around, there was no loud music, there was no laughter. The small terraced house had the atmosphere of a library reading room. Their house had four small rooms. Two bedrooms upstairs, a living room and a parlour downstairs. The kitchen was a tiny lean-to structure. There was a backyard which housed an outside toilet and a shed. As Irene used the downstairs parlour as her bedroom, Miss Warburton was perched on a chair in the living room, next to a small side table containing a tray with tea and digestives. She sat, bewildered how anyone could manage to bring up four children in such a tiny space. She looked at Irene with some sympathy, a single mother, with a full-time job, living in such a poor area of town. It was no surprise to her that David had issues.

"Where to start?" said Miss Warburton, emphasising the aitch in *where* and the t's in *start*. Irene looked at her, and gave her no clues.

"David hasn't settled in very well at school Mrs Watson. I'm afraid to say. He doesn't seem to have the ability to concentrate on basic tasks in the classroom. Why do you think that is Mrs Watson?"

"Why don't you tell me," Irene said, "tell me what you think the problem is and I'll tell you how things look from my point of view."

Miss Warburton was heartened by this approach and she launched into her assessment of Mrs Watson's youngest son.

"There are a number of issues really. He seems to talk a lot, to nobody in particular. We find that *very* worrying. His language is very mature but he doesn't seem to engage with the other children, at any level. I find it difficult to persuade him to concentrate on the tasks I have set him. He seems uninterested in the graded readers we give him and he won't take books home. I'm unsure why that should be." She paused at this point, as if she thought that Irene might offer some explanation. She paused in vain, so carried on with her analysis. "He often takes no notice of what we're doing in class but occupies himself, drawing and talking and writing. He writes a lot but won't form his letters properly and he doesn't write in any organised way. He mixes numbers and letters with small drawings, it's like trying to read hieroglyphics. What I would like to do is to go back to basics with his letter formation and numbers. I know it's difficult, in your situation, but if we can count on your support in this, I'm sure we can help David to take a more cooperative approach in the classroom, going forward."

There was a long silence.

"We think a more organic approach might help," she added, just to fill the vacuum.

Irene took a deep breath and gave her considered response, "I don't know what you mean by *my situation*, or why my situation should make things difficult. I'll let that go, for the moment. Concerning his reading, he could read at the age of four. He has read all his brother's and sisters' graded readers right up to a reading age of eleven plus. Perhaps that's why he hasn't shown any interest in Biff, Chip and Kipper, in the Floppy's Fun Phonetics series you keep putting in front of him. His handwriting is difficult to decipher, impossible for people with only a passing interest in what he's trying to say. However, I did send you some samples of his work that he did on the computer which you claimed had been done by his older brother. I also wrote to you about the bruises on his legs from that big oaf who sits across from him in class. Nothing was done about that."

Miss Warburton did open her mouth at this point, but no sound came out before Irene continued.

"As far as his talking in class is concerned, David has an imaginary friend who he talks to. He's told me all about him. His brother and sisters know all about him, his name is Henry. Henry is one of the many men from this area who fought in the First World War. My husband did a lot of research on all the men who were involved in the war from the local area. He looked up the names of the men on-line and visited the relatives and downloaded all their army records. He even visited some of their regimental museums. If you had asked David about it, he would be able to tell you the names of the men my husband researched. He has taken a particular interest in Henry Bradshaw who lived in the next street. That's who David talks to, an imaginary friend. If any other child in your reception class is capable of reading well enough to understand my husband's files and books, I would be very surprised. There's no need to go back to basics with David. He's a very gifted child. He's being bullied, which is something I have repeatedly complained about. So, I will tell you what I will I do Miss Warburton, I will tell David not to talk to Henry outside the four walls of this house. That should help. And if you could move him off the remedial table away from that moron Wayne, I think we have ourselves a deal. Going forward!"

"Mrs Watson, there isn't a remedial table in my
class."
"Call it what you like. I want him moved."
"Well. I'll have a word with the Headmaster and see
what he has to say."
"Good. I'll have a word with David, and I shall tell
him that if you sit him at that table on Monday to
come straight home from school and we'll teach
him at home."
"I don't think that's very wise Mrs Watson."
If Irene was at all concerned what Miss Warburton
thought, she didn't show it. Instead, she thanked
her for her visit and showed her to the door.
        Irene spoke to David the next day. "I want a
word with you David, it's about your friend, Henry."
David looked at her with the intensity that only five-
year-old children are capable of. The intensity that
they start to lose about the age of seven.
Irene looked at his face, so full of concentration, so
innocent and trusting, she struggled to control her
laughter. She couldn't help smiling. "Now you know
that Mrs Warburton visited us yesterday?" David
nodded his assent. "Well, we agreed that you
wouldn't talk to Henry again while you are at
school. Mrs Warburton doesn't like it."
"Her name's Miss Warburton mum."
"Miss Warburton. My mistake David."
"I don't like her."
"Yes I understand that but you don't have to like her
but you must do as she tells you and you have to be

polite to her."
David gave her a nod of agreement.
"Now I want you to promise that you won't talk to Henry while you are at school. You can talk to him at home but not at school. Is that alright?"
"Why can't I talk to him at school?"
"Because it disturbs the other children and Miss Warburton doesn't like it."
David thought about it for a moment but then said, "Can I still talk to Francis?"
"Francis? Is Francis in your class?"
"No, Francis was at school with Henry."
Irene suddenly felt cold and her stomach felt sick.
"Do you talk to Francis David."
"No," he said, "but she talks to me sometimes, but only when we're in the playground. She never comes into the classroom. She says she doesn't like coming to the classroom. I don't think she likes Miss Warburton either. Francis told me that her teacher hit her with a leather strap because she spilt some ink. I asked her what ink was and she said everyone knows what ink is but I didn't but I do know now. Miss Warburton isn't the teacher that hit her with the leather strap. Francis was in the same class as Henry a long time ago but she died of a bad cough when she was seven."
"I don't want you to talk to Francis at all David, not at school and not at home either."
"Why not mum?"
"Never mind why not. Just do as your told."

"But I can talk to Henry at home mum, can't I?"

"Yes David, you can talk to Henry at home, but not at school."

"Alright mum. I'll not talk to Francis and I'll tell Henry not to talk to me at school."

"You're a good boy David."

David smiled at her and went up the stairs to his room to talk things through with Henry. His mother stayed where she was and wiped her eyes. She didn't really know what to do about David and his imaginary friends. She had talked to the doctor about it and he said imaginary friends were nothing to worry about. Irene wasn't so sure.

Chapter 2.

When the 999 call was received from the two workers, the Police Station in Padiham was alerted. The desk sergeant received the news of a potential suicide with a degree of scepticism. Ever since the poor man who had thrown himself off the cliff two years before, the police had received regular reports of potential suicides from the public. You only had to have a picnic somewhere near the edge for someone to raise the alarm. A dog walker peering over the edge because his Yorkshire Terrier had gone missing had caused the last emergency only two weeks earlier.
"Thompson, just drive up to the quarry will you and check out this report of a jumper. It's probably nothing but just have a look and see if there's anyone up there." Trainee PC Thompson had only just arrived on his first posting a few weeks earlier. He had joined the police straight from school at 16 and although he had not shone brilliantly in any of the more academic tests during his training, what he lacked in intelligence he made up for with physical strength, fearless determination and a willingness to succeed as a trainee constable.
"Right Sergeant, I'm on my way."

David didn't talk to Henry in school after Miss Warburton's home visit and this was seen as a turning point in his development. Miss Warburton was rewarded with an increased salary scale point and the teaching staff no longer thought he was schizophrenic. David was moved away from Wayne. Wayne still kicked him but less often, because he now had to walk across the classroom to do it. As he progressed through the school, year by year, David became more confident, especially with the teaching staff. He had a long discussion with Mrs Wood, his year 2 teacher, about triangles. She told him he had drawn his lines too thick and needed a sharper pencil. He thought that lines only had length, no thickness or height, and were therefore invisible, as were triangles. He thought it didn't matter how thin the lines were. She told him that triangles were visible. He thought only pyramids would be visible because pyramids had three dimensions and triangles only two. She smiled at him and told him to get on with his work. Wayne, who overheard the conversation, told David that he was 'fick if he 'fought' triangles were invisible'. "Cos, I got one in my book", he said. David thought Wayne might have missed the point of his conversation with Mrs Wood but didn't pursue it because whenever he tried to answer Wayne, Wayne would kick him. Wayne kicked and punched David whenever the mood took him, which was most days. There was a constant stream of threats, and not just from Wayne. Wayne recruited a group of followers who joined him in his campaign of bullying, the followers feeling that while David was being victimised, they were feeling safer. David wasn't the only child in the class who feared Wayne. A year later David's class teacher was Mr Prendergast. It was when Mr Prendergast had been teaching them the Easter story that David became fascinated by God's ability to bring back the dead. He first asked Mr Prendergast why God didn't bring back Dismas, who was crucified along with Jesus. David said that he'd read that Dismas was innocent of any crime, just like Jesus, and he thought God might have brought him back from the dead too. Mr Prendergast said that Jesus was the son of God and Dismas wasn't. David said that Dismas was someone's son, and it seemed to him, a bit small minded of God just to bring back Jesus and leave poor Dismas dead and buried. Mr Prendergast said that God worked in mysterious ways and David couldn't disagree with that. God had allowed his Dad to die in a road crash for no good reason and he hadn't brought him back to life either. David wondered if God had brought Jesus back to life properly or if he'd just appeared like Henry. He would have liked to ask Mr Prendergast about that but his mother had told him not to mention Henry outside the house, so he kept quiet about it. Most of the children in the class disliked David because he was different, because he didn't often talk to them and because he didn't want to join in with their games. They didn't like him because he seemed aloof and too clever by half. And they didn't like him because Wayne didn't like him and they were very frightened of Wayne. One exception to this rule was Jenny. Jenny Simpson was a red headed girl with freckles and bright emerald eyes, she was a bundle of energy and enthusiasm. A constantly busy, Jenny Wren. Jenny would ask David why he thought triangles were invisible and was fascinated by his explanations. She didn't think he was weird because he preferred reading to playing football. She wasn't frightened of Wayne, something that impressed David and filled him with envy.

In his final year at Primary School David's teacher was Mr Tillotson. Known, to the children as 'Tilly,' he seemed to take a special interest in David. He was impressed, not only with his academic progress in school, but the fact that he was teaching himself Spanish so that he could converse with the locals when he visited his aunt who lived in Almeria. Tilly asked David what other interests he had, and David told him that he was interested in how cuckoos knew how to lay their eggs in other birds' nests. He wondered how salmon could find their way back to where they were born. He wanted to know why there was still so much fighting going on in the Holy Land. There was no end to David's curiosity and Tilly, unlike most of the teaching staff, was always happy to listen to David's stories.

"Mrs Wood told me why you thought triangles were in invisible David."

"Yes sir. She said I was wrong about that."

"Well, it is an unusual idea."

"My mum said I should listen to Mrs Wood."

"Well, I'd say that your mum knows best David."

"Yes, that's what my mum always says."

One of David's fascinations, that he didn't mention to Tilly, was Amanda. Amanda was the most beautiful girl in the school. He enjoyed Jenny's chatter and friendship but he adored Amanda. Jenny was just a girl he talked to. Amanda was an angel, the object of his awakening sexual desires. In his final year at the school, he became obsessed by her and the more he worshipped her the more impossible it became for him to speak to her. If she happened to speak to him, he became flustered and confused. His pituitary gland would ring like a bell and he became hot, flushed, and his tongue would swell up and render him speechless. Amanda was perfect in his eyes. Her flawless pale skin. Her small mouth with perfect red lips. She always seemed to be absorbed by what she was doing, not looking around for approval. Every boy in the class was in love with Amanda and every boy in the class dreamed of being her boyfriend. Not one of them had been brave enough to ask her. David decided that he would be the first to try.

He asked Henry about 'girlfriends' that night in his bedroom. Henry seemed reluctant to discuss the subject.

"You must have had a girlfriend Henry?"

"Not at your age. Not until I went to India. I was twenty by then. Not exactly innocent but not exactly experienced either."

"Well, tell me about your first date, your first girlfriend, how did you get on?"

"It was different back then David. I was in the army. In Meerut. The army arranged everything for us, including girls."

"Do you mean the army found your girlfriends for you?"

"Well, sort of. I mean the officers had their wives with them but the rest of us, well, we were all young men."

"So what was your first date like? Did it go well?"

"It wasn't really a date as such, we didn't go dancing or owt like that, the army just arranged girls."

"That was nice of them."

"Yes. I didn't hear any of the lads complain."

"What was your first girlfriend's name?"

"I didn't have a proper girlfriend in India. I met a lot of girls there, but, well there was nobody special, so to speak. I met a girl when I got back from India. She was very special. We shipped back in October and they gave us a few weeks leave before we went over to France. There was a girl in our street called Mary. Mary Kelly. She was just a child when I joined up but when I came back, after five years, she was a beauty. I suppose I looked like the returning hero, *still in uniform. She said she'd always liked me, even before I joined the army, schoolgirl crush. She was just an innocent girl and I fell in love with her. She said she loved me; I knew I'd soon be going to France. Anyway, one thing led to another, it wasn't my finest hour. But I did love her."*

David pressed Henry for more information, but he couldn't be persuaded. When he didn't find the help he was looking for from Henry, he just decided to go ahead and ask Amanda if he could go out on a date with her. Even if he didn't really know what a date might involve.

The next day in school he asked her. It was in the dinner hall. Her friends had disappeared and she was sitting alone.

"Can I have a date?" he asked.

She looked up at him, but didn't speak.

"A date Amanda, can I have a date?"

"What for?" she asked.

"To go out with you. On a date. To be your boyfriend?"

She let out a little scream, stood up and sent the bench falling backwards. It hit the floor with a crash. Everyone in the dining hall was now looking their way.

"No!" She shouted. "I don't want a date with you! You're the last person I want a date with. I hate you." She then burst into tears and ran out of the hall. David might have been embarrassed if he wasn't so shocked. He thought a simple 'no thank you' might have been sufficient, and he was prepared for that, he expected it. It wouldn't have surprised him. But why did she hate him? Perhaps for the same reason that Wayne and his friends hated him. No reason at all.

When word of this episode permeated into the brains of Wayne and his gang, they decided that they should meet David at the end of the school day and beat him up. Wayne informed him of this decision in the playground.

"You're for it after school," Wayne prodded David in the chest when he spoke to him, not just on this occasion but every time he spoke to him. David had tried, once or twice, to prod Wayne when he answered him but it hadn't ended well. "We're gunna get you. Me and the lads'll be waitin after school." All the boys in his class seemed to have seen this radical act, asking Amanda for a date, as a personal insult to their manhood. They were stirred into a lather of aggression. Even Raymond, who had never said a harsh word to David, who had come to David most days and received help with his work, even he threatened to 'get him' after school. David had been threatened many times but it seemed more serious this time. Every male member of his class had spent the day taunting him and promising him various punishments they were going to inflict on him when school was over. Orchestrating this maelstrom of abuse was Wayne. His romantic overture to Amanda seemed to have brought

22

everything to a head. When he saw the group of boys waiting for him, he had that metallic taste of fear in his mouth and a numb empty feeling in his gut. The fear rendered him incapable of retaliation or even or rational thought. He was like a rabbit in headlights; unable to think, unable to run, just waiting helplessly, waiting for whatever they wanted to do to him. It was Jenny who saved the day. She had informed Tilly of what was being planned and as David approached the group of boys, at four o'clock, Tilly appeared and gave Wayne a good talking to. David was able to walk home in safety. He was extremely grateful to Jenny and Tilly for this reprieve. Having been rescued by Tilly, he thought that Wayne and his gang wouldn't dare to attack him again now that their plan had been discovered. When he went back to school the next day it was as if nothing had happened. He felt safe. There were no threats, no evil glances, no subtle punches on the arm as he walked along the corridors or in and out of class.

A few days later, as he was walking home, his wildest dream was realised; David was approached by Amanda.

"Can I walk along with you David?" She seemed almost shy as she asked him.

David nodded. He was thrilled at the prospect of walking with Amanda but he was too excited to speak.

"Are you going home?" she asked.

He nodded again. He knew he would have to speak sooner or later but for the moment nodding was all he could manage.

"Why don't we go through the park?" she said.

"I don't go that way," he said, without thinking. She looked at him as if he had stabbed her with something. Looking at her pained expression, it occurred to him that she may have had a change of heart about the offer of a date. He collected his thoughts quickly, "We'll go through the park," he said.

They turned back and walked up the hill to the Memorial Park. They walked in silence and David racked his brain for something witty and charming to say to her. This was his big chance to impress her and he could not think of a single thing to say, witty or otherwise. However, as they walked towards the War Memorial he was inspired, "Keep her banners free from stain. Lest we should dream that we may die in vain," he said to her.

She looked at him as if he were a bad smell.

"That's the inscription at the base of the Memorial," he said.

She didn't respond. They walked on past the memorial and into the park. He started humming a tune to break the awful silence. Then he stopped because he thought it was a really stupid thing to do. Which it was. She walked down past the bandstand and down towards the shelter where she stopped and sat on the bench. He followed and sat beside her. David was slightly worried about what might happen next. Amanda looked nervous but started talking about her holiday in Greece. She talked about the hotel, the hotel food, the hotel pool. She told him the waiter's name, the name of the village near the hotel, how long the flight was and how short the transfers were. He would normally have preferred to throw himself under a bus than listen to such monotonous tripe but this was Amanda, and he was entranced.

"It was all inclusive too," she said proudly.

"What does that mean?" he asked. Glad to be part of the conversation at last.

"It means all your drinks and food are paid for. *Everything* is paid for."

"Do you pay for your food and drinks at home?" he asked.

"Of course not."

"So your whole life is all inclusive?" He laughed. He thought it was quite a funny joke but judging by the silence and the look of disgust on her face it clearly wasn't as funny as he had hoped.

There was another long silence which was broken by a familiar voice.

"Look who it isn't." It was Wayne. He had his gang with him and they stood behind him looking on in silence.

"Wayne!" said Amanda in surprise and alarm.

"You." Wayne pointed to Amanda. "Get lost."

Amanda protested in rather melodramatic fashion. David thought she was going to swoon. She kept putting her hand up to the side of her face as if she had a toothache. "Oh Wayne," she kept saying, "Don't Wayne! Leave us alone."
"Amanda, get lost."
She didn't swoon, she gave David a little peck on the cheek and then stood up and walked off.
"Just me and you now Watson," Wayne said, apparently forgetting his gang who stood behind him.
David felt so disappointed by Amanda's treachery that he seemed to lose his fear of Wayne. Even though David was still sitting down and Wayne was towering above him he showed no sign of fear. Wayne looked uncertain about what to say next. David looked at the smirking crowd of boys all standing, trying to look as menacing as possible. Boys he had known since the age of five. Boys who had constantly ridiculed him, taunted him, punched him as they passed him in the corridor, written the most awful things on the playground walls about him, about his mother and brother and sisters. Five years of torment, still they hadn't had enough, they wanted more. Wayne stood right in front of him, his small platoon of thugs in a semi-circle behind him. David had no experience of fighting, he had been punched often enough, but had never fought back. Looking at Wayne and his entourage in front of him he realised this was the time to strike back. As

David got up from the bench, he swung a punch at Wayne. It wasn't a particularly powerful punch but it was a lucky one. He hit Wayne in the most painful place the male of the species can be hit. Fist to Scrotum. The pain radiated from Wayne's gonads to every part of his anatomy. A flame of pain exploded into his abdomen and radiated down his lard-barrel legs, right down to his toes. As Wayne doubled up in agony, he presented David with another target. Wayne's face was now at the perfect height to be kicked. Not that David was a footballer, he hated the game, but had he any idea of the game at all, he would have seen the fat face of Wayne appear at the perfect height for volleying. David didn't want to hurt Wayne at this point, he wanted to kill him. He saw that big fat face looking down at the floor in front of him, and he kicked out at it. Never having volleyed anything in his life before, it was no surprise that he missed the target. He had flung his foot with such venom that as his foot flashed past Wayne's right ear and into thin air. Both his legs were flung upwards and his body made a half back-somersault which saw him land on the concrete floor with a sickening thud to the back of his head. David lay there seeing stars and a few blurred images. Wayne was out of the picture, clutching his family jewels and moaning. David came-to slowly. He had no pain but felt sick. His vision was blurred and he was aware of some blows to his body. He was being kicked. In a sort of feeding frenzy, the gang had set upon him and had started to kick him as he lay on the ground. They kicked him tentatively at first but slowly the group gained momentum and David was being beaten and stamped on. He managed to get to his knees, still being kicked, and he knew he had to get to his feet and with one tremendous effort he stood up and ran. He made off in the direction of the woods, towards the railway embankment. He didn't look back to see if he was being chased, he just ran for survival. Pure instinct took him across the park, over the stone wall and into the woods. Like an injured bear he climbed into a tree, and climbed up as high as he could, until he was swaying in the breeze looking down on the leaf-strewn floor of the forest. His tormentors were nowhere to be seen. They had stayed with their injured leader. Wayne.

David should have run home, had he known that the gang would stay with Wayne he could have made it back safely. However, now that he had managed to scramble up the silver birch he just decided to stay there. He was sore now. He was in pain; he was angry and he started sobbing. His whole body heaving so violently he thought he might shake himself free from the slender trunk of the very top of the tree. "What a mess." He whispered. "How stupid." David had often climbed trees as a child and climbing made him exhilarated, gave him a feeling of superiority; looking down on everyone and everything. However, as his sobbing subsided and his vision began to clear he looked across the skyline of Padiham, at the sleeping factory chimneys, the rows of terraced houses, the railway and the river and he felt wretched. The view seemed to match his mood. Grey and colourless dereliction. Why was he always the victim, always the target, never appreciated? It didn't seem fair. He could hear the baying mob assembling below him. He couldn't hear what it was they were shouting up to him. He just heard their stupid laughter and their stupid voices. He knew they would be spewing out the familiar diatribe of sad abuse. Mob law; if you feel weak, pick on a victim and the whole group feels stronger.

On the ground Wayne was walking in circles, still clutching his groin, muttering invective to nobody in particular. His acolytes stood around in a circle and some of them shouted up towards David, the usual comments but some of them seemed unsure of themselves. Some of them were thinking treasonable thoughts, could David slay Goliath, could Wayne be beaten, need they fear him at all? Their thoughts were interrupted by a sudden noise of snapping branches and a very loud dull thud as David hit the ground. They stared at the body in bewilderment. Not least because he had landed among them but miraculously had hit none of them on the way down. The body had appeared suddenly, as if by magic, without warning.

"He's dead!" said someone, breaking the awful silence.

"No, he's not, he's breathing, he's breathing. Look he's movin." This was Raymond, David's 'friend' from school. Raymond who could never keep still. He was the only one of the gang who *was* moving. All the rest of them were staring, like statues. There were more signs of life from David now as he started to make a high-pitched wheezing sound. "That's death throes that is," said Raymond, "me grandad did that when he died, I could hear him, mum told me to gerrout a house but I didn't. I stayed and listened. I stayed and listened to him wheezing and sort of screeching, it went on for about ten minutes. Then it stopped, and he were dead." After Doctor Raymond's diagnosis of the situation, there was only one thing for the gang to do and that was to run. Nobody gave the signal. It just happened. They all ran off, like a flock of birds spooked by a loud noise. But the only noise was the wheezing from David who struggled slowly to his knees and then tried to stand but failed and fell back again.

"You're just winded lad. You've knocked all breath out of your lungs. You'll be right as rain in a minute." David was pleased to see Henry standing there. It did occur to him, for a moment, that he might be dead, like Henry, but he had too much pain to be dead. He felt like he'd been run over. His face and

arms were all scratched and there was bruising
already visible on one side of his face.
"Nothing broken then?" Said Henry as he watched
David struggle to his feet.
"No, I don't think so," David said running his hands
over each limb in turn. "I slipped," he said.
"Did you slip or just let go?" Henry looked worried.
"No, I just slipped."
"You sure?"
"To be honest Henry, I'm not sure what happened."

Chapter 3.

"What's the situation Thompson?"
"Well, he's sat right on the edge of the quarry but I know who he is sergeant, his name's David Watson."
"That name rings a bell."
"I know him from school, he lives in Altham Street."
"That's right. There was an incident in the park a few weeks back, and wasn't his father killed in an RTA years ago? Listen, stay where you are and keep an eye on him. Let me know if anything changes. Don't let him see you watching him. Don't, whatever happens, approach him or try and talk to him. Understand? That's very important. I'll get someone to contact his mother and I'm going to contact Hutton to get some help on this one. I have a bad feeling about this."
P.C. Thompson didn't feel it necessary to inform his sergeant that he had already approached and spoken to David Watson. If it came out, he might fail his probationary period. That was a worrying thought but it occurred to him that if David jumped, nobody would ever know, and if he didn't jump nobody would take David's word against his.

September came and David was due to start his secondary education at Gawthorpe Academy. It was a large Comprehensive School and took in students from many different primary schools in the area. He had passed the holidays healing; his bruised ribs, sternum, carpals, metacarpals, tibias and fibulas. He had been sent to the doctor who shone a light in his eyes and told him not to climb trees. During the holidays, Irene was delighted when Jenny came to visit David. His fall from the tree had increased her worries about him. He was still talking to his imaginary friend and she thought that a real friend, like Jenny, might persuade him to leave the imaginary friend behind.

"I came to see if you were okay David. I heard about your accident. Are you alright now?"

It seemed to David that Jenny had grown a year older since he had seen her a few weeks before. He had been so besotted with Amanda at school, he hadn't really taken much notice of Jenny, or any other girl there. Jenny was a very slim girl; she had a pale complexion with ginger hair that she called auburn. Her eyes were green and always bright. She had a bubbling energy and enthusiasm that attracted people to her, both young and old.

"I was just bruised, nothing broken," he said.

"What made you climb to the top of that tree? Raymond showed us which one you fell out of. It's a wonder you weren't killed."

33

"I was running away from Wayne and his gang. I'd hit Wayne. I don't think he was too pleased."

"He's a bully."

"Did he ever bully you?"

"I wouldn't let anyone bully me," she said proudly.

"How did you stop him?"

"I just showed him I wasn't frightened of him. I never did what he said. I stood up to him."

"Maybe that's what I should have done a long time ago."

"It's not so easy for boys, is it?" She asked, kindly.

"I don't know."

"Raymond told Ian that you hit him."

"I was disappointed so many of them joined in with Wayne, I didn't realise so many of them hated me."

"They only follow Wayne because they're frightened of him. He's twice the size of any of the other boys. Anyway, according to Raymond, you hit him hard. He said you hit him where it hurts."

"In the nads," David said.

"Is that what you call them?" she giggled.

"There's lots of names for them."

"Yes I suppose there is."

"Some more descriptive than others."

"Tell me about all your pictures," she said, in an attempt to move the conversation away from genitals. There was a dozen or more pictures of men in uniform, from the First War, on David's bedroom wall. "Most people have footballers or pop stars on their wall," she said.

"They're pictures that my Dad collected. He was writing a book about the First War and he collected a lot of information about men who lived in Padiham and fought in the war. He never got chance to finish it."

"Did they all die in the war?" she asked as she looked at each photograph.

"Not all of them, he was looking into the men who survived as well as those who died. He wrote about how they got on when they got home from the war, as well as what they did in the war."

"Oh look, there's one called Tillotson."

"He *was* killed, he lived on Stockbridge Road. He was 21 when he died."

"And this one looks a bit like you David."

"I don't think so Jenny. He's no relation anyway but my Dad has a lot more detail about him than anyone else. That's Henry Bradshaw. He survived. He fought in the second battle of Ypres. He was a prisoner of war. He lived in James Street. That picture is a postcard he sent from the prison camp. If you look closely you can see his prison number over his jacket pocket, 580." David was pleased that Jenny seemed interested in his father's pictures.

"Are you looking forward to starting at Gawthorpe?" he asked her.

"Yes, we start soon, don't we? I'm *really* looking forward to it. I'm looking forward to doing Chemistry and Biology. I've decided. I'm going to be a doctor."

"That's good."

"My mum's a nurse and she always wanted to be a doctor. I'd like to be a surgeon."

"A surgeon? I've no idea what I want to be."

"You're so clever you could do anything you want."

"You think so?"

"Yes."

" If I could get through the next school without being picked on every week that would be something."

"My mum says you're eccentric."

"Is it such a bad thing, to be eccentric?"

"No!"

"So why do so many people think they need to pick on me then?"

"I don't know. My mum says people don't like it if someone is different from them. You're clever, and they're jealous."

"Amanda's clever and everyone seems to like her, except me now."

"And me."

"That's two of us then. Everyone else thinks she's the bee's knees."

"Well she *is* clever, but not like you. You think in a different way, in a special way."

"Special needs?"

"No, just special," Jenny said in a quiet almost embarrassed voice.

"Do you remember," David said, "when I asked Tilly if I could dismantle the Climbing Frame."

"Oh yes." Jenny laughed.

"Ian and Simon used to do it all the time, and they would climb up and fall back and at the last minute, jump down and catch the climbing frame just before it landed on them. So eventually Tilly let me have a go and I just fell backwards with the climbing frame on top of me?"

"Yes, I remember!"

"That *was* special."

"Yes, me and the girls couldn't stop laughing. Sally said she thought you were trying to commit suicide and that made us laugh even more. Tilly told us off and said we should be more sympathetic but it looked so funny the way you just leaned back and fell flat on your back with the climbing frame on top of you."

Jenny visited him several times during the holidays and her visits were welcomed by David and his mother. Irene tried to persuade David to visit Jenny in her home but he was reluctant to go. "I'll see her when term starts," he said, "I'm not sure her Dad approves of me."

"Don't talk rubbish David."

When David started at the Academy his plan was to blend in, to go unnoticed. The plan went well for a week. It suffered a major setback on his first visit to the football field. David had never really shown any interest in football. He thought about asking the sports teacher if he could do something different but he stuck to his plan to blend in, to conform. Conformity in this case, meant getting changed from warm clothing into thin cotton shorts and a sleeveless shirt and running around a field in the cold and rain. It was a horrible day as the Sports Teacher, an enthusiastic young man with blonde hair and a sun tan, explained to Group Four that football was for 'everyone', which meant girls and boys. Group Four was what was left after all the children with any athletic ability had been put in other groups. Quite how the more able boys and girls had been creamed off was a mystery to David but he was content with the group which consisted of children who were either grossly overweight or unenthusiastic about sport, or both. As he stood there in line, wondering how cold you had to be before you could be classified as hypothermic, he slowly became aware that he was being addressed by the Sports Teacher. He was called Mr Coffey and he was from Ireland. David became aware that the teacher was talking to him but had no idea what he had been asked, so he replied, "Yes Sir." This tactic had worked in the past with teachers who had woken him from one of his daydreams. It didn't work with Mr Coffey. It seemed to have a devastating effect on him. He found out later that the question had been the last in a series of questions aimed at David, the last of which was; "Are you deliberately ignoring me?" In defence of

Mr Coffey, he had only singled David out because he had put his football boots on the wrong feet, his left on his right and his right on his left. Mr Coffey's first question had asked David if he might go into the changing room to check his boots. Mr Coffey was a nice man and didn't want to embarrass the boy. However, Mr. Coffey now exploded: "Look at your boots lad! You'll run like a duck! Get them changed!"

David looked at his feet and saw his laces neatly tied in a huge bow on his shiny new boots. His toes did seem to be pointing in the wrong direction so he preened himself, and waddled away to change them. David had been noticed! He was known as Donald from then on. The football match proceeded, with minimum input from David. He did run around, but only to keep warm. He had little interest in making any contact with the ball. After half an hour of his meanderings Mr Coffey blew the whistle, stopped play and gave a little talk. It was about tactics. None of the talk meant anything to David. He had never read a book about football. Towards the end of the talk he asked David what position he thought he was playing. David had no idea.

"I haven't really given it any thought Sir."

"Well I think it's about time you did." Mr Coffey seemed annoyed about something.

"What positions are available?" David asked.

"What positions are available? Are you trying to be funny lad?"

David was shocked. There was nothing further from his mind. The only thing on his mind was how to get through the next half hour without being noticed and without freezing to death.

"Well, Donald. You can play striker. Get up the field."

The circle of shivering pupils found this funny. David had no idea what a striker was. He had heard the term, but had not bothered to ask anyone what it meant.

"Go on, get up the field, right up, as far as you can without being offside." Mr Coffey was really furious with him now.

David assessed the slope of the field and moved up the slight incline, towards his own goalkeeper.

"That's enough Donald. Take a detention!"

David never knew if Mr Coffey had called him Donald on purpose or by mistake. Whatever the reason, he was known as Donald for the rest of his school career. For the next five years he would be referred to, by all pupils as Donald. Having a nickname wasn't unusual. There were other pupils with worse names than Donald but David worried that his stupidity on the football field might be sufficient reason for the bullying to start again. Only Ian, Jenny and Amanda were in the same class as David from his previous school. The Academy streamed the pupils by ability and Wayne was in a lower stream. He hadn't been a problem so far but the laughter on the football field was the first stage, he thought, of the inevitable slide back into becoming the target of more threats and violence. 'Is it me?' he thought, 'or is it a crime to have zero interest in football?'

That evening he asked Henry if he had ever been bullied.

"Some of the officers seemed to enjoy bullying the lads. There was a subaltern in India. Ponsonby something or other, he seemed to enjoy making us suffer. He'd make us run races in the heat, climbing over ten-foot fences with full pack and rifle. He'd bring out all the wives and children to watch us, like we were race horses, or dogs. He had a few lads that he picked on constantly, he'd put them on a charge for no reason, tell them there was some of their kit gone missing, or hadn't been cleaned properly when it was obvious there was nothing wrong with their kit. It got worse when we got to France."

"So, what did you do about it?"

"Not a lot we could do about it really."

"Why not?"

"Well it didn't matter how stupid a thing they asked us to do, if we didn't do it, they could have us shot."

Jenny was even less helpful. "Even I know what a striker is David. She's the one who scores all the goals. They stay up front and poach."

"Oh I see. That's cleared a lot up that has. So, I should have gone up, and poached?"

"Yes."

"It's a complicated game football. I thought going up the field meant going up the slope but apparently you go down the slope to go up and poach."

"It's not complicated. It's simple. You always seem to get the simple things wrong."

" I can't believe he put me in detention for not knowing about striking or poaching. They wrote mum a letter and told her I'd be kept in for an extra half hour after school. I wasn't going to tell her. Then she got mad I didn't tell her about it. She said not telling her was the same as lying. I don't think it can be the same, otherwise we'd use the same words to describe both things."

"Don't talk stupid David. Not saying anything is the same as telling a lie."

"Is poaching the same thing as striking?"

"More or less."

Chapter 4.

On the telephone to the police Headquarters in Hutton, the Inspector at Padiham police station made his request for support for the situation at Hambledon quarry.

"We have a car up at the quarry but we've made no approach to the boy at the moment. We had a uniform visit the mother and she's in a state. She rang his mobile but he's left it at home, which she says is unusual. The boy's home from university and not happy. Mother and son had a falling out yesterday. The boy went for a walk, promised to be home for five, never late usually, he's still up there. If he set off walking now, he'd be an hour late. It doesn't look good sir."

"Right! I'm ordering a full response team right away. Why do we get so much joy and peace every Christmas? Keep your officer up there but don't make a move until we get a team there. It could take a while to get a specialist negotiator. We don't want to take any chances on this one, not after that fiasco two years ago. Hopefully the lad will have seen sense and walked home before we get there."

"I hope you're right sir. One last thing though. I remember about twenty years ago this lad's father died in a road traffic accident, the coroner ruled it accidental death, but I attended the incident. He

***drove into a Motorway bridge, no other vehicle
involved."***

After the debacle on the football field, David
worried that the bullying might start again. It didn't.
David successfully blended into the background. He
kept quiet in class and spent most break times on
his own. He did his work, read his books and was
largely invisible in the vast ocean of the two
thousand pupils who attended the academy. Wayne
hadn't come near him. He was in a different class
and their paths never crossed. Perhaps Wayne had
found someone else to pick on. Or maybe Henry
was right when he told David that some lads see
things more clearly 'when they've had a good kick in
the balls'.
As the years progressed David found that he was
much happier at the Academy than he had ever
been at primary school. He came top in every test,
in every subject. Even if he didn't appear to be
listening in class, he always seemed to have a good
answer if a teacher asked him a question.
Sometimes he would come back with an answer
that showed far more understanding than his
teachers thought possible. He was an enigma. The
Language department said he was a prodigy. His
Science and Maths teachers were suspicious of him.
Most other staff thought he was very clever but
complained about his handwriting and general

chaotic presentation. The Sports Department thought he was an idiot.

At home he missed his brother and his sisters, who had all flown the nest. He had no real friends apart from Henry and he enjoyed occasional conversations with Jenny. His mother still complained about his long evening talks with Henry, and about his lack of friends, but as time passed, she began to accept what she couldn't change.

He occasionally got into trouble with the teachers at school. In Physics he got a detention for arguing with the teacher about Newton's first law of motion. When David got enthusiastic about something he often started shouting and that's why the teachers tended to give him detention. The problem David had with Newton's first law of motion was that it stated that 'a body would remain at rest or continue to move at a constant velocity unless acted upon by a force'. David asked the teacher, quite politely, if he could think of anywhere in the world where a body wouldn't be acted on by a force. The teacher told him he was missing the point of Newton's first law of motion. David suggested that if there was nowhere in the world where the law applied, it was the law that was irrelevant and it was Isaac Newton who was missing the point. The discussion developed and the watching class enjoyed the spectacle. David ended up raising his voice and ended up in detention. He won another detention in Maths for revisiting the invisible triangle discussion. Everyone seemed to think that triangles existed, even if by textbook definition they didn't. 'If triangles exist why not Henry?' was a thought often on his mind.

However, the real crisis came in year 10, in the History lesson. It was a few weeks into the first term of his fourth year at the academy that Irene got a phone call from school. They called her at work and she took the call in the supervisor's office.

"What's wrong? Has he had an accident? Is he alright?"

"Nothing like that Mrs Watson, don't worry, he's not hurt or anything but we would like you to come and collect him if that's possible?"

"Is he sick?

"Not sick, as such, but he got very upset, well excited, in the History class. He was very vocal, and aggressive towards Mr Pointer. Mr Pointer wants him excluded. He says David attacked him."

"He attacked him?"

"We're looking into it, Mrs Watson. It isn't clear what happened or why. David's such a quiet boy normally. He's clearly very upset, as is Mr Pointer, but if you could come and take him home, we think that might be helpful."

"Of course I'll come. I'll come straight away."

Mr Pointer had given his class the task of writing a story about the First World War. There was to be a competition and the best story would be read out in front of the whole school at a commemoration service. It was one of the many events being arranged to mark the 100th anniversary of the start of World War One. Mr Pointer was not the most inspiring of teachers, the only ambition he had left was retirement. Most of his class took no notice of him whatsoever and as long as the class remained reasonably quiet, he took no notice of them. It was an arrangement that satisfied everybody. When Mr Pointer told the class about the competition, David was one of the few students who was enthused by the monotone announcement.

"Don't make it too long. It can be fictional but must be Historically accurate. Five hundred words describing conditions in trench warfare. Hand it in next week."

"I don't know which story to tell Henry," he was looking through the War Diary of Henry's battalion. "There's this attack on the 1st of March, in front of St Eloi. Your Battalion was ordered to take German trenches and hold them until relieved. When you took the trench, it was full of corpses. Do you remember that one?"

"Not really."

" Then on the 11th of March, with a new officer, who'd just arrived, he led you to the sunken road between St Eloi and Shelley's Farm."

"Oh I remember him alright, he got us completely lost. Well, he was lost, we all knew where we were but of course he wouldn't listen. He led us the wrong side of St Eloi, and the Germans opened up on us

from three sides. What a shambles. They were bombing us and putting down a lot of accurate fire. We had no cover and there was only one thing to do. Officer was waving his arms and screaming like a lunatic, so we took off and headed off back to our own lines."

"It says in the Battalion history that there was a 'somewhat hasty and quite uncontrolled advance, on the part of some troops holding St Eloi, in a rearward direction'".

"Well that's one way of putting it. An advance in a rearward direction. Sounds about right. We ran off before we were all killed."

"It says in this diary that the officer had just come out. Is that true?"

"Yes, he'd just arrived from England. He didn't have a clue what he was doing. There's lots of attacks to choose from lad, try and find one that succeeded in gaining a bit of ground."

"That's not going to be easy Henry."

"Well do your best."

"I think I'll combine a lot of attacks from the diaries and make one good story out of a lot of different events."

"I'll look forward to hearing it."

It was a few weeks later when David was informed that his story had made it onto the 'short list'. The whole school had taken part in the competition and there were ten students who were to read their stories in front of a panel of teachers. They would decide which student would be chosen to read at the Commemoration service. The judging was to take place in the main hall and each of the ten students took it in turn, to stand on the stage and read their story to the panel of judges. David was the youngest of the finalists but many of the older students seemed much more nervous than he was. Eventually it was his turn to read.

He stood up on the stage and read it out with confidence, "My name is Henry Bradshaw and I was born in Padiham in 1890. I joined the 4th Battalion Kings Royal Rifle Cops in 1909 and served in India until 1914. In October of that year we sailed back in convoy from Bombay to Plymouth to join the fighting in France. The voyage taking just over a month. After some leave and training I arrived in France on the 20th of December 1914 and I shall describe one attack we made on the 11th of March 1915. We were to advance from Bellewarde Wood on the Menim Road under the cover of darkness and take the German lines between Shelley's Farm and St Eloi and hold them. There was a full moon, and although we moved slowly and with great care, we did not hold out much hope of getting to the first German trench undetected. Our company was the first to arrive in the trench which had been abandoned by the Germans, who had moved to higher ground. At the entrance of the trench there were the corpses of two corporals from our own regiment. They stood upright, with their fixed swords shining in the moonlight, as if they were standing guard. When we entered the trench, it was filled with corpses of many different regiments and nationalities. The filth and stench were awful and the only way to avoid sinking waist deep in mud and slime was to step on the bodies of the dead. There were more dead from our division further along, that the Germans had stacked like sandbags to support the walls of the trench. We waited in the trench for further orders from our officer in charge. We should either have pressed forward our attack from there, or withdrawn. But our officer, who had just come out from England a week before, insisted we stay where we were and consolidate our position. The Germans, who often seemed to know when an attack was coming, had a habit of vacating their first line of trenches and wait for us to assemble there. They would then open fire on us from their deeper and better defended second line of trenches. After nearly all the companies involved in the assault had arrived and we were crowded into the stinking trench, the Germans bombed us and hit us with very accurate fire from higher up the slope. Our officer in charge who had, so far been pleased with his first taste of action, began to wave his arms and cry and shriek like a lunatic. The trench was emptying fast as we all tried to escape back towards our own lines. This is what is known in the regimental diary as a hasty and largely disorganised advance in a rearward direction. But we were just running for our lives. I had only covered a few yards when a shell burst close to me and I was knocked off my feet with a terrific hammer blow to my head. When I woke up, it was daylight and the attack was over. I was shivering with either cold or shock and I was covered in blood and fragments of blood-stained khaki but I was unhurt. It was the blood of my comrades that I was wearing. I sat in a shell hole for the rest of the day. It would have been certain death to try and move before dark. I was very close to the German lines. I could hear someone shouting just to my left. I could tell by the upper-class accent and the pathetic wailing noises that it was our officer in charge. I wanted to shoot him myself, for getting most of my company killed unnecessarily but instead of that, when darkness fell, I crawled over to him and dragged him back to our own lines. I thought the army might shoot him for what he did, but they gave him the D.S.O. for a leading a brave and successful assault of the German lines at St Eloi. They gave me a lesser medal, the D.C.M., for saving his life. This brave and successful attack gained us no ground and we lost 2 officers and 64 other ranks. That's the end Sir."

"Thank you, David. You read that very well." That was the only comment he received. "Mr Pointer will let you know the result in due course."

David was summoned to Mr Pointer's classroom one lunchtime, to hear the results of the competition. After a long preamble about how difficult it was to separate all the excellent entries and how highly they regarded his work, how grateful they were, he was told that he hadn't won the competition.

"I'm sorry David. You did very well. Do you want me to explain why you weren't successful?"

"No sir, it's okay. I'd like to know who won though."

"I can't tell you that, at this stage."

"Oh well, I suppose I'll find out in time."

"Yes, it will be announced in morning assembly."

"Well thank you for letting me know sir."

"Just one thing David," he said, as David stood up and was about to leave. "I just wanted to mention about the swords." Mr Pointer laughed. David had never seen him laugh before. "You said in your story that the soldiers had swords."

"They had fixed swords."

"Yes, you should have said bayonets."

"Should I?"

"Yes, and I thought the part where the officer got the DSO was far-fetched."

"It's okay Sir, I don't need to know why I didn't win, really, it doesn't matter."

"You see David the story was meant to be historically accurate and also, if you are going to read out at a commemoration service, well, the part you said the Germans used corpses like sandbags was, I thought, unnecessarily gruesome."

"Did you?"

"Yes, and the two corpses standing up at the

entrance of the trench, how could they stand up if they were dead?"

"I don't know sir, but everything I described was taken from the war diary of the King's Royal Rifle Corps and those two corporals *were* dead, and they *were* standing at the entrance of the trench when the men from the 4th Battalion entered."

"Well that's as maybe David but you must admit the part about the swords was a mistake. They didn't use swords in the first world war."

"I think you'll find that the cavalry regiments were issued with swords in the First War and the King's Royal Rifles used a fixed sword, a long, curved blade. If you bothered to check the references I quoted you would find that the details in my story were all historically accurate."

"Don't you raise your voice at me boy! Just because you didn't win doesn't mean it wasn't a good piece of work but it's important that you are clear about the historical inaccuracies."

"It all came from War Diaries written at the time!" David was shouting, his enthusiasm had turned to anger. "They called them fixed swords because that's what they were, they were longer than a bayonet. And bayonets were straight but the fixed swords were curved. If you study those diaries you will find that everything I described actually happened. Why don't you people ever listen?"

"How dare you talk to me like that, get out, go on,

get out of my classroom." He was pushing David towards the door now.

"Who do you think you are? Do you think Henry Bradshaw is a liar? How do *you* know how Henry got his medal? You don't! You wanted historical accuracy but now you think it might be too upsetting to hear at the commemoration ceremony. Well, I'm sorry, but that's what it was like."

"You will go and stand outside the Headmaster's office this moment young man."

"No, I won't," and he pulled himself away from his teachers grasp and Mr Pointer stumbled slightly, recovered his balance and slapped David hard, across the face.

"You're just a boring old fool!" David shouted, almost in tears with anger.

Pointer shouted some more instructions about going to the headmaster but David just walked away.

When Irene arrived at the school, she was ushered into the Head of Year's office to find a tearful David, not crying but clearly upset, and the Head of Year Mr Carrol looking stern and Mrs Davies, looking conciliatory.

"What's happened?" she asked.

Mr Carrol spoke first. "Mr Pointer has complained that David attacked him in his classroom. Mr Pointer was giving David the result of the competition. David didn't take the news well and according to Mr Pointer, David started arguing and eventually attacked him, at which point Mr Pointer slapped David to calm him down. I must say, right at the beginning, that we do not condone any physical punishment of pupils and Mr Pointer has apologised for slapping your son but says that he was provoked. Mr Pointer is of the opinion that David should be expelled from the Academy."

"And what has David said about all this?" she asked, looking at her son.

"He hasn't said a word about what happened as yet," said Mrs Davies.

"Did you attack this Mr Pointer David?"

"No Mum. I didn't."

She looked at David's accusers. "Were there any witnesses to all of this?" she asked.

"I think, Mrs Watson, until everything has calmed down, you should take David home. We can discuss the matter when the dust has settled, so to speak."

"So nobody saw David attacking this Mr Pointer?"

"As I say...."

"Well either there was a witness or there wasn't."

"They won't listen to you mum," David said, "They're all the same. I never attacked anyone. Mr Pointer started pushing me and he nearly fell over and then he slapped me across the face. He lost his temper because I told him he didn't know what he was talking about. It was the same in Maths and Physics, if you ask a question or disagree with something they say, they put you in detention. I got my first detention for putting my football boots on the wrong feet. I'd be glad to get expelled. I don't want to come back here again. I can do much better on my own."

"As I said Mrs Watson, perhaps if we can meet in a few days when everything has calmed down?"

David had to describe to his mother every detail of the incident when they got home. It was a more intensive interrogation than his teachers had managed and he told her everything about the story, how he had researched it, how he had kept the historical accuracy but mixed details from several attacks.

"So, you called your teacher an old fool? And now you might get thrown out? You're going to have to apologise David. You can't go around calling your teachers fools. He shouldn't have said you attacked him though, if you didn't, it sounds more like he attacked you, thought a good slap never hurt anyone as far as I'm concerned."

"He's lying mum. He lost his temper and slapped me and then made up this story that he was trying to calm me down."

"You seemed so happy there. You were doing so well. You're going to have to go back you know. All this nonsense about not going back. You can forget about that!"

David was given a week's suspension by his Head of Year but he was determined never to return to the Academy and he refused absolutely to apologise to his teacher Mr Pointer. His mother, on the other hand, decided that he would return to the academy and that he would apologise to Mr Pointer, the Head of Year, and that nice lady she met whose name she couldn't remember. David was brave enough to argue with his teacher and his Head of Year, but he didn't have the courage to argue with Irene. He spent the week's suspension moping around, lying on the bed in his room, thoroughly depressed by everything and everybody.

"Did you ever get down Henry? I mean, with everything you went through, did you ever think that it just wasn't worth carrying on?"

"Everyone gets down now and again, I was no different."

"But really depressed, so that you couldn't see any good in anything. As if everything is pointless and worthless. Did you ever feel like that?"

"When my eldest was killed. Well, after we found out. I got right down. I never felt that bad before. Even right through the war. I think I'd buried all the bad things that happened, I never talked about them, never thought about them, but when we got the news about Alan, it was like I remembered all the things that I'd forgotten about. It's as if they came back to haunt me."

"How did he die?"

"He was killed in Italy, Salerno, at the beach landings. It was the strangest thing. My wife woke me up in the middle of the night, she was terrified. 'It's our Alan,' she said, 'something's happened to

*him. He came and stood at the bottom of the bed
and smiled at me, as if he was saying goodbye.' It
made me go cold when she said that. That was the
Thursday night, the 9th of September 1943, he'd
been killed that day. We got the telegram a few
days later. As soon as we heard I just shut down, I
just wanted to lie in bed, I couldn't work, I couldn't
sleep. I was useless. I was depressed I suppose."
"Did you get help? Medical help?"
"No I wasn't that bad, it wasn't like shell shock, once
I'd spent a week doing nothing, I just decided to get
up and get on with it. I had a wife and a daughter
still at home, I had to get back to work, otherwise
we'd have nowt to eat."
"I suppose getting a slap from the teacher isn't
worth getting depressed about really, is it?"
Henry didn't comment.
"The thing is, the harder I try, the worse it gets. They
think I was annoyed because I didn't win the
competition but it wasn't that. It was the fact that
Pointer said everything I wrote was inaccurate. He
said they didn't use swords in the first war. He was
laughing when he said that, and whatever I said, he
just didn't listen."
"They never do, teachers, officers, they always think
they know best. Those fixed swords weren't much
use in narrow trenches, they were too long, kept
getting caught on the sides of the trench, they were
a right nuisance."*

Irene made sure David went back to school after the week's suspension and he was under strict instructions from her to apologise to Mr Pointer, to get on with his schoolwork and to keep his opinions to himself. As she left the house for work that morning, she added, as a parting shot, "And for goodness sake try and make some friends and cheer up. This is the best time of your life if you all but knew it."

Chapter 5.

The two workmen who had called the emergency services were consulted by the police inspector, who wanted to know how his vehicles and staff could approach the top of the quarry without being seen from the cliff edge.

"You'll need to go up the back way, it's steep and lots of potholes but it's doable in a car and in a four-wheel drive it's not a problem." He pointed down the hill, "You'll need to go back down there and take the first left after that clump of trees. It's a long way round but there's only one track, you can't go wrong. There's a hut on top. If you park behind it there's plenty of room."

"Right. Get these vehicles turned round and make a start. We'll wait here for the negotiator and bring her up when she arrives."

"You'll not get that caravan up there." The workman said, pointing to the blue caravan being bounced down the track by a police Land Rover but the Inspector had already moved on to more important issues.

"It looks like they're setting off for a week's holiday up there, all the vehicles they're taking."

"Well they must know what they're doing."

It was Jenny's mother who suggested that she invite David to her 16th birthday party. Irene had shared her worries about her son with Sandra. "I don't think he has any friends at school, if he has, he never talks about them." Irene told her. "Your Jenny seems to be the only person he'll talk to and she calls in occasionally but he never seems to go out anywhere. I mean that's not normal is it? He's nearly 16 now and he never goes out. If he does go out, it's to the library or one of his solitary walks."

"He'll grow out of it Irene. It could be worse. He could be doing drugs and staying out all night. You shouldn't worry so much. If you like, I'll tell Jenny to invite him to her birthday party."

"Oh no, not if she doesn't want to."

"She likes David, she always has. She'll probably invite him anyway, but I'll mention it to her just in case."

When Jenny called at David's house to invite him to her party, he didn't want to go. Not many other sixteen-year-old boys would have refused the invitation. Jenny was now slim rather than skinny, her hair was golden rather than ginger, her childhood freckles were fainter. Her smile was as childish as it had always been but everything else about her had left childhood behind. Had you asked David what colour her eyes were, he would not have known. Every other boy who knew her, knew they were green, the irises large and the pupils dark.

David was oblivious of Jenny's attention. She would call occasionally and chat to him at school, but it never occurred to David that she might be anything more than a friend. It wasn't as if he didn't value her friendship, he did. She was really the only real friend he had. When she invited him, he protested.

"I won't know anyone," he said.

"Well, you'll get to know them if you come along."

"I'm not really a party animal."

"It's my birthday David, it's important to me."

"You'll be with all your friends, they won't like me."

"How do you know if you don't come?"

"But, why do you want me there?"

"It's important to me!"

"You'll have Ian there."

"I want *you* to be there."

"Will Raymond be going?" David asked. "I haven't seen him for ages."

"No Raymond won't be there."

"Well, can I think about it?"

"What's to think about?"

"Well Jenny, there's all sorts to think about. What have I got to wear? I don't really have any smart clothes apart from the school uniform and I don't suppose many of your friends will be wearing school uniform, will they? Then there's alcohol. I don't drink alcohol. I tried it once and was very sick. Then what do you talk about at parties? I always upset people when I try and make conversation for no reason."

"David, I want you to come to my birthday party. Wear what you're wearing now, that's fine."

"It's not the height of fashion though is it? Will people be taking drugs? I'm not keen on pharmaceuticals, I won't even take Paracetamol when I get headaches."

"Christ David. Stop making such a fuss. It's a party. What's so difficult?" She had raised her voice now and David couldn't ever remember Jenny shouting at him before. Everyone else he knew, had shouted at him on a regular basis but not Jenny. He looked at her eyes, and thought she might be going to cry. Jenny never cried. She was always cheerful. He wondered if there might be something wrong at home, or whether she was not feeling well. She did look rather pale.

"Are you feeling alright Jenny?" he asked.

"Yes, I'm fine."

"It's just that you don't look very happy."

"Don't I?"

"No."

"Well you can't be happy all the time, can you?"

"No, I don't suppose you can."

They sat in silence for a while. David tried to think of something cheerful to say that might brighten the mood.

"I'll tell you something that will cheer you up Jenny!" he said at last.

"What?"

"I think I'm in love."

"What the hell are you talking about?"

"With a girl, at school. Maria."

"What?"

"She's from Madrid originally, and she has long dark hair and large brown eyes."

"Yes. I know the one you mean. Ian's very keen on her."

"Everyone likes her Jenny, all the boys I mean. She's very quiet and I think you might say she was an introvert. She seems to spend a lot of time on her own and I think we might have a lot in common."

"Oh please, don't say there's another one like you David."

"She's different, not one of the crowd, doesn't quite fit in." David wasn't listening now, he was only talking."

"She's a misfit in other words," Jenny said.

"Her mum died when she was young, I think. Either that or her parents separated. Could be both I suppose. If she's dead and he's alive. You can't get more separate than that can you? Like me and dad. She's good at languages, she's in my class for French and German. We both get top marks."

"How wonderful."

"I think you'd like her Jenny."

"Well, you must bring her over to my house and introduce her."

"I haven't really spoken to her yet, well not more

than a few words."

"Why does that not surprise me?" David didn't see the disappointment in Jenny's face. He didn't see much beyond the end of his nose as he eulogised over Maria.

"She's a very good swimmer apparently. All the boys like her."

"She's a very lucky girl."

She is *very* pretty Jenny." David said this with a wistful smile and his head tilted upwards, as if he was looking into the face of an angel hovering above Jenny's head.

"Yes, I've seen her around."

"I think she is my perfect woman. They say there's someone in the world that is the perfect partner for you, don't they? An ideal."

"Just like Amanda then?" She was angry now. David looked at her with a surprised expression, "What is wrong with you?"

"Oh, nothing David. Absolutely nothing. I invite you to my party and you make all these excuses and then start banging on about Maria. I've just met a girl called Maria! I'll bet you haven't even spoken to her, have you?"

David didn't reply.

"No, I didn't think so. You live in a dream world, you really do. Oh, I can't come to your party because I've nothing to wear, I don't drink, I don't take Paracetamol. Well it didn't stop you falling in love with Maria did it? My ideal. My perfect woman.

65

Never had a conversation with her. How do you know she's so perfect if you've hardly spoken a word to her?"

"Well I'm sorry Jenny. I thought you'd be pleased."

She swore at him and left him and thundered down the stairs and out the house. A few minutes later his mother appeared at his door. "What was all that about?" she asked.

David held his arms out in a gesture of innocence. "I don't know. I just told her about me and Maria and she swore at me and ran out."

"Are you going to her party?"

"No, I don't really want to."

"You idiot, David. Go after her and apologise!"

"I haven't *done* anything!"

" Jenny invites you to her party and you turn it down? What is wrong with you? Go after her and apologise."

He went, but it was too late. She was gone.

Jenny avoided him at school and didn't speak to him for several weeks. He tried on several occasions to ask her what was wrong, he apologised but she would have nothing to do with him. He missed the brief conversations he would normally have with her as they moved from class to class. He missed her birthday party too. He was saddened by the situation but had no idea how to fix it. His mother told him to buy her a birthday present and, as you might expect, he did as he was told.

He had no idea what to buy Jenny but when he saw what looked like a silver ring with a green stone, in a charity shop, it seemed to have her name on it. He walked through the park to the estate where she lived. Her house was an imposing structure and had a huge front garden and a long drive.

"I've got you a birthday present," he said when she opened the door.

She smiled, and he was relieved. He feared she might shut the door on him.

"It's very small," she said, looking down at the box he held out to her.

"I'm sorry," he said.

"Come in. Idiot!" She smiled again and welcomed him into the house, her anger with him apparently subsided.

"I'm sorry I missed the party. This is your birthday present. I didn't get a card. I thought it was too late for a card."

"Thanks," she said.

They sat in the living room and she unwrapped the gift. It was a tiny box with a bow."

"It's beautifully wrapped," she said.

"They wrapped it in the shop. They said do you want it gift wrapped and I said yes, then they charged me an extra two quid for the wrapping."

She laughed. "No expense spared then?" she said.

"I'm sorry for what I said, whatever it was. I didn't want to upset you."

"I know David," she said, slowly unwrapping the gift.

"My mum said I should tell you how important you are to me," he said.

"Your mum?" She looked annoyed again.

"You *are* important to me Jenny. It's just that my mum said I should tell you."

"That's alright then." She smiled at him, and everything seemed ok.

She unravelled the wrapping paper and looked at the tiny box. She opened it and looked at the ring he'd bought her. "David! You've bought me a ring?"

"I hope it fits. I couldn't remember whether you had thin fingers or fat fingers."

"David, boys buy girls rings, when they want to marry them."

David looked shocked. "I don't want to marry you!" he said, rather too earnestly.

She laughed again. "I sort of guessed that."

"Well is it alright? Does it fit?"

"It fits my little finger," she said, putting it on. "I must have fat fingers."

"Do you like it? Is it alright?"

"I *love* it David, and I'll treasure it always. Thank you!" and she leaned across and kissed him.

"I've never been kissed before," he said.

"You'll have to get Maria to kiss you."

"I don't suppose that will ever happen." He looked at her and something in her demeanour told him that she didn't really want any more detail on Maria. He felt Jenny might be the best friend he would ever have. He looked at her admiring her birthday present and felt proud to be her friend. He wanted to tell her about Maria but she would only get angry again. He thought he might tell her about Henry. Henry was his only other friend. It seemed odd not to share him with her. He knew his mother had told him not to tell anyone else but surely Jenny was different. He could trust Jenny not to go and tell anyone else. It seemed to him that if he told her about Henry, it would make his friendship with her even more special. He felt sure that she would understand and believe him when he told her that Henry was real and not just a voice in his head. "Can I tell you a secret Jenny?"

"If you like." She was holding her hand in the air and waving it slightly to admire her new ring.

"You promise you won't tell anyone about it?"

"I promise."

"It's Henry," he said, "I have another frien...."

"You can't tell her about me David!" It was Henry. He was in the room behind Jenny. It was unusual for Henry to appear like this.

"Why?" David asked. Jenny looked at him like he'd suddenly gone mad.

"You need to keep it secret, you promised your mother. If you tell her you won't see me again. That's just the way it is David." He was dismayed by Henry's sudden appearance and, even more sudden,

69

disappearance. He was so used to chatting to him in his room, it seemed so normal, so commonplace that he didn't really think of Henry as anything but a real friend. To see him appear like that and speak and then instantly vanish was disorientating for him.
"David what's wrong? You look like you've seen a ghost."
David collected himself and tried to think what to say next.
"What's the matter with you?"
"Nothing, nothing. I'm sorry. I should probably go."
"You've only just got here and you started to say something."
"Yes. I shouldn't have. Will you meet me after school tomorrow? I'll buy you a coffee at Costa."
"Well yes, but why go so soon? And what's this secret?"
"Oh, it's nothing important. Nothing of any real interest." David stood up to leave and she thanked him for the jewellery and asked him again, to stay longer. He left quite abruptly but thought that things were back to normal or would be if he could meet her for a coffee the next day. He was sure everything would be alright.
Henry showed up as usual after David went to bed that night.
"Why can't I tell Jenny about you? Why is it such a secret?"
"Why do you want to tell her?"
"I don't know, it's just something I thought I could

share with her. I thought she would understand and it would make our friendship closer."

"I hope I can be of some use but I can't help you if you go telling everyone you're talking to a dead man. You'll end up in an asylum. Once you get into them places there's no getting out."

"My mum knows I talk to you; she hears me all the time."

"That's different. Your mum isn't about to go and tell anyone. As far as she's concerned you've an imaginary friend and that's just a bit eccentric. Not mad. A lot of people would think you'd got a screw loose."

"Jenny wouldn't tell anyone!"

"You don't know that David."

David let it go but Henry reassured him that if he did spread their secret more widely, he wouldn't hear from Henry again. He wanted a closer friendship with Jenny but not at the expense of losing Henry.

A week later David was walking through the park during his lunch hour. He frequently came to the Memorial Park to eat his lunch but he had never seen Maria there. She was all alone and he thought that this was a chance for him to speak to her, having been too timid to speak to her in school. As he approached his confidence started to ebb away. She seemed to be talking to someone, although there was no one else there, her arms were moving in conversational gestures. He thought it looked very odd. Maria, he knew, had held herself aloof

from all the boys in school who had approached her and that made the thought of starting a conversation with her all the more terrifying. The closer he got the less confident he became. He decided to walk off the path and walk behind her so that he could go past her without being seen. As he was stumbling through the bushes behind her, like a blundering spy, he could hear her conversation. She was speaking to someone in Spanish. He had longed to speak to her in Spanish. Actually, he had longed to speak to her in English or any other language come to that. He hid in the bushes and listened. It took him a while to tune into the language but after a few minutes he started to understand the occasional phrase: "Deberías hablarle a tu madre sobre nosotras. Si no se lo puedes decir a tu padre, díselo a tu madre. Te quiero, Marta."
(You should tell your mother about us. If you can't tell your father tell your mother. I love you Marta.)
David struggled to follow the conversation. He could follow quite complex conversations when he was in Spain but Maria was speaking at an impossible speed. He was tempted to ask her to slow down but as he was eavesdropping, he thought that might be inappropriate. He understood *te quiero,* she was in love with someone! That wasn't good news. *Marte or Madre.* Her mother. She loved her mother. That was better news!
"Por supuesto que quiero seguir viéndote. Eres la única amiga real que tengo, pero no podemos

mantener nuestra relación a escondidas por siempre, cariño. Llevamos juntas ya dos años y quiero decírselo a todo el mundo."

(Of course, I want to carry on to see you. You are the only real friend I have but we cannot keep our relationship secret for ever my love. We have been together for two years now and I want to tell everyone")

David couldn't understand everything that was said, he couldn't hear clearly and thought he should move closer. He knew that Maria wanted to uncover some secret but her mother didn't. That much was clear to him. However, someone had told him that she had lost her mother when she was young, her father had moved to England to marry a local girl, Maria's step mother. He always knew he had something in common with Maria. Both of them had lost a parent in early childhood. The germ of an idea started to grow in David's head.

"Se que es difícil, pero puedes hacerlo. Eres mayor que yo y más fuerte que yo. No creo que tu madre se enfade y si lo hace, nadie va a morir por ello."

("I know it's difficult but you can do it. You are older than me and stronger than me. I don't think your mother will be angry and if she is, nobody is going to die.")

David's thoughts ran away on a trajectory all of their own; "She's not talking to herself; she's talking to a missing mother or even a mother who has died! She was talking to the ghost of her mother!" He grew so excited that he nearly fell over and the bushes behind Maria's head were shaking and rustling as if possessed. Maria however, was engrossed in her one-sided conversation and didn't notice.

"El próximo año estaremos en el mismo colegio, Marta, juntas todos los días. ¡Ser lesbiana ya no es un crimen! Todo el mundo lo sabrá cuando nos vea todo el rato juntas. ¡Alguien se lo dirá a tus padres! Es mejor que ellos se enteren por ti. Cuando se lo dije a mi padre fue difícil, pero él acabó aceptándolo. Ni siquiera parecía disgustado."

("Next year we will be at the same college Marta, we will be together every day. Being Gay is not a crime. Everyone will know when they see us together. Someone will tell your parents. It's better they find out from you. When I told my father, it was difficult but he just accepted it. He didn't even seem disappointed.") Maria's speed of delivery was at such a fever pitch David could follow very little but picked up the odd word here and there. It was like trying to catch bullets from a machine gun. There was a long silence as Maria listened to whatever voices were inaudible to David.

"No estoy enfadada contigo, mi amor, sino con lo ridículo de la situación. Te quiero; siempre te he querido desde la primera vez que nos conocimos."

("I am not angry with you my darling but with the ridiculous situation. I love you. I always have since the first time we met.")

There was another pause while Maria listened and
then she said,
"claro, podemos quedar mañana..."
("of course, we can meet tomorrow........")
It was at this point that David leaned forward in the
vain hope that he might be able to hear more
clearly and understand more of the conversation. It
was also at this very point that he fell out of the
bushes, hit his head hard on the back of the park
bench and fell to the ground behind, and almost
underneath Maria.
Maria was obviously startled, said a hurried
goodbye to her friend and stood up, putting the
phone and the earpiece away in her pocket, more or
less, in one swift movement.
David looked up through the gap in the park bench
but could only see Maria's magnificent legs.
"Hola," he said in what he thought was a perfect
accent, "Esa Es Maria?"
Maria didn't speak. Probably couldn't speak. She
just looked at him with a death stare.
David stood up slowly. "Como estas?" he said.
"I'm fine," she said. "Have you lost your mind?"
"No, lo siento." (I'm sorry)
"It might be better if we continue in English."
"Si, you're right."
"What the hell do you think you were doing?"
"I'm sorry, I really am but I was walking past and I
overheard what you were saying and....."
"You didn't understand it. Did you?"

"Not all of it but I think I got the gist of it."

"Well you shouldn't go around hiding in bushes listening to private conversations, it's insane!"

"I'm sorry."

"So you keep saying."

They stood for a while just looking at each other wondering what to say next. Maria looking immaculate as ever, David with a cut lip that was bleeding and large bruise on his forehead and some leaves in his hair.

"Whatever you heard me talking about," she said, "you must realise that it was a private conversation between me and, well it doesn't matter who it was, you must not tell anyone about it under any circumstances!"

David reassured her that he wouldn't tell anyone.

"You can trust me Maria. Honestly. I won't tell a soul. I mean, I wanted to tell a friend about my situation but I can't."

Maria, bewildered, shook her head.

"Let's just say that I think I have the same sort of relationship with a special friend and I can't share it with anyone. If I did tell someone, well it would cause problems." David gave her what he thought was a significant look and nodded his head to emphasize the point. The effect was spoiled somewhat, by several leaves that fell out of his hair and floated slowly to the ground.

"What do you mean?"

"I mean, I have a *special* friend, you have a *special*

friend. So, we are both in the same situation, so to speak."

"So, you......"

"Yes. Does that surprise you?"

"Well I suppose not. You seem to find it difficult to find friends and......"

"We have a lot in common Maria."

"We do?"

"I would love to tell the world about my friend Maria. He's been my constant companion for years now but I just don't think most people would understand. I wanted to share the secret with someone just the other day but he stopped me and said if I did, I would never see him again."

"That's awful!" she said.

"I think," David said and paused to add melodramatic affect, "I think that *you* may be in a similar situation."

"You seem to have understood quite a lot of my conversation." she said.

"Thank you," he said proudly.

Maria seemed reassured. "Your lip is bleeding," she said.

"I think I fell for you," he said.

She laughed. "It's no bad thing that someone knows about my 'special relationship', as you call it. Shall I tell you who it is?"

"No! Don't do that. I can't tell you about my friend so I don't think you should tell me about yours. I can't tell you who he is, but just the fact that you know he exists makes things seem better. It will be good to know that there is someone in school who shares the same, the same situation."

"Well that's an odd way of putting it but you're right. It feels good that someone knows she exists, even if you don't know her name."

Why don't we sit down and eat?"

"That would be lovely."

The two new friends sat and shared a lunch together. David had found a friend and fallen deeply in love with one of the most beautiful girls he had ever seen. Maria had found a friend that she felt comfortable with in the sure and certain knowledge that, like her, he was gay.

Chapter 6.

The Inspector greeted the negotiator who had arrived from Hutton. "Fifteen minutes!" she said with enthusiasm, "blue lights all the way. What's the situation now?"
"He's still up there, we haven't approached him. His mother is in the car over there."
"I'll chat to her while we travel up to the scene. Have you got the scene secured?"
"That's pending. Go and have a chat with his mother and we can set off in a few minutes."
"No, we need to set off now. It's going dark Inspector."
"I can see that but there's an access situation."
"Meaning?"
"The incident unit caravan, it's stuck on a bend half way up, and nobody can get past."

David was about to go up to his room after tea one night but his mother stopped him. "I want to have a word with you David," she said. "There's a couple of things." She had him sat down at the dining table now. "First, you're sixteen next month and I think you should have a party."
"I hate parties."
"I know, but it's time you grew up a bit and got to like them. Liking parties is part of growing up. You need to learn to socialise more."

"Mum, I'll do anything, but please don't make me have a party."

"David you are nearly sixteen, you're no longer a child. It's time you learned to mix with people and make more friends."

"I am, I am. I've even got a girlfriend!"

"This is Maria I suppose. The Maria we've never met."

"Well. She lives miles away."

"There are buses."

David squirmed in his chair, and looked even more miserable than he felt. If he stayed silent long enough, perhaps his mother would let him go.

"Does she even exist David?"

"What do you mean?"

"We've never seen her. She never calls you on the phone. What kind of girlfriend is that? Your brother's girlfriends were never off the phone. Same with your sisters' boyfriends, we could never get rid of them. This girlfriend of yours hasn't shown her face, she's never phoned you. Do you ever call her?"

"We spend a lot of time together at school."

"I'm worried about you David."

"But why, I'm happy mum. Happier than I've ever been. Everything's going well at school. Nobody bothers me. I talk to the teachers now. I talk to Jenny and I spend a lot of time with Maria."

"And every night you go upstairs and talk to your imaginary friend."

"Not that again."

"You're nearly sixteen now David not a child. Small children have imaginary friends. I know you've never known your father. I know it's *good* to have a father substitute as you're growing up but..."

"But what?"

"I think Maria is imaginary too."

"She's not mum, she's real. Honest! Cross my heart. I'll prove it."

"Alright, alright. But if you have real friends, this Maria at school, Jenny, why do you persist with this other friend? He's not real."

"He's real to me mum. I know everything about him, where he grew up, what boat he shipped out on to India, where he was based. I've got his whole military record. I know the dates he was in hospital with a gunshot wound. Where he fought, where he was captured. I know the names of his parents, his brothers and sisters.

"David, you're describing Henry Bradshaw. Your Dad found out all that information about him. He got his war record from the internet. He visited his family. He even went down to the museum in Winchester. Your Dad recorded all those details for the book he was going to write. You've read all that stuff in your Dad's files. It isn't Henry that told you. It's all in your head David. He isn't real. It's time you let it go. You spend hours talking to this ghost from a hundred years ago. I can hear you upstairs at night. I have the TV on loud to blank it out but I know it's going on. It's not natural."

"But what's natural mum? Some kids at school are on cannabis, cocaine, painkillers and inhalants, even during the lunch break. Some of them will drink vodka at the weekend until they collapse. What's natural about that? There's one of everything at that school, bisexuals, transexuals, homosexuals. That's all natural. You've got a son that doesn't do drugs, doesn't drink, doesn't wet the bed, he gets a bit down and lonely sometimes, and talks to an imaginary friend most nights. Is that so unnatural?"

"No. I'm not saying you're a bad lad. I'm just trying to help David." She pulled her mouth into a tight-lipped pout. She was trying to hold back her tears.

"I'll talk quieter if that helps mum."

She smiled at him. "You're a good lad. I know that. But what do you talk about?"

"He tells me stories about the war. How he was captured and sent to Chemnitz in the East near the Polish border. How he was punished in the camp for answering back, had his head shaved and put on bread and water for two weeks. In the middle of winter half-starved he tried to escape but was recaptured, hung up by his thumbs and whipped with wire. Another time he was put in front of a firing squad, blindfolded, and the order was given to shoot. He heard the firing pin hit the chamber on the rifle, but nothing happened. The guards were all laughing at him as they took off the blindfold. He only weighed seven stone when the war ended, they didn't send him home straight away because he was so sick and thin. He didn't get home until 1919."

"It's not like that in the films is it?" Irene said. "I thought they all vaulted over boxes and dug tunnels and dropped the soil down their trousers and called each other 'chaps'. It all sounds a bit grim to me David. Does he talk about anything else, or is it always about the war?"

"No. He told me about his girlfriend who he met on leave. About his brother who emigrated to Australia. About his wife and his children. I even know where he's buried."

"He didn't tell you that I suppose?"

"I found it in the Parish Records."

"You never cease to amaze me David." She was silent for a moment. "How does all this help you though? All this terrible stuff he tells you about the war? What good does it do?"

"Well, it helps me when I get down, if I feel a bit depressed. I think of everything that happened to him and how he managed to carry on. How he managed to have a life and wife and family after being shot and captured and beaten and he never seemed to get depressed. So, if somebody picks on me at school, it doesn't bother me anymore, it used to get me down, Wayne and his gang. I was frightened of them but when I listen to Henry's stories, I can see that I've nothing to be frightened of."

"I can tell you David. Your father would be very proud of you, you know. I'm sure he's looking down on you. I like to think so anyway."

"I often wonder what he was like," he said, glancing at the black and white photograph in a frame on the shelf.

"He was a lovely man, best thing that ever happened to me."

"What exactly happened mum? In the accident? You never talk about it."

"I wonder why?" she asked with a cheerless laugh. "It was just a stupid accident. Just bad luck. Just one of those tragedies that happens every day. The sort of thing that you read about in the paper in the morning over breakfast and have forgotten about by dinner time. Just another road accident. Just something that turns your world upside down in an instant and breaks your heart every day for the rest of your life."

David could see that his mother was beginning to get upset again so he left it alone. He knew his Dad had died in a car on the motorway travelling back from work. That's all he knew, because that is all he'd been told.

"Well think about that party," she said and left him alone, walked down the stairs and switched on the TV.

David looked forward to going to school with even more enthusiasm now that he could spend time with Maria. He wasn't actually dating her in the true sense of the word but she seemed to want to talk to him in between lessons and during the break times. Their relationship caused some consternation among the other boys in the school and even some of the girls seemed surprised. Amanda wanted to know all about Maria. Jenny, on the other hand, seemed to have no interest in the girl at all. The most severe reaction came from Ian Jones. Ian had always been pleasant to David, or at least he'd never caused him any problems. The fact that David had befriended Maria seemed to annoy him. He started to make cruel comments about David's appearance and his clothes and the fact that he lived in a terraced house on the wrong side of town. Ian lived on the same fancy estate as Jenny but that had never been an issue before. Jenny told him that Ian had asked Maria out on a few occasions and had always been turned down. Ian Jones didn't often hear the word 'no' when he asked a girl for a date. David's relationship with Maria moved slowly. She agreed to help him with his Spanish and he helped her with French and German. They talked about college and what subjects they thought they might do at Advanced Level. Maria wanted to do languages at University. David wasn't sure what to do.

"You get top marks in everything," she said to him. You could do anything you want but I think you should do languages. You could be an interpreter. That would be so cool."

"My science teachers tell me I should do a science
degree, but I particularly like Maths."
"Mathematics is difficult."
"So are languages."
"Not for you," she said, "it seems to come so easy to
you."
"You don't see the hours I put into it," he said.
"Everyone says it comes easy to me but I've never
really had any friends, even at primary school, my
friends were all on the library shelves. My
conversations were with books, tapes and CD's"
"You have your *best* friend," she said
conspiratorially.
"Yes, I suppose so."
He thought he ought to ask her out for a date but
what form the date would take and how to arrange
it was, despite his great intellect, way beyond his
capabilities. The more time he spent with her the
more he desired her. He had kissed her many times,
but only in his imagination and his night time
dreams. He understood the mechanics of sex but
how to overcome the logistical difficulties of getting
started on the process, were a complete mystery to
him. His mother had tried to start a safe sex
conversation with him many times but it was
inevitably Jenny who he turned to for advice.
It was over one of their many meetings in the Costa
Coffee shop that he broached the subject.
"Jenny can I ask you something?" That's the
question that always appears just before a really

embarrassing or inappropriate conversation.

"You're going to ask it anyway."

"It's about Maria," he said, and paused to see how she would react.

"Go on."

"Well we get on ok, I mean we talk a lot in school, it's difficult because she lives at the other side of Preston you see."

"End of the earth then."

"I help her with German and French and she helps me with Spanish."

"It sounds like a very passionate relationship, I hope you don't get her pregnant."

"That's just it Jenny."

"She's not?....."

"No."

She looked at him with sympathy and sadness, "You haven't got past first base have you David?"

"I wish I was approaching first base. If I could see it in the distance, I would be happy. Getting to it would be great. Getting past it is beyond my wildest dreams."

"David, why are you telling me all this?"

"I thought you might be able to advise me."

Jenny shook her head in disbelief. She looked at him with concern. "You did this with Amanda. You fall for someone who had no feelings for you. It's almost as though you are too frightened to have a real relationship with a girl. It's as if you want to fail. Like succeeding is far too worrying. Sex is a two-way thing. There has to be mutual attraction. All you ever do is have this daydream romance that doesn't really exist, because you have no relationship at all with this girl of your dreams, because deep down you're too frightened of having a real relationship."

"I think she likes me," he protested.

"It doesn't sound like it if all she wants is help with her schoolwork."

"We talk about other things!"

"Like what?"

"Chemistry."

"Christ David. You'd be better off dating a text book."

David stirred his coffee and looked at the swirling liquid for inspiration.

"Do you have a boyfriend Jenny?"

"Do I have a boyfriend? What a question. You'll be asking me next if I have sex."

He wanted to ask her that, very badly, and nearly did but drew back from the precipice just in time and said nothing.

"David, can I ask *you* a question?"

"Anything Jenny."

"Do you think you might be gay?"

David looked as if he had been stung. "Gay?" He said this far too loudly and he attracted stares from a dozen coffee drinkers at nearby tables. "What makes you think I'm gay? He whispered. "Do I look Gay?"

"You don't have to mince about like Alan Carr and

Julian Clarey to be gay David and there's nothing to be ashamed of. It's not a crime anymore. Just admit it to yourself if you prefer boys to girls. "
"But I don't!"
"Are you sure?
"Of course I'm sure."
"You sounded ever so gay when you said that," she said, laughing.
"Stop messing about. I'm not gay. If I was, I would tell you."
"Well if you *really* like the girl you are just going to have to bite the bullet and ask her out. Nobody can do it for you."
He stared at her in silence.
"You haven't even kissed her, have you?"
"It's difficult."
"No it isn't David. German French and Chemistry is difficult. Kissing is easy."
"It might be easy for you..."
"That's enough David, you need to grow up and stop thinking and start acting. Just do something. Ask her out. Take her to the movies. Jump on her in the bike sheds. Just do something and stop dithering. Why can't you do the easy things when all the difficult things come so easy to you?"
"If I were in love with you Jenny it would be easier, I can talk to you, I'm relaxed with you. With Maria, I'm on edge, I never know what to say."
"If you love someone David, you always know what

to say, you even know what the other person is thinking, without them saying a word."

"Do you really think so?" he said with genuine curiosity.

She looked at him, but didn't say a word.

"You really do, don't you?"

"Yes David. I really do." She moved back in her chair and stood up. "I have to go. I'll see you later."

"Yes, thanks Jenny. I'll call you tomorrow."

She smiled at him, called him an idiot, and left.

It was in the Academy dining hall that David took the plunge and asked Maria for a date. After his dining hall proposal to Amanda in the Primary School it was a brave decision to choose such a crowded venue.

"Maria, could I take you out one night?" He tried to speak calmly, as if asking a girl our for a date was something he did all the time.

"Yea, cool," she said. She had developed a habit of saying 'cool' every couple of minutes for no discernible reason.

"So, is that a yes?" He hated it when people started a sentence with 'So'. He was always shouting at the radio when people answered a question and started the answer with the word – 'So'. Now he had started doing it too. It always drove him mad when people ended a sentence with so, but starting a sentence with so was even worse.

"So, when and where?" she said.

"So, where would you *like* to go?" he said.

90

"So, there's like a really good club I know in Preston."

"So, we could go there?"

"Cool," she said.

He wondered why it had taken him four months to pluck up the courage to ask her out. It wasn't like he had to go over the top and walk slowly towards a machine gun. He sat there in a daze. Jenny was right. These things were easy. Not like Chemistry at all. Perhaps kissing might be next. He had left the trench and moved forward. With any luck the artillery would have blown large gaps in the wire.

"Bring your friend if you like," she said, giving a little giggle. She giggled a lot these days. Maybe she was happy. It was more of a nervous laugh than a hearty belly laugh. Almost a cough. Sometimes she would start a sentence she thought was funny and start laughing half way through, which made the second part inaudible. He didn't comment on it because he was so pleased when she spoke to him that he didn't want to interrupt her and halt the flow of her conversation. He also liked the lilt of her Spanish accent and the small grammatical mistakes that sounded cute from her but would have been really annoying from someone less glamorous. Despite the taunts from some of the boys, this was the best of times for David. He had a date with the most beautiful girl in the school. He hoped it might go better than his date with Amanda.

His mother was delighted that he was going out. Most mothers worry when their children decide they are going out for the first time on a Saturday night but she was pleased for him, not least because the mystery girl Maria might be real after all. Not only did she seem pleased to have him go on a date, and all the way to Preston, she stopped badgering him about having a birthday party. She helped him get ready for the great event and bought him a new white shirt. "We don't want you going looking like a tramp, now do we?"

He had arranged to meet Maria at the bus station and he arrived far too early. It was a concrete shrine to the sixties. It was a huge multi storey car park with a concourse on the ground floor where the buses came and went. It was like something you might find in Eastern Europe, built in the Soviet Era. A monument to the glories of reinforced concrete. The concourse was a depressing mixture of metal railings and concrete pillars. It was the sort of scene you might choose to make a film about drug abuse and street crime. David stared with some trepidation at everything going on around him. He had never been out on a Saturday night before. He found it slightly alarming. Everybody else seemed relaxed; young people walking around, meeting friends, standing in groups laughing and joking. He felt like an alien in a strange land. He sat on a bench and waited for Maria. He wondered what she would be wearing. He had only ever seen her in school uniform. She looked so much more glamorous than the other girls in school. They all wore extremely short skirts and black stockings or bare legs. Maria was no different but she had beautiful legs, long, slim and tanned. If you've got it you should flaunt it and if you haven't you should cover it up. Her school blazer and blouse were always immaculate and she wore her dark hair long and flowing down her back and occasionally tied up into a ponytail. Her skin was flawless and always tanned, even in winter. She was, David thought, just the most perfectly beautiful girl on the planet.

As he sat there in a reverie, he was approached by a girl in fish net stockings and boots with platform soles and long thin heels. He could see her walking towards him but he looked the other way. He thought she might be a prostitute. From the corner of his eye he could see she had a tiny black leather skirt, more fish net over her abdomen and a black bra that had metal studs and little tiny mirrors that caught the light. She had blonde hair with tight curls and a white face and dark purple lips. She looked like a walking cadaver.

"You cool?" She said to him.

He looked up. It was Maria. He couldn't find words. "You have not brought your friend?" she said. The voice hadn't changed but everything else had. She was wearing a dog collar with spikes on it. Everything she wore was black except her skin which seemed to have been bleached white. Her

eye make-up started at her eyes but continued
down her face in thick triangular shapes like black
starfishes or explosions. There was a blood-red line
on her eyelids which made her look very ill. Her
eyebrows seemed to have disappeared altogether
and reappeared further up her forehead, almost
touching the hairline of her blonde curly wig. She
had an industrial looking bolt in one ear.
"Your hair?" he said at last.
"Yea, I hate it. This is really cool though." She
moved a hand towards the wig. All her finger nails
had turned black.
"You've never seen me all dressed up before."
David's mouth moved but words wouldn't come and
he mouthed in silence like a goldfish stuck in a bowl.
"Let us go down to the club." She seemed happy to
see him. That was something, so he left the bench
and followed her. He in his best jacket and trousers,
new white shirt, polished shoes, hair brushed. They
walked side by side, the clean-cut kid and the Goth.
He resisted the temptation to hold her hand.
"You're quiet," she said, "I think you'll like a lot the
club. We go most weekends."
"Ama Zombie," he said.
"That's right. Not far now."
When they arrived, they joined the queue. Most of
the people in the queue seemed to be dressed for
one of those bars you see in the Star Wars movies.
There were lots of boys with make- up, some with
ear rings, some with nose rings, several with both.

Extremely tight jeans were common, as were designer underpants that showed above the waistline of the jeans. David's underpants were from Marks and Spencer and he would never dream of having any part of them on show. There were lots of the girls wearing similar outfits to Maria's and some dressed in men's suits. He couldn't help but stare at one boy who had the longest ear lobes he had ever seen outside of a National Geographic Magazine. They had been stretched by enormous button like devices that he wore in each ear. He stared at him and the boy caught his eye and gave him an extremely friendly smile. Most of the queue stared back at David as if he was some sort of oddity. As they waited in the queue, he heard the word 'geek' uttered in his direction several times. The club was down steep stone steps that Maria negotiated with ease despite the thin sixteen-centimetre heels that looked like polished spikes. He was given a queer look by the bouncer who seemed reluctant to let him in, dressed as he was, like a normal human being.

"I said I'd meet Marta inside!" Maria seemed excited as they entered the club itself. They walked towards the bar, Maria confidently walking like a model on a catwalk. David followed like a hunted animal with his hand pressed against his jacket to make sure his wallet was safe.

"Maria!" A short girl in tight black jeans and enormous boots came running over towards Maria.

The girl in the jeans, like Maria was all in black, but her hair was black too, and short. David thought she looked more like a boy than a girl and that thought was reinforced when Marta and Maria greeted each other with a passionate kiss that seemed to go on for ten minutes. This was no peck on the cheek. David stood there and watched. It was like something from a porn film. He could see the short girl firing her tongue into Maria's mouth. Maria was moaning like an injured bear. David couldn't decide whether to have an erection or throw up. He did neither but couldn't take his eyes off his 'girlfriend' snogging with the short girl in the tall boots. They finished eventually and Maria said, "This is Marta." The girl stepped towards David, who took a step back. He was half expecting a similar greeting to the one Maria had received but Marta only shook his hand and said, "Hola!"

When he heard her voice, he decided that she was definitely female.

"This is my *special* friend David. You meet her at last."

"You didn't bring your friend David?" Marta asked.

"No, no I didn't." David felt humiliated but the dim lighting in the club hid the colour coming to his face. Maria's special friend was Marta not her dead mother or *madre muerta*. Jenny wasn't the only one who thought he was gay.

"Let's get a drink, "said Maria and walked towards the bar.

They found a booth at the back of the club and
David watched the dancing while Maria and Marta
spoke in Spanish. His desire to progress his fluency
in the language had temporarily left him. He was
fascinated by the club and its clients. Most of them
were adults, only a few around his own age. There
was a bearded man wearing a dress, serving behind
the bar. Marta said he was called Penelope. The two
girls had spent the first half hour alternatively
laughing, chatting, and stroking each other. With
the preliminaries over they started snogging in
earnest. David thought they might have sex right
there in the booth and he couldn't help speculating
on what form the sex act might take. There was a
lot of moaning and groaning but eventually they
came up for air and Maria set off back to the bar.
Their heavy petting was clearly thirsty work. Left
alone with Marta he thought he might try and make
conversation but Marta beat him to it. She leaned
towards him and shouted in his ear, "When did you
come out David?"
Even David knew that she didn't want to hear what
time he left the house.
"I'm not gay." He shouted back.
She laughed at him. It was hardly surprising that she
thought he might be joking.
"You're transgender?"
David shook his head. "No," he said. He almost felt
like crying. He stared at the crowded bar and the
gyrating dance floor and wondered what on earth

he was doing in Ama Zombie. "You couldn't make this stuff up," he said to himself. He watched Maria waddling back from the bar in those ridiculous boots and that outfit that had transformed her, from one of the prettiest young girls he had ever seen, into a walking cadaver in fish net tights. That's when he started laughing. Once he'd started, he couldn't stop. The girls seemed pleased that he was having a good time at last. He thought of himself, hiding in the bushes and listening to Maria. He thought of Jenny calling him an idiot. What kind of idiot is it that tells a girl that he has a special friend who visits him most nights in his room? "I can't tell you about him!" he'd told her. He started laughing again.

"Do you remember what I said Maria? I wanted to share the secret with someone but *he* stopped me and said that if I did, I would never see him again. That's what I said. It's priceless!"

"What's he on?" asked Marta.

"Cannabis, got to be. He certainly has the giggles. He always seems so straight at school. I thought he was a strait-laced geek. His mother's cool too. She lets them make out in his room most nights."

"Cool!"

"It wasn't your mother you were talking too," he said, almost breathless with tears in his eyes, "it was Marta and I thought it was Madre!" His laughter subsided at last and he held his tummy as if he was in pain.

It was later that a young man, with half his head shaved and the other half glued up in Spikes, came over and asked David if he wanted to dance. That set David off again. He roared with laughter and tried to stop but couldn't and he kept waving his hand at the lad as a sort of apology but more tears came and he was helpless.

"What's wrong with him?" the grim looking youth said to the two girls.

"He's just high," Marta said.

David nearly screamed with laughter at that "I've had two lemonades!" he roared. The girls laughed too. It was contagious. The grim looking youth with the glue in his hair didn't laugh. He just grunted and walked away.

"It's great here isn't it David?" Maria said, when he'd recovered.

"Yes, it's fabulous," he said, "thanks for letting me come and meeting me at the bus station. It's been a great evening but I'll go now. I've got a bus to catch."

The girls protested that it was far too early to think about leaving but David left anyway. He was still smiling when he sat on the top deck of the number fifteen bus back to Padiham.

Chapter 7.

The negotiator walked towards the police car, for a chat with David's mother. She opened the car door, smiled and was nearly knocked over as Irene got out of the car.

"Mrs Watson, please, just wait a moment," she said. A constable stepped in front of Irene to halt her progress towards the quarry.

"Mrs Watson, can I call you Irene?"

"You can call me what you like love, if David's up there I'm going to get him down."

"I seriously, would not recommend that Irene."

"Well what would you recommend? Get out of my way you great oaf!" she said to the constable who was standing with his hands up, as if someone had pulled a gun on him. "I've been in that car long enough watching this pantomime, they set off half an hour ago with half a dozen vehicles and a caravan, now the fire brigade's arrived. What do you think he's going to do? Set himself on fire? If you don't get out of my way this minute you great lummox, I'll land you one, God help me if I don't."

"Mrs Watson, Irene, please wait, have you perceived any signs of Suicidal Ideation?"

Irene hadn't heard the negotiator's question. She had already set off up the quarry road. The negotiator ran behind her, asking her more questions.

The week after David's visit to the club, he was keen to see Jenny and tell her about his date. He knew she'd find it funny. He saw her in classes and they exchanged some brief conversations but there was never an opportunity of sitting down with her in private. He was a little disappointed that she hadn't asked him about it. His mother had asked him, of course, but he had only told her that he had enjoyed it. He didn't tell her why. He sent a couple of texts inviting Jenny to join him for a coffee or visit him at home but she answered that she was busy, swatting for the end of year exams. At the end of the week he mentioned his frustration to his mother. "I thought Jenny might have called down to see us."

"Well why don't you call on her for a change? You never visit her and she's always calling here."

"It's Friday night, she'll be out."

"Well call her."

"I did there was no answer."

"Well If she's revising for exams her phone might be switched off. Go up and see her, you don't have to stay long. Her mum was only saying you should call on her sometime. It's always Jenny who comes to see you. It's about time you returned the favour."

He set off down the street and along the footpath to the park. Up the hill to the top of the town and onto Woodlands Estate; a prestigious development of executive style properties. A world away from Altham Street but only a ten-minute walk. The house had a fountain in the front garden. Jenny said that the sound of running water was very therapeutic but it was switched off at bedtime. She said the noise caused her Dad to keep getting up in the middle of the night. He knocked on the door. Her father opened it. "It's you!" he said. Jenny's father thought David was weird and didn't like him. Jenny's family lived in the best part of town and he thought there were more suitable boys her own age on 'Woodlands', with its mature trees and walled gardens. He couldn't understand why she kept up a long-standing friendship with someone who lived on a terraced street, overlooking the railway and Green Street Mill.

"Is Jenny in?"

"No."

"Do you know where she is?"

"She's gone round to Ian's."

"Ian Jones? Could you tell me where he lives please?"

"Shenandoah."

"Seriously?"

"Shenandoah, big white house at the end." He gestured towards the end of the avenue.

"Thank you, Mr Simpson." He headed in the direction of the gesture.

He found Shenandoah, it was a large white American Ranch style house with a steep roof and an attic window. It had a large front lawn, but no fountain, no rolling river. He walked up the path and knocked on the door. There was no answer. He knocked again, louder this time. Still no answer. He found the doorbell and tried that. He heard the sound of cow bells from inside. Eventually, Ian came to the door.

"Hi Ian," he said, trying to sound friendly. "Is Jenny with you?"

Ian looked surprised. He looked rather flushed and disorientated. He was normally so calm and self-assured.

"What do you want?" Ian seemed annoyed.

"I want to see Jenny."

Ian turned round and shouted, "Jen! David Watson's here!" A few moments later Jenny appeared behind Ian. "What's wrong David?"

"Nothing. I just came to see you. I wanted to have a chat. Mum said I should call on you."

"What about? Has something happened?"

"Well," he said smiling, "I had a date with Maria."

"What?"

"A date. You know you said I should do something. And I did."

Jenny seemed less self-assured than usual. "Did it go okay?"

"Oh no. It was a complete disaster."

"Well you seem very happy about it," Jenny said.

Ian made a loud tutting noise, turned on his heels and swore on his way back into his house.

"What did Ian say Jenny?"

"Something about not being able to make this shit up, I think."

"He seems to be in a mood."

"David. Ian and I are *babysitting*," Jenny said.

"Babysitting?"

"Yes."

"Has Mrs Jones had a baby?"

"There is no baby David."

"No baby? How can you be babysitting without a baby?"

Jenny gave him one of her significant looks.

"Oh. I see. I shouldn't have come, should I? I'm an idiot. I can't do anything right. It's just that the date was such a disaster but so funny, I wanted to tell you all about it. And I also wanted to tell you that you were right about what you said about me. I have been in denial. You could see it but I couldn't. I'm amazed it took me so long to work it out. You were right. I thought you'd like to know. Anyway, I'm going now. You need to look after the baby. It'll need a nappy or a bottle. Tell Ian I'm sorry. I'm off."

And he went. Jenny closed the door slowly after watching him disappear down the avenue.

It was harder for David to see the funny side of his date after his visit to Ian's house. He felt himself slipping into depression but was pushed out of the house by his mother who told him to go for a good long walk, which was her cure-all for melancholia of any kind. Exercise or work, that was her prescription for lethargy or despondency and syndromes and isms of any sort. David could always find solace in Henry and as he walked over the hills alone, he was never really without company.

A long walk and a chat with Henry helped him to avoid the 'Black Dog' of depression and he set off to school on Monday feeling better than he had at the weekend. His mother had given him his new white shirt to wear. It was a perk, for the boys in their last year at the academy, to wear a white shirt rather than the regulation grey that the younger boys wore. David was one of the last in the year change from grey to white. His mother didn't approve of unnecessary expense. His new white shirt helped to lift his spirits. Ian Jones glared at him when he arrived in class but when Ian noticed how pleased David was with his new shirt, he couldn't resist making fun of him.

"Your mum won the Lottery Donald? Expensive looking shirt." Ian didn't normally call him Donald. He never called him Donald when Jenny was around. David listened to the taunts all day but didn't react. Ian was probably annoyed about his visit to his house. David was able to chat with Maria and that made up for the taunts from Ian. She had metamorphosised from the black larva back into the beautiful butterfly and her attituded towards David hadn't changed since the night out. She still asked him about his special friend, and said she was keen to meet him. Everything was 'cool'. The last lesson

of the day was Geography and David was seated quite close to Ian. Before the teacher arrived, Ian couldn't resist one more effort to provoke David. "Hey everyone! Look how good Donald looks in his new shirt. His mum bought it for him at the jumble sale, and he's finally dumped the grey one."
There was a ripple of laughter from the class.
For once David reacted; "The problem with you Ian is that you confuse having money with having sense. Your Daddy might have money but that doesn't mean you're clever. It just means your Daddy has money. You would understand that if your IQ ever got above room temperature." David's comment brought a roar of approval and laughter from the class and Ian looked humiliated. He just sat in his seat and fumed. The teacher arrived and the lesson began, something about Winnipeg.
During the lesson David noticed spots of black ink appearing on his desk, on his hands and his exercise book. He glanced across at Ian, to see him waving his fountain pen that his dad had bought him for not coming bottom in the end of term exams. Ian's face was a picture of delight as he flicked the pen again and again in David's direction. He felt the ink hit his face and his neck and Ian couldn't help laughing out loud as he made a direct hit on David's new shirt. David glanced down at his shirt to see the polka dot effect. He had been so delighted to wear his white shirt for school and now it was covered in spots of black ink. The shirt was ruined. For once in his life

he didn't think, he just reacted. He picked up his Geography text book, walked the short distance across the aisle to Ian's desk and hit him in the face as hard as he could, with the book. It was a hard-backed volume entitled 'The World'. It probably weighed nearly a kilo. The weight of the book added significant force to the punch that hit Ian's left eye. David just hit him once and stood there, staring at him and shaking with emotion. Ian stood up with his hand over his injured eye. He looked unsure of himself as if he had just realised that David, who had been much smaller than him at the age of ten, had grown in height and strength to match the sixteen-year-old Ian. He moved towards David and swung a haymaker and missed. David pushed him away. Ian's attack petered out and the Geography teacher had arrived by now and was remonstrating with David.

Ian's eye was soon badly swollen, it looked like a blue egg. From the side he looked like one of those Aliens found in the Arizona desert. "I can't see!" he kept saying, even though his right eye was undamaged. Because he kept on saying that he was blind, which was clearly not true, they sent him to hospital as a precaution. He was later diagnosed as having a black eye. David was sent to see the Head of Year who wanted to know what had made him behave with 'such unprovoked violence'. "Unprovoked?" David said, "Just look at my shirt. It's ruined!"

"Don't you take that tone with me David. It's just a shirt. Ian is in hospital. You need to learn to control your temper." David's defence was his ruined white shirt but the Head of Year was unimpressed.

"You will be suspended from school with immediate effect. You can come in to take your exams, but at this stage I don't think you should come back to school other than to take the final exams."

"Well what about Ian?" David asked. "What are you going to do to him?"

"You can leave my office now David." The Head of Year was all professional and calm, which made David even more furious.

David explained to his mother what had happened when she got home from work and later that evening, she got a phone call from the Head of Year. David was surprised how calm she was about the whole incident. She didn't exactly congratulate him on what he'd done but he detected a small element of pride in the fact that he had fought back for once. Even when Ian's father phoned, even later in the evening, threatening legal action she still remained calm and told him, "You can sue us if you like but we've no money and you can't take off us what we haven't got, so if I were you, I wouldn't waste your time."

"Don't get down over this David. I know what you're like. Sounds to me like Ian was asking for it. He's made a right mess of your new shirt."

"I'm sorry mum"

"It's alright David. It'll all come out in the wash."
Being prohibited from attending school was not a
punishment for David. He was quite happy studying
on his own. It's what he had done most of his life
and he knew he would do much better in the final
exams without the distractions of school. What
made him unhappy was the fact that Jenny and Ian
were now going out together. Not only that, he had
given Ian a black eye. She wouldn't be pleased with
him. He also realised something else. Jenny had
been right about him always chasing dreams. She
was also right about the reasons for it too; it was
fear. He was frightened of what would follow if he
found a real girlfriend. Of all the girls in the school
Maria was the most unobtainable. Everyone had
failed to attract her so she was the one David
decided to fall in love with. It had been the same
with Amanda at Primary school.

*"It wasn't love at all," he said. "It was just stupid. I
was frightened Henry. Of a girl!"*

*"They're frightening things women." Came the reply.
"It's nowt to be ashamed of. We all get frightened of
women."*

David was embarrassed that he had been unable to
see what must have been obvious to the people
around him. He was supposed to be so clever, so
quick to learn. Why had it taken him so many years
to learn what was blindingly obvious? He was
immature, he was weak, he had lied to himself. It

wasn't Amanda or Maria that he had wanted. It was Jenny! He had always felt close to Jenny, always knew what to say to her, always enjoyed being with her, he felt comfortable in her company. He had no secrets with Jenny, apart from Henry.

"Why was I so stupid not to see it before?" he asked." And now it's too late. She's Ian's girlfriend now, and I've just smacked him in the eye. What a fool I must have looked, calling at Ian's house. And to tell them about my stupid date with Maria." He didn't know whether to laugh or cry, so did neither.

"I'll probably never see Jenny again." he moaned.

"Don't talk soft," Henry said. "Go and see her now, if you want to see her. If you don't want to see her, stay where you are."

"I will," he said. "I'll go and see her. But I'll ring her first. If she doesn't want to see me, well, at least I will have tried."

To his surprise Jenny agreed to meet him in town.

"I heard about you being suspended," she said after they had sat down with their usual Cappuccinos, "it seems a bit harsh."

"I'm not that bothered about that," he said, "I'm really sorry about coming to Ian's house though, and about hitting him. I shouldn't have done that."

"He shouldn't have been flicking ink at you. It was childish of him."

"What did he say about my visit, and about Geography?"

"Nothing worth repeating. I think he thought you

could have used a smaller book to hit him with."
"Yes, the Head of Year said he could have lost his
eye."
"It's not that bad. He made a fuss about it. He'll
survive."
"I thought you'd be angry with me?"
"No, not really. You were going to tell me about
your date with Maria," she said trying to lighten his
mood, "you said it was funny?"
"It was at the time, but it doesn't seem so funny
now."
"Why not?"
"Well Jenny, what you said about me, you know the
last time we met for coffee? Well I have thought
about what you said and I think you are right about
me. I mean, I couldn't see what must have been
obvious to everyone else but I see it now. I can see
it clearly for the first time."
Jenny looked shocked, "Have you told anyone else,
have you told your mum?"
"No, why should I tell my mum?"
"David, it's really important when you realise
something like that about yourself to share it with
people close to you. I'm pleased you shared it with
me first David, I really am."
"That's alright Jenny."
"No, I mean it. It means a lot to me."
They were silent for a while.
"You look lovely in those jeans Jenny and that top,
the colour suits you."

"Wow! She said, "This is the new David. You've come out and suddenly you're flirtatious."

"I wasn't flirting, I was just saying as I see it."

"Well you've either never seen it before, or you've seen it and never bothered to say it."

"I never saw it before Jenny."

"Well, it doesn't matter now, does it?"

"No, I suppose not."

He stirred his coffee again and looked sad so she asked him about his date with Maria. He told her in detail, how he met her and didn't even recognise her, how the people at the club were dressed. How shocked he was when Maria met Marta, when he realised that she was gay. He told her about the boy with the blonde hair that was half glued and half shaved and how he had his dance card marked. "I had my best jacket and trousers on, a new white shirt, my school shoes polished up. My mum wanted me to wear a tie but thank God I didn't. They kept staring at me Jenny because I looked weird!"

She laughed with him, and everything was good between them again.

"So, was it a gay club?" Jenny asked.

"I suppose it was."

"So are you going back?"

"Back? Why would I go back?"

"Well, because you're gay."

"I'm not gay!" He said in a very loud voice that caught the attention of most of the other coffee drinkers.

Jenny shook her head in disbelief, "But you said I was right about you. I asked you the last time you were here. I said I thought you might be gay. You just said you'd thought about it and realised you'd been in denial."

"No, Jenny, you were right about me being frightened, frightened of a relationship with a girl, that's why I was always chasing the unobtainable. Chasing what I couldn't have because I was too scared to get what I really wanted."

Jenny sat quietly for a moment to get things straight in her head.

"So, you're not gay?"

"No."

"Well that's good to know." She drank some of her coffee and then asked, "And what was it that you *really* wanted?"

"It was you Jenny. It was always you."

Jenny laughed with delight, "Well that's really good to know."

"Better late than never, eh Jenny?"

"It's never too late David."

"What do you mean?"

"What do you think I mean? You can ask me out. Ask me for a date if that's what you want."

"But you're going out with Ian, and you've been babysitting together."

"I'm not married to him," she said.

"Did he ask you?"

Jenny took hold of his head and pulled him towards her and kissed him. He pulled his head back in surprise but she pulled him back towards her and kissed him again. He didn't resist this time. She kissed him hard and passionately and he responded and held her close and felt her neck and her hair and her soft skin. He forgot completely about the other coffee drinkers, and the Costa staff, and the small crowd gathering in the street, looking at them through the shop window.

There was a ripple of applause when they'd finished and a shout from the back of the cafe, "He's not gay then?"

"What about Ian? David asked, when he'd recovered his equilibrium.

"You leave Ian to me," she said. "Come on let's get out of here." She stood up to go.

"I can't leave just yet Jenny."

"Why not?"

He glanced down at his trousers by way of explanation, she followed his glance and said, "Ooh, you're definitely not gay. Come on, hang your jacket on it, and let's go."

Jenny and David spent the whole summer together but much to David's dismay the relationship didn't change as much as he would have liked for the first few weeks. It developed. They held hands, kissed, talked. Mainly talked though. He had imagined that the relationship would instantly transform from a happy friendship, into an uninhibited relationship of wild passion. Full of moans and groans and rather sweaty and sticky struggles with clothes being ripped and inhibitions abandoned. Not so. Jenny, despite her earlier predictions found it difficult to end the relationship with Ian.

"I don't feel comfortable, you know, until I've broken up with Ian. It's difficult, we were only going out together for a few weeks, and now he won't take no for an answer. He said I hadn't given it a chance, which is true. He said we'd always got on well together, which is also true. I mean, I told him straight away that I wanted to finish it but he kept on asking me to give it another go, give him more time and I felt sorry for him. I thought he was going to cry."

"Ian, cry? I didn't think anything would make Ian cry but what does he think about us, spending so much time together? Isn't he jealous?"

"No, he's working a lot of hours at the supermarket, he's saving up for a motorcycle, so he doesn't have a lot of free time to go out. He isn't at all suspicious."

"But he must suspect that something's going on between us, I mean, we're always together."

"Yes, well I meant to tell you about that."

"About what?"

"He thinks you're gay."

"Did you tell him I was gay?"

"No, it was Amanda apparently, but everyone else is convinced you're gay as well. Someone must have seen you dancing with that blonde guy with the glued hair."

"I didn't dance with him."

"Well Amanda told Ian you did, and you were snogging him too."

"That's just a lie!"

"Well they say you shouldn't let the truth get in the way of a good story and apparently you are the talk of the town, well the talk of school anyway. That's why Ian isn't worried about us spending so much time together."

"So you didn't contradict him then?" David was getting agitated.

"Calm down David, I'm doing my best here. What was I supposed to tell him? I know he's not gay because I snogged him in Costa?"

"Well when are you going to tell him?"

"Like I said, I've told him and I'll just have to keep telling him until it sinks in."

David enjoyed the first weeks of his new relationship with Jenny. He had always enjoyed her friendship and company but the physical closeness and the sense of belonging was something new to him. He became aware of her sensuality, her smile had always cheered him, but now it provoked deeper feelings. In the past he had been happy to be in her company whereas now he felt pride just to be walking down the street with her. Previously he had valued the time he spent with his friend but without the aching and longing he now felt when they were apart. He had thought himself in love with Amanda and then with Maria but he had never before experienced the euphoria that his first real feelings of love had brought him. His mother was pleased to see the change in him but had no real idea what had caused it. She thought perhaps his exam results, which were excellent, had caused the change in his demeanour. She was certainly delighted and proud of her youngest son. There was a photograph of him in the local newspaper with a half a dozen other delighted students waving bits of paper. David hated the picture because he was standing next to Maria but his mother thought it was wonderful and ordered a print from the newspaper. She had it framed and hung in the hall so that everyone coming into the house would see it. "Oooh is that David with his exam results?" they would say, "And who's that very pretty girl beside him? Is that your girlfriend David? She looks lovely. What's her name David?"

"She's Maria!" his mother would say, with a surreptitious wink to her son.

The bonhomie at 29 Altham Street was ended by an unexpected visitor. David was in his room upstairs when the knock at the door came. He could hear voices downstairs and although he couldn't hear what was being said he could detect an atmosphere of unpleasantness. After a short while he was called down by his mother. He found Jenny's father sitting in an armchair, with a sour look on his face. He rarely smiled, in David's experience, but now he looked like he'd swallowed vinegar. He was a stocky little man and he sneered at David as he walked into the room.

"Well Stephen Simpson, you can say what you came to say to his face."

Jenny's Dad looked surprised. He'd said his piece and didn't really see why he should repeat it. David supressed a smile when he suddenly realised that Jenny's father's initials were SS.

"Well it's nothing to smile about lad," he said suddenly. "I've told your mother what I think and I'll tell you. I don't want you messing about with our Jenny any more. You're not to keep seeing her."

This did take the smile off David's face.

"Tell him, what you told me." David couldn't decide if his mother's anger was aimed at him or at Jenny's Dad but he suspected that they were both in big trouble.

"Well," started Jenny's father, less confident now. "She was seeing that nice lad Ian, and he's a good lad. I play golf with his dad. Jenny likes him and everything was going well until *he* came along. I won't have our Jenny seeing someone who bats for both sides, he's not wired up right he's not. I won't have it and that's an end to it. Worlds gone mad, all this gender chopping and changing from one thing to another. It's not right."

"Oh for God's sake man, stop your blather!" David's mother took over; "He's heard you went to a gay

club David, and danced with a lad and was snogging him too. He doesn't want his daughter seeing a homosexual. Is that right Stephen Simmons?"
Jenny's Dad nodded.
David laughed. "That's just rubbish." He said incredulous.
"Young Ian told me all about it. *He's* not a liar!"
"Neither is David. He's not gay either."
David shook his head slowly and looked at the two adults who were staring at each other. His mother had one of those expressions he'd seen in Clint Eastwood movies where Dirty Harry asks the paedophile weirdo if he's feeling lucky. Jenny's father had that rigid dumb expression of someone who has less imagination than the below average sheep.
"You're not gay, are you David?" his mother asked.
"No, I'm not gay," David said, "I've never had the slightest inclination or thought of being gay. I went on a date with a girl called Maria. She took me to this club called Ama Zombie, there were lots of gays there and Maria is gay too. I didn't know that when I asked Maria out for a date. I didn't dance with anyone and I didn't kiss anyone, I certainly didn't kiss any boys. Where the stories came from, I have no idea. I *have* been seeing Jenny and she told me she had told Ian that she wanted to finish with him but he wouldn't accept it. She told him several times but he wouldn't take no for an answer. That's

the truth. I'm not gay. I don't know how many times I have to say it."

"Well you're not to see Jenny again," was Mr Simpson's considered response.

David's mother had rather more to say; "You never told me that this club was a gay club David Watson." She only ever used his surname when she was completely furious with him. "You told me you'd had a good time when you got back."

"See. I told you," said Jenny's dad.

"You shut up. You've said quite enough for one day. Now, David, what else haven't you told me?"

"Well I didn't want to tell you about Jenny and me because she said to keep it quiet until it was all sorted out between her and Ian. I didn't tell you about the club because I knew you wouldn't like it, and I'd no intention of going back anyway. I didn't lie to you I just didn't tell you about it."

"Same thing," she said, "but Jenny is your girlfriend now, is that bit true?"

"Yes."

"Well that's good news. She's a lovely girl. Always cheerful and well-mannered, unlike her father," she said glancing across at Stephen.

Jenny's Dad opened his mouth at this point but David's mother was having none of it. "You be quiet Stephen Simpson, you always were as thick as two short planks when you were at school, why that wife of yours agreed to marry you I'll never know. It's easy to see who Jenny takes after. You should be ashamed of yourself at your age spreading second-hand gossip."

"Well he's not welcome at our house."

"Don't talk soft! If you tell Jenny she can't see David it'll just make her all the more determined to keep seeing him. You haven't got sense you were born with."

He looked at her with an angry scowl on his face but couldn't find a response.

"Go on, you can go home now. And don't forget your hat!"

Stephen left, with a look of relief on his face.

"I'm disappointed you didn't tell me the truth about that club David. It's not like you to be dishonest. Anyway, forget about it now, but keep away from Jenny's Dad. He's a bit of bully he is. Always was. You'll have to invite Jenny round here. She's always welcome."

"I always seem to attract bullies," he said to Henry later. "Why is that do you think? I'm like a magnet for morons. I never seem to get anything right. Everything's a mess."

"Don't get so down. It'll work out. She's a clever lass that Jenny. She won't let her Dad stop her seeing you. She'll find a way."

Chapter 8.

The Chief Inspector from Hutton had now arrived at the quarry and was having a hard time understanding why all his officers were at the base of the quarry when the potential incident was at the top.

"I was led to believe that you had an officer up top."

"Yes, PC Thompson. We called him down when we arrived. He's a trainee and just arrived this week. We sent vehicles up there as soon as he got down."

"But there's still no officers up there?"

"There's two access roads but only one out of sight of the boy."

"That doesn't tell me why we don't have anyone up there."

"It's the incident caravan sir, it's stuck on a bend and we can't get anything past."

"It's not possible to walk?"

"It's several miles, the road goes around and to the top of the quarry from the North side."

"Which idiot decided to send the caravan up there?"

"I'm looking into that as we speak, sir."

" Well get rid of the caravan, tip it over if you have to but get it off the road."

"I'll get onto that straight away sir."

"Where's the negotiator? I'll travel up with her."

"She's walking up the road sir."
"And why, is she walking up the road?"
"The boy's mother set off up the road, she refused to stay in the squad car any longer."
"I'm glad there's someone around her with a bit of initiative. I'll pick her and the negotiator up on the way. Make sure you get rid of that caravan. I want to be up there A.S.A.P."

When David told Jenny about her father's visit, she couldn't believe it. It took confirmation from Irene to convince her. "I can't believe he would do something like that," she kept saying. "He hasn't been his normal self recently. Mum says he's under pressure at work." Although Jenny was surprised and upset by her father's visit to his house, it didn't stop her seeing David. They spent the rest of the summer together but David stopped his visits to her house.

When the time came to move from the Academy to the college for Advanced Level studies, David was determined to make a good impression. He had been encouraged by Jenny to be more sociable. She told him that the secret was to 'show an interest in people'. David thought that sounded simple enough. He promised to try and not withdraw into himself. He didn't want to cut a solitary figure at the College as he had done at the Academy. The college was an opportunity for him to find new friends, students who hadn't known him before. He was looking forward to a fresh start. Now that his relationship with Jenny was well established, he seemed to have more self-confidence.

Mixing with students out of school uniform for the first time David was acutely aware of his lack of style. The first day he wore his best jacket and his old grey flannel school trousers. He stood out like the black face in a cathedral choir. Most of the girls wore tight jeans or just tights that hid no anatomical detail. Many of the boys had jeans that hung precariously low, just hanging on for dear life to their thighs leaving a large display area for designer underwear. There was a lot of jewellery on ears, through lips, chins and cheeks, and clipped into eyebrows, and to David's horror, he saw one boy with a ring threaded through his eyelid.

"That's got to get infected," he said to Jenny.

"You don't need to shout David." David had a habit of shouting when he got excited about something. The first day he found himself in the canteen, not a venue where he had always triumphed. He was sat around a large circular table and as usual Jenny was involved in animated conversation and seemed to know everyone. He looked across the table at her, she was laughing and gesturing with her arms as she spoke. There must have been half a dozen conversations going on at once and he was involved in none of them. He smiled occasionally and nodded his head to give the impression that he was listening in, on one of the many conversations. He felt disappointed that he wasn't contributing to any of the discussions. He thought he might have success with a tiny girl with green hair and blue lips, called Tamsin. In a brief moment when she wasn't involved in any of the conversations, he took his opportunity and 'showed an interest'.

"Do those ever get infected?" he asked her.

"What?"

"Those metal studs in your ears, and the ring in your eyebrow. I should think they might be possible sites for infection?"

She looked offended, but didn't respond.

"Are you new to the college?" he asked. As soon as he'd said it, he realised it was a stupid question because everyone at that table was new to the college. They'd all signed up that morning. However stupid the question she seemed to take it better than his first question, which he thought she would have found more interesting.

She answered him with a tiny thin voice that rose in pitch to the end of her reply as if she was asking a question, "This is my first day?"

"I don't know if it is or not," said David with an attempt at a smile, "that's why I asked you."

"It's my first day?" she said, in an even more timid voice.

David's first reply was an attempt at a joke and his second reply continued in the same vein. "Are you sure?" he said with an exaggerated crescendo.

"You're very rude?" she said tentatively.

David was surprised by that response but persisted.
He was determined to show interest. "What
subjects are you studying?" He asked.
She ignored him.
"I said, what subjects are you studying?" his voice
was a little too loud, as if he thought she was deaf.
Several of the group at the table looked in her
direction now and she felt under pressure to
answer.
"So, I'm doing media, fine art, and History?"
David thought she wasn't too sure about History but
decided to let it go. "What's your favourite era? In
History?"
"My favourite era?"
"Yes."
"So, I don't really have a favourite era?"
 "What about Modern History; first war, second
war, cold war, Gorbachev, Glasnost, Perestroika?"
David was speaking far too loudly now.
Tamsin muttered something inaudible.
"Why don't you leave her alone? Can't you see
you're upsetting her?" came a voice from the group.
He could see a circle of faces staring at him, like a
jury convinced of his guilt before the trial had even
started. Only Jenny's expression seemed mildly
sympathetic. Sympathy or disappointment? It was
hard to say.
"I was just making conversation." He said, rather
pathetically.
"You were making her cry." Said the voice. "Look!"

He looked, and the voice was right. There were tears in her eyes.

"I'm sorry! I really am." He had no idea what he was sorry about. In his mind he was showing interest. The trick Jenny had of showing interest and gaining friends was beyond him. The harder he tried the worse things got. It seemed to be a vicious circle from which there was no escape.

Jenny was able to explain it to him in simple terms. "You should have asked her questions she could answer, where do you live, what subjects are you doing?"

"I did, I did ask her what subjects she was doing."

"Then you made a joke that she didn't understand, then you asked her about Perestroika. She probably didn't know what Perestroika was, or Glasnost. She probably felt that you were trying to make her look stupid in front of the group. She was embarrassed."

"Well, if she didn't know what Glasnost meant she could have asked. Couldn't she?"

"And how would that have looked? In front of all those people she'd met for the first time? And you were shouting at her."

"I wasn't!"

"You're shouting now."

"Am I?"

"Yes."

"It's very difficult," said David, "being nice."

"It's not difficult at all and you are nice David. You just keep it very well hidden."

David and Jenny's relationship progressed as they worked through the first year of college. David struggled with his social skills but Jenny helped and advised him and David helped her with Chemistry and Biology. Jenny's father couldn't be moved on his low opinion of David but his wife Sandra was more sympathetic. Jenny wanted to be honest with her father rather than lie all the time about where she was going and who she was seeing but her mother persuaded her against it.

"Your father doesn't need to know that you two are going out together. We'll tell him you're just friends and see each other at college. He won't ask who you are seeing at weekends and if he doesn't ask, we don't need to tell him. You'll make things worse if you have it out with him Jenny. He's not the sort of man you can persuade once he's made his mind up, you just have to work round him. He'll come round in the end, but not if you try and force the issue. You see David at college and you spend a lot of time at David's house. Be satisfied with that. I know it's not easy love."

After several months of seeing each other they became more intimate and more adventurous with each other. David had asked Jenny frequently about when they could have 'full sex' as he called it. It was Jenny who controlled the level of intimacy and David who followed her lead.

"The main problem David, is where, not when."

"Here's the obvious place," David said, glancing around his bedroom, as if assessing the suitability of the fixtures and fittings for intercourse.

"Your bedroom?"

"Why not?"

"Well your mother sitting downstairs could be one reason."

"She always has the telly on loud."

"Oh well, that's alright then, all we need to do is check the schedules to make sure we do it when there's something good on, so doesn't notice the noise from upstairs."

"We could keep quiet."

"David, I'm not having sex upstairs while your mother is sitting downstairs, it's disrespectful!"

"Would it be disrespectful if she went out?"

"She never goes out."

"But if she did, would it be disrespectful then? I mean from an ethical point of view. Is it disrespectful to have sex in your mother's house when she's there but respectful when she's not there? In a way it seems more disrespectful to do it behind her back. I mean if you did it while she was down the shops, it's like you don't respect her at all."

Jenny waited until he had finished his philosophical analysis before she replied, "Shut up David. I'm not having sex upstairs while your mother watches Come Dancing downstairs. But you *have* given me an idea."

David waited, and camping trips, park shelters and bike sheds in the college grounds flashed through his mind.

"My bedroom!"

"In your house?" David was incredulous.

"It would be so romantic. It would be perfect."

"What about SS and your mum?"

"Don't call him that. They go ballroom dancing every Friday."

"And we go out every Friday."

"Yes, but I could I tell them I'm staying in now and again, or we go out as normal, go back to the house and, well, we can be gone before they get back at eleven. They're regular as clockwork. I don't know why I didn't think about it before. It's perfect!"

"It's not disrespectful then?"

"Of course it's disrespectful but what's the alternative?"

"Your Dad will murder me if we get caught."

"We'll both be dead if we get caught, so we've nothing to lose."

"Like Romeo and Juliet, thus with a kiss I die." David kissed her.

"Juliet's father didn't approve either, did he?" Jenny said.

"No, and look how that ended."

The problem of the venue having been sorted by Jenny she left the issue of contraceptives to David. He came back from the pub toilet in a panic and with bad news. "It's empty," he said. "I couldn't get

130

my pound back either. I was bashing the machine with my fist when someone came in. I think he thought I was a vandal."

"Calm down David, and stop shouting, you can go to the supermarket on the way, they sell them there."

"Do they? Which aisle?"

"Frozen food, what do you think? They're in the medicine aisle, next to the pain killers, get some of them while you're there."

"There's no need to be like that, I've never done anything like this before and the idea of sneaking into your house makes me nervous."

"Don't be such a wuss. Come on, they'll be doing the Rumba by now."

David entered the supermarket like a hunted animal. Clutching his basket, he bought some crisps and soft drinks to hide the condoms at the checkouts. He walked up and down the Hygiene aisle six times before he could be alone in front of the display. He glanced to his left and right to make sure nobody could see him and then looked up at the display. He was shocked to see so many options. "Durex Close Fit" sounded ok. Durex Ultra-Thin, too risky. Durex Thin Feel, might be too small. Durex Comfort XL, might be too large. He didn't know what size he was or even what constituted extra-large or how to get measured. "Durex Pleasure Me Ribbed and Dotted" was downright weird. He was just about to reach for his first choice, Close Fit, when a familiar voice said, "Doing a bit of shopping David?"

Horrified, he looked round to see a neighbour from Altham Street. Mrs Derbyshire from three doors down.

"Can't find what you want?" she continued.

"No, no, I'm looking for toothpaste."

"Well you'll not find it there, it's further down look."

He followed her down to the dental care section.

"Doing a bit of late-night shopping for your mum are you?"

"Yes," he said as he grabbed the first tube he saw and dropped it in his basket with what he thought was nonchalance.

"You're a good lad David. I never believe what folk say about you."

"Thank you."

"Your mum showed me that photograph the other day, that your girlfriend next to you in the picture?"

"No."

"Ah well, never mind. I'll get going now. You take care lad."

David nodded.

"Oh, and don't forget your condoms," she said, laughing as she walked away.

"What took you so long?" Jenny asked, when he eventually emerged from the supermarket. She looked at the bulging plastic bag in his hand, "and what the hell have you bought?"

He rifled through the crisps, various drinks, pain killers and toothpaste and showed her the pack of "Close Fit".

"You bought a pack of forty! How many times were you thinking of doing it?"

"I'm not sure I'll be able to do it at all after that. I bumped into Mrs Derbyshire when I was looking at the condoms, she lives in our street, and when I eventually went to pay it was Ian on the checkout. Of all the people to be on the checkout."

"Well why did you choose his checkout?" She was laughing now and the more she laughed the more agitated David became.

"I didn't. I was heading to the automatic pay when this woman stopped me, she had a sign saying 'I'm here to help' and she said this checkout's free. I told her I didn't need her help but she didn't listen and pushed me toward this checkout. I never saw Ian until my things were on the belt. He didn't look pleased."

Jenny tried not to laugh too much because she could see David had lost his sense of humour.

"What did Ian say?"

"He asked me if I needed any help with my packing and wished me a pleasant evening."

"Well that was nice of him."

The rest of the evening did go well although the stress of the situation didn't help the love making. Over the following months as they worked their way through the forty-pack of 'Close Fit' their Friday night trysts became a routine. With each successive Friday night, the stress of the situation dissipated and the pleasure from their love making increased. Jenny, who had found lying to her parents about her whereabouts stressful and shameful, found that over time the lies came more easily. David inevitably found lying to his mother more difficult but he did it all the same.

The crisis came towards the end of the forty pack. They were still in bed together, one Friday evening, when they heard the front door bang. David sat up in bed and had a mild conniption fit. Jenny was frightened but outwardly calm and started to get dressed. She opened the door and shouted, "Are you back?" Then whispered to David, "Get dressed and hide!" He looked around the room for a hiding place. Spotting his clothes, he grabbed them into a bundle. Jenny dressed quickly and headed downstairs. He could hear their voices, there was no shouting. He strained to hear what was being said, but all he could hear was his heart beat thumping in his chest. He glanced under the bed but there wasn't room. The built-in wardrobes were crammed but after getting back into his clothes, he jammed himself between shoes, dresses and overcoats and tried to close the doors. He couldn't move and could barely breath and he thought perhaps he should go downstairs and face the music but it was a fleeting thought. Instead he crouched down in the dark, it seemed inevitable that he would be found out. He didn't want to be murdered by Jenny's Dad but at least that would prevent him from facing his mother after all the lies he had told her. After what seemed like an hour Jenny returned. She opened each door of the fitted wardrobes until she found him. "Are you ok?" she whispered.

"Can I come out now?" he whispered back.

She moved back to the bedside table and switched on her radio. "I've told them I didn't feel well and came back early. Mum said she felt sick too, she said there's a bug going round. My Dad's out back having a cigarette and mum's coming up to see me with hot milk and a biscuit. I'm going back to bed and you'll have to stay there. Don't even breath when she comes in."

"I've got cramp and need the loo. I'm desperate."

"You'll just have to stay desperate. It's probably nerves. Try and stay calm. I'm getting into my pyjamas and waiting for mum to come up. I'll close the door. You can leave when they're asleep."

"I could die in here."

"You'll die if you come out. Now shut up." She closed the door. It was much darker now that the doors had been closed properly. He was aware of Jenny tidying the room and undressing and sitting up in bed in pyjamas and dressing gown like the good, brave little daughter, making light of her stomach bug. After what seemed like another hour – time moves slowly when you're locked in a wardrobe – Jenny's mother appeared, bearing hot milk and biscuits.

"There you are dear."

"Thanks mum."

"Everything will be alright dear, don't worry. Your Dad and I will be in bed soon. You'll probably hear him snoring."

"Thanks mum, I hope you feel better in the morning."

"Yes, I will. You too."

"Goodnight."

"Goodnight dear."

David breathed a large sigh of relief as the door closed. He sat in the dark and waited. Eventually the radio was switched off. He thought he might be rescued at that point but was disappointed. Eventually Jenny's parents could be heard settling down for the night. He listened to the usual noises and was in agonies when the toilet flushed several times. Still there was no rescue, until the noise of snoring came from the bedroom next door. It started slowly like a big-cat growl, in short bursts of noise but then built into a regular rhythm. David had never heard anything like it. It was almost loud enough to rattle the windows. Soon after the snoring started Jenny rescued him. He couldn't actually move and Jenny had to prise him out of his hiding place.

After some remedial massage he was ready to make his escape.

"Can I at least go to the loo?" he whispered.

136

"No, just follow me downstairs. Make sure we take each step together, so it sounds like one person going down. I'll have to switch the alarm off when I get to the bottom so I'll need to go first. As soon as it's off you can slip out the front door. Don't leave until the buzzing stops, otherwise the alarm will go off and wake everybody up."

It was a plan and they silently slipped out of the bedroom with David following slowly in Jenny's footsteps. They continued their strange silent dance down the stairs and reached the bottom without incident. David couldn't help thinking that they looked like Groucho and Harpo Marx as they crept down the stairs together.

"That's strange," Jenny whispered, "the alarm usually makes a buzzing noise."

"I've switched it off Jenny," said Jenny's mum. She was looking at them from the living room door.

"Mum! What are you doing down here?"

"Waiting for you two. Do you think I was born yesterday?" she looked surprisingly calm.

David made a strange noise. It's the sort of noise you make when you've had a terrible shock with an overfull bladder.

"You can go now David," Sandra said.

"I'm really sorry Mrs Simpson I....."

"Just go David. It's alright."

David left, still in agony, with a hurried apology to both mother and daughter he set off into the night.

"I'm really sorry mum," Jenny said, close to tears.

"There's no need to be sorry love, just be careful. If your Dad finds out what you get up to every Friday, I don't know what he'll do."

Jenny was shocked by her mother's calm matter of fact tone. "How long have you known, about him coming here I mean?"

"Since it started Jenny. I'm your mother."

"And you don't mind?"

"I don't like it. But if I tried to stop you, you'd find somewhere else to do it. At least I know you're safe here. Until your Dad finds out at least.

"I do love David mum, it's not just sex."

"There's nothing wrong with sex Jenny. I loved your Dad once, believe it or not."

As Jenny hugged her mother in the living-room she could hear the lion growl of snoring coming through the ceiling.

David and Jenny's relationship continued but without the passionate intensity that the Friday night ballroom dancing at the town hall had brought them. It was after several weeks of chastity that David and Jenny were shocked to hear that both their mothers had got together and agreed that they could continue to meet in Irene's house. The arrangement meant Irene going out every Friday evening and Jenny and David could 'revise' in David's bedroom. The two mothers seemed quite calm about the whole business. The two lovers were less comfortable with the conversation. Jenny was

more embarrassed than David and he was more
shocked than Jenny.

"When you said that we could carry on *revising* like
we used to do before. You know, we didn't really
get a lot of work done when we met up in your
house Mrs Simpson."

"Call me Sandra, David. I've never liked being called
Mrs Simpson. It always makes me think of King
Edward's abdication.

"Yes, and King Edward was very friendly with the
Nazis, wasn't he? He and Wallace met Hitler I
believe. It was quite a scandal at the time. Did you
see that film of the queen giving the Nazi salute? I
can see why you might prefer Sandra"

"Why don't you keep quiet David, and just listen,"
his mother said.

David nodded, Jenny's face was the colour of
beetroot.

Sandra continued, apparently unperturbed. "I've
discussed all this with Irene and we're not happy
about what you two got up to, especially lying to us
all that time. But we both think that as you're nearly
18 now, and you've been going out for nearly a
year, if you *are* going to have sex together it should
be somewhere safe. So, Irene's happy for you to
meet here every Friday.

"I'm going to go out every Friday," Irene said, "It'll
do me good to get out, I should have done it years
ago."

Sandra continued, "There are two conditions. We want you to go to the family planning clinic to get some professional advice. They'll tell you about the risks of pregnancy and sexually transmitted diseases."

"We use condoms," David said. His mother told him again, to shut up. Jennie's face turned to whatever colour comes deeper red than beetroot on a colour chart. Something approaching purple. There was also perspiration on her forehead.

"They'll explain at the clinic that there is a risk of pregnancy whatever form of contraception you use. No method is a hundred percent safe. They will also talk to you about sexual health. There's a clinic at the Hospital I can give you all the details but I'm sure you can find it online. It doesn't do any harm to know the full facts. The other condition is that we tell my husband that you two are seeing each other." David became pale at this point. "There's been too many lies already," Sandra continued. "Are you going to tell him about us *revising* on Fridays?" David asked.

"That's exactly what we're going to tell him if he asks, which he will. I know I just said there's been too many lies but there's no need to tell Stephen everything. If I have to, I'll tell him that Irene will be here every Friday. He doesn't need to know about the sex.

"So, what exactly are you going to tell Dad?" Jenny asked.

"That David and you have become good friends at college and have started dating."

"That could be construed as a lie," David said.

"David, I won't tell you again. Be quiet."

"Yes mum."

"Well what do you think?" Sandra said, "Are we all in agreement?"

"I'm delighted!" David said with rather too much enthusiasm.

"I can't thank you both enough for being so understanding," said Jenny, "I'm sorry we didn't talk to you earlier. I never thought you would react like this. I thought you'd be really angry about us, you know..."

"Having sex," David added.

"Your generation didn't invent sex," said his mother.

Jenny's father didn't take the news of Jenny and David seeing each other at all well. Sandra made sure Jenny was out when she confronted him.

"Over my dead body!" he shouted. "I won't have him seeing our Jenny."

"Don't be such a fool Stephen. They get on well together, there's nothing wrong with the lad."

"He's a bloody weirdo, and I won't have him in my house and that's the end of it."

"It isn't your house Stephen, it's in joint names if you remember, and if I want to invite him here I will."

"Well I won't put up with it."

"You won't will you?"

"No!"

"Well what are you going to do? Hit me again? If you do, I'll have you put away. You see if I don't." He was shaking with fury and he raised his fists, but thought better of it and dropped them again.

"His Dad committed suicide, is that the sort of person you want for our Jenny?"

"You don't know that. It was an accident."

"He drove straight into a motorway bridge. What else do you call it? He was as nutty as a fruit cake and his son's the same."

"You really are a vindictive man Stephen. Nobody knows what happened to David's father and don't you go spreading that poison around. If you try and spoil this for our Jenny I'll be out of that door and I won't be back. And Jenny will come with me." While Jenny's parents were having their frank exchange of views David and Jenny were making their way to the hospital for their first family planning consultation.

"You're sure we don't need an appointment David?"

"No, it's a walk-in clinic. It's all there on the internet. Services are free and available for everyone, regardless of sex, age, sexual orientation or ethnic origin.

"I'd just feel better if we had an appointment."

"Stop worrying Jenny, I've researched all the alternatives, there's the coil or IUD, which I wouldn't recommend. They don't prevent ovulation so I'm not sure you'd be happy with the ethical aspects of that. Plus, the diagram I looked at about how they are inserted was eye watering to say the least. Combined oral contraceptives, now they do prevent ovulation and then there are Progesterone only pills, condoms and spermicides." David had also done some research on abortions but he thought it might not be the best time to share his findings with Jenny.

"What about a male pill?"

"I didn't look into that"

"No I don't suppose you did."

"Are they available?"

"Not yet. What about a vasectomy?"

When they arrived at the clinic, it was called clinic 21, which they both thought was an odd sort of name for a family planning clinic.

"I think they use it for different things on different nights," said David confidently, "It's not contraceptive night every night of the week. Just Thursdays."

They walked down a narrow corridor and through a door marked "Clinic 21 Please Walk In".

"See, walk in, like I said Jenny."

At reception they were each given a card with a number and asked to sit in the waiting room which was at the end of another narrow corridor.

"She didn't even ask us our names David." Jenny whispered, even more nervous now that they had arrived.

"That's because it's confidential. Stop worrying. It'll be fine."

In the waiting room there were six men and a woman who looked like she had been a man quite recently. Two of the men looked quite old to Jenny, certainly older than her parents. There was a boy, similar age to David and Jenny. He smiled as they sat down opposite him, but it wasn't a welcoming pleasant smile, it was more of a sort of disparaging sneer. They sat and waited. David looked at the information posters. Jenny looked at the men, with suspicion. "There's something wrong David," she whispered into his ear, "they're all men."

"Stop worrying Jenny," he said, without bothering to whisper, and he continued to examine the posters.

"I'm just going to have a closer look at that poster, it looks interesting."

"Don't you move," she whispered urgently, "stay where you are!"

"Alright," he said, "I was just curious what STI meant."

"You can get a leaflet on the way out," she said.

The feral looking men disappeared one by one and were replaced by equally sinister looking newcomers. They waited in silence for nearly an hour. There was little conversation between them

but David was aware that Jenny was feeling more and more uncomfortable as the time dragged on. "This wasn't one of your mother's best ideas," he said, in a failed attempt to lighten the mood.
"Just shut up David," she said. Not bothering to whisper for once.
"Number 13 please!" A middle-aged woman in a white coat called David's number. David jumped up and Jenny with him but the lady in the white coat explained that they would be seen separately. David started to argue but Jenny told him to be quiet again. David had never seen her in such a dark mood, so he followed the white coat towards the consulting room. It was a small room with more merry posters on the walls advertising Syphilis and Chlamydia, HIV and AIDS. It was just like his doctor's GP surgery, only much smaller.
David started the conversation, to the surprise of the small Asian doctor who was sitting behind the desk. "I thought my girlfriend Jenny should come in too, we wanted to listen to your advice together but the lady said we should come in on our own. I think the Combined Oral Contraceptive Pill might be an option, we've been using Close Fit up to now. I've looked at the options on the internet and IUD's look like they are reliable but they don't prevent ovulation, do they? Do you think that's ethically sound? I'm not sure Jenny would agree anyway, it doesn't look comfortable, having it fitted I mean. Would it be you that fitted it? Jenny asked me about

the Male Pill but I didn't think that was available yet. Is it?"

The doctor seemed relieved when David's soliloquy had dried up and he asked him to sit down. He then started to ask him questions about his sexual history, how many partners, male, or female, or both.

"We just want contraceptive advice," David said, "Jenny's my first girlfriend. Her mum's a nurse and she suggested we come here."

The doctor smiled, "This is a Sexual Health Clinic young man, we give advice on sexually transmitted diseases. Family Planning is on Wednesdays."

"Oh! That would explain all the posters on syphilis and chlamydia. S.T.I. that means Sexually Transmitted Infections?"

"That's right."

"I don't think my girlfriend and I will have contracted anything like that."

"I very much doubt it."

"I'd better go back into the waiting room and explain that we've got the wrong night."

"Good luck with that young man. It's been a pleasure to meet you."

They parted on good terms but David was not looking forward, for once, to meeting Jenny. When he returned to the waiting room, he saw Jenny sitting in the same seat where he had left her but his seat was now occupied by his old schoolmate Raymond. Jenny was close to tears and when she

saw him, she jumped up and with a hurried wave
towards the still chattering Raymond she walked
towards David.

"You're a moron David, a bloody lamebrained idiot.
Bringing me to the clap clinic!" She pushed him
towards the exit door and hurried him back down
the narrow corridor and out of the clinic.

"We can come back next week Jenny, it was silly
mistake, I just got the wrong night, I bet loads of
people have done the same thing."

"No David, loads of people could not make the same
mistake. Just you. Only you could mistake Sexual
Health for Family Planning. Only you could stare at
posters wondering what STI meant without realising
it meant sexually transmitted infections. Only you
could leave me in the waiting room so that bloody
Raymond could come in and talk to me about his
bloody penis and how swollen it is, and his
discharge. Only you could do that to me. It'll be all
over the town now that we have gonorrhoea or
syphilis. I'll never live it down. My Dad thinks you're
a homosexual, when he hears about this, he'll think
you've infected me with AIDS."

"You're not going to tell him are you?" When David
asked this, he instantly realised that he should have
just kept it as a silent, passing thought, instead of
vocalising it.

"Oh. Am I going to tell my father that I've spent the
evening in the special clinic? Now let me think. Do
you really think I'm that stupid? You're supposed to

be so clever David. Why do you say and do such ridiculously stupid things? I don't know why I bother with you, I really don't. I don't think I can carry on seeing you anymore. It's just all too much!"
This outburst silenced David and she was sobbing now. He put her arm round her but she pushed him away and sobbed the whole way home.

Chapter 9.

When the Chief Inspector took over the situation at the quarry things began to happen. He set off in his car and picked up the negotiator and Irene. He apologised to Irene for the debacle and assured her that things would improve 'going forward.'
The negotiator chipped in with some helpful statistics about the percentage of suicide attempts that failed and the average hospital stay after a failed attempt or parasuicide as she called it. "In the UK, their average stay is 79 days," she said.
The chief inspector was able to change the subject before the negotiator quoted the percentage of parasuicides left permanently disabled.
"We'll soon be up there Mrs Watson. I'm confident of a positive outcome."
Irene wasn't impressed with his easy optimism. She was developing a low opinion of the Lancashire Constabulary. Her opinion of the Chief Inspector changed however, when they arrived at the blockage caused by the large blue Incident Caravan. As they drew to a halt there was a crowd of policemen waving their arms and arguing about whether to tow the thing up or down. Some were pulling on ropes attached to the caravan, most of them were stood watching and offering contradictory opinions of the way forward. The Chief Inspector jumped out of the car and ordered

them to disconnect the caravan from the Land Rover. He then gathered his forces, all on one side of the incident unit, and on the count of three they heaved it on its side, leaving the road clear. The manoeuvre might have been a complete success had the Incident Unit Caravan not slid over the edge of the precipice to fall to the bottom of the quarry, some forty metres below. The Chief Inspector feigned indifference to the calamity and got back in the car, ordering the driver to move on.

Jenny had told David that she had 'had enough' after the fiasco at the Sex Clinic. She said she wanted 'space'. David wasn't sure what that meant but he found out at the college during the week because she wouldn't talk to him and wouldn't listen to his apologies. He kept trying to tell her that it was a simple mistake, that anyone could make. She didn't agree and he thought it best to give her the space she wanted, until she had calmed down. David's mother knew something was wrong when she heard the sound of his one-sided conversation coming from his room. "Henry's back again," she muttered. "I thought we'd heard the last of him." Jenny's mother was even more concerned as Jenny moped around the house, staring at nothing and doing nothing, quite out of character for a girl so normally full of enthusiasm and energy.
"Why don't you go and talk to him love? I'm sure you can sort it out, whatever it is that's bothering

you." Jenny didn't respond. Mothers never understood these things.

"I've made a mess of everything with Jenny," he said to Henry, who was sitting on the edge of his bed, *"she won't even talk to me at college, she won't come round to see me and I can't visit her with that moron of a father there."*

"You shouldn't talk like that about her father. I hope you don't talk like that about him to her."

"Why not?"

"Well how would you like it if she called your father a moron?"

"I don't normally call him a moron. I normally call him SS."

"Oh well that's nice."

"Did you ever fall out with your girlfriend Henry?"

"You mean Mary? No. We didn't fall out as such."

"What happened, you never told me why you never saw her again."

"Well, like I told you, we met when I got back from India, we only had a few weeks together before I had to go back to the regiment. Those were the most wonderful weeks. She was such a sweet girl. After I left her, I wrote to her every day and she wrote back, such lovely letters. I kept them all, nearly wore them out reading them over and over again. Just after we arrived in France her letters stopped. I kept on writing but got no more replies. Then my mother wrote to me to tell me that Mary was pregnant. My child, obviously. I wrote to her

151

again and said I would marry her but her family had moved away and my mother could never find out where they went. I never saw her again but years later, I found out what happened to her. Her family had the child adopted, I never knew if it was a boy or a girl and Mary was put in an asylum. Some families did that to girls who got themselves 'into trouble'. They were embarrassed and couldn't cope with the disgrace. She spent the rest of her life there. Place called Brockhall, not far from here."

Whenever David talked things over with Henry it could only make him feel better. His problems didn't seem so serious when compared with what Henry had suffered.

It was a Wednesday evening when Jenny called at David's house. Irene answered the door and was delighted to see her standing there. "Come in love, come in! I'm so glad to see you. We've missed you, David's missed you." They walked into the living room. "Whatever did he do to upset you so much? He'll have said something outrageous, that's normally what happens when he upsets someone. It's got worse since his brother and sisters left home."

"Is he in Mrs Watson?"

"Yes, he's upstairs love. Do you want to go up?"

"I will in a while. Did he tell you what happened?"

"He told me you didn't want to see him anymore. He didn't say why."

"I told my mum what happened last night. I think I

should tell you too. It'll be all round the town anyway so it's best you hear it from me, rather than anyone else."

"What did he do?" Irene asked, concerned and a little frightened about what she was about to hear.

"Well, you know we agreed to go to the Family Planning Clinic, to discuss contraception?"

Irene nodded.

"Well he took me to the wrong clinic. He took me to the sexual health clinic."

Irene nodded again. This time with a more vacant expression on her face.

"The sexual health clinic is a special clinic for people with sexually transmitted diseases, AIDS, gonorrhoea, syphilis. I bumped into Raymond there, in the waiting room, he told me about his infection and asked me about mine."

"Oh no! David never said a word. You poor thing." As she sympathised with Jenny, whose face was deadly serious, Irene couldn't help smiling.

"It's not funny Irene!"

"No, you're right, it's not," she said, still smiling.

"My mother thought it was funny too. I can't see the funny side of it, actually."

"Well you will in time dear, now go upstairs and see David and I'll bring you both up something nice.

Jenny was in no mood to listen to David, she wanted to do the talking. When David saw her, he was delighted but launched into a fast-flowing monologue about the chaos theory and the

153

interdependence of events in a deterministic nonlinear system. She interrupted him and was determined that she would be heard.

"I've heard it all before David, how a butterfly can land on a rose and a chain of events causes you to mistake a sexually transmitted disease clinic for a family planning clinic. It's all very clever and interesting but it's about time you realised that you need to get your head out of the clouds. You need to come back to earth occasionally and deal with the real world."

David's mouth opened as if he was going to reply but she held up her hand like a policeman stopping traffic and his flow of conversation was halted.

"I know it was a mistake and I know you've apologised a hundred times and said that anyone could have made the same mistake but that's not true, is it David? Most people look at the schedule of the clinics and make a note of the times and days the clinic is on. You read the clinical papers on oral contraceptives and agonise over whether the progesterone only pill reliably prevents ovulation and whether that means it's a less ethical alternative to the combined pill. And that's all very interesting and that's part of the reason I love you but it's the simple things you need to get right before you fly off on an intellectual tangent. Checking the times of the clinic is easy. Anyone can do it. Raymond managed to do it, so why couldn't you? Look at what happened with Maria, you spend years writing love poems or whatever you spent five years doing before you decided to ask her out and then find out she's gay. That turns my Dad against you and you end up hiding in a wardrobe in the middle of the night waiting for him to fall asleep so that you can sneak out of the house."

David thought that validated the chaos theory about how one small event can lead to a more significant chain of events but Jenny didn't seem in the mood to be contradicted.

"Look at the conversation we had on the way to the clinic. You didn't ask me if I was feeling nervous, which I was. You didn't ask me what I thought about going on the pill. No. You launch into this big diatribe about the Virgin Birth. How Mary got pregnant while Joseph and Mary were still engaged and what Joseph's mates would have said to him when he told them the Holy Ghost was the father and not him. And instead of asking me how I felt about discussing my sex life with a complete stranger you just wanted to know whether I thought that Jesus would have had the same hair colour as Joseph or whether he would take after the Holy Ghost."

"I was just trying to make you laugh Jenny."

"And you did and it was funny but all the fun went out of it when Raymond started telling me about his willy, in that bloody waiting room, surrounded by all those creepy looking men. If you can't start focusing on the silly little important details in life, then you'll always be surrounded by chaos and I can't cope with it. You're going to have to change."

David lowered his head, guilty as charged, waiting for the verdict; "So where does that leave us?" He said at last.

"I think if you can try hard to think about what you say, before you say it, and focus more on the simple, practical issues. If you could just try to take your head out of the clouds, or your books, or wherever it is most of the time. If you could just focus on everyday issues, and stop rubbing people up the wrong way. Like when you told Ian the other day that his mother was morbidly obese. Why did you tell him that?"

"Well, because it's true."

"People don't want to hear the truth all the time David. It's depressing."

"Well Jenny, I'll change. I won't tell people the truth. I'll be more practical. I'll look after you. I love you Jenny. I really do, and I don't know what I would do without you."

"Well, we'll give it another go then, shall we?"

"That's great Jenny. That's just great!"

"Good. Come here then, and give us a kiss."

As Jenny and David were repairing the damage done to their relationship, Jenny's mother was trying to heal the rift between herself and her husband Stephen. Stephen was a man with a high opinion of himself. He had built a successful career, he had a large expensive house and a large expensive car. He

had strong opinions about people who had not
managed to achieve similar success. Many of his
colleagues at work found him cold-hearted and
ruthless but Stephen was proud of his intimidating
persona. He thought it was the reason for so much
of his success. His wife was frightened of him, he
was short tempered and he was a bully. To his
daughter Jenny however, Stephen was a loving,
gentle, and caring father. She was an only child, and
Stephen loved her more than life itself. She lit up
the room when she walked in, her smile made him
smile, her laughter brought him joy. There was no
coldness in his manner, no sneering remarks to his
wife, no threats of violence when Jenny was in his
presence.

"Stephen, I want to have a word with you about
Jenny, and I want you to listen and let me finish. I
don't want you going off the deep end."

"What is it? I'm busy!"

"Jenny thinks the world of you, you know that don't
you? You were always her favourite when she was
small. She always went to Daddy when she needed
help or advice." Stephen listened with pleasure. He
would have preferred to listen to more flattery but
his wife's conversation moved from the rose-tinted
past to the harsher reality of the present.

"Stephen, I have to tell you this, and I don't want
you to get angry about it because it will just upset
everyone, especially Jenny, and if she doesn't do
well in these exams, well you know she's set her

heart on being a doctor."

"What are you talking about?"

"Right. Well. When you went and told David Watson that he should keep away from our Jenny, it really shook her, frightened her. She told me that she thought it was not like you to behave like that, that maybe you weren't well. She was worried."

"Well he's not right for her."

"Just listen Stephen! If you start getting angry again, you'll lose Jenny for good. I mean it. She's eighteen now and she's not a little girl anymore, and if she loves David Watson, you're just going to have to accept it."

"She doesn't love him. She can't. That nerd from the arse end of Padiham? That pompous little good for nothing?" He banged his fist on the table and hurled more insults at David and his mother, his brother and sisters, the house he lived in, the street and the whole area at the wrong end of town. And finally, his dead father who had also been a 'useless good for nothing', a 'dreamer' like his son.

Sandra waited for the storm to subside and then said quietly, "You need to accept the situation for Jenny's sake. You need to calm down or you'll lose her for good. You need to talk to Jenny and apologise for warning David off. You need to tell her that she can see him with your blessing. You need to invite him to come to the house."

She stood over him as he sat at his desk, his powerful frame was pulsing with emotion. He looked at her with an expression of either pure terror or rage. She couldn't decide whether it was fear of losing his precious child or anger at the thought of her being with David.

"I mean it Stephen, you can rant and rave and shout and scream blue murder all you like but if you don't want to lose your daughter, you're going to have to swallow your pride and back down. It's up to you. Talk to Jenny. Listen to her. The more you try to drive her away from David the closer to him she'll become."

"You bitch!" He was on his feet now and Sandra took a step back. She knew what was coming but her nerve held.

"Go on!" she shouted, "Hit me again! We'll tell Jenny I've had another fall. She might believe you, but then again, she might not. She's not a little girl anymore. She's not as naïve as that little girl you used to twist around your little finger."

Stephen stared at her with pure hatred, but he unclenched his fists, and sat back in his chair. He didn't speak. His wife sat down on a chair at the other side of the room.

"You need to think about things Stephen," she said, "about how things are between us. About how things are between you and Jenny. It can't go on like this for much longer. Jenny's got her final exams soon and then she'll be off to University. I think you should talk to her about David. Apologise for the way you threatened him, you could invite him up here for dinner, get to know him, he's a good lad really. Jenny and David have been going out for a while, she likes him a lot, and if you try and break up the relationship, you'll just make their relationship stronger than it is now. I'm trying to help you Stephen. If you don't change the way you treat him you risk losing Jenny for good."

David and Jenny resumed their happy relationship with only the rapid approach of the final examinations and the gossip circulating the college, about their appearance at the sex clinic, to disturb their equilibrium. It was Jenny who suffered most from exam worries. David continually told her that the less she worried the better she would do in the examinations. "If you get stressed you won't be able to think straight, so in the exam room just tell yourself that staying calm is worth at least one higher grade. If you think like that, you'll be fine." It occurred to Jenny that if she didn't manage to stay calm in the exam room that might result in at least one grade lower. Somehow that prospect had never crossed David's mind. He was free from exam worries himself and underestimated Jenny's difficulties. On the other hand, Jenny was largely unaware of the amount of gossip and malicious comments about her and David's visit to the clinic. It was David who was the target of teasing abuse. Ian Jones, in particular, seemed to take great pleasure in asking David about his condition and his orientation. He would call him gay boy as he passed him in the corridor, he and his friends would blow kisses across the dining hall. They made comments about him being infectious. Ian was his normal pleasant, nice young-man self, when Jenny was around. However, when David was alone Ian became a hectoring sore, a pale shadow of Wayne, the bully from David's primary school days. However, what caused David more concern was the dinner invitation that Jenny said had come from her father. After the exams, he was to visit the Simpson house for dinner. He'd always thought dinner was something that happened at noon, but apparently at the top of the town it was something that happened in the evening, about six or seven hours after lunch. It seemed incredible to him that her father would want to invite him to his house for any reason other than to kill him. Jenny was so delighted about the whole thing. She couldn't stop talking about how Daddy had changed, he was 'back to his old self'. David found it difficult to believe that this 'old self' was a kind and gentle loving father, rather than the squat, angry little bull of a man that David knew. The man, who seemed to him, to threaten violence with every small gesture.

It was a pleasant walk from David's house to Jenny's. Along the railway path, past the bowling green, over the river bridge and through the park. Jenny had told him not to worry. Her father's attitude towards him had changed, he would be welcomed like the prodigal son. He felt more like

the fatted calf on the way to the welcome home
feast. His mother had warned him about Stephen.
She had grown up with him, been to school with
him. Henry had warned him about Stephen, quite
where Henry had got his information from was a
complete mystery.

"Just come with an open mind," Jenny had told him.
"Don't go off on one of your tangents when you're
talking to him. Try to be nice. Don't swear. Try and
think things through before you say anything. Don't
mention sex. Certainly, don't mention clinics or
forms of contraception or sexually transmitted
diseases."

"What am I allowed to talk about?"

"Football or fishing, you can ask him about his work.
He loves his work. But try and keep away from
politics and religion."

"I don't know anything about football or fishing or
his work."

"You'll be fine," she said.

He arrived at the house early, so walked around the
block a few times so that he would arrive on time.
Jenny's father watched him go by three times, and
shook his head in disgust, every time he passed.
After three laps of the avenue he walked to the
front door and knocked, ignoring the bell push.
While Jenny and her mother fussed over the meal in
the kitchen, Stephen studied David from behind the
curtain. He wasn't going to answer the door until
the bell rang. David knocked again, a little harder

162

this time. Stephen watched, and waited. David
looked at his watch, looked up at each window,
thought about turning for home but knocked again,
really loud this time.

"Stephen is that the door?" came a voice from the
kitchen.

"I didn't hear the doorbell, darling," he chimed.

"Darling!" His wife said to his daughter. "He *is* in a
good mood."

Eventually David saw the little white button sitting
to the side of the immaculate white door and he
pressed it. The chimes rang out and Stephen moved
to answer the door.

"Come in David. Come in!" Stephen seemed pleased
to see him.

David looked at him and waited for a moment
before he answered. "Thank you, Mr. Simpson.
Thank you."

"Stephen, call me Stephen, don't stand on
ceremony lad, come in," and he stepped to one side
and David walked past him.

"You have a lovely home Stephen," he said as he
walked through the door.

"You haven't seen it yet. Wait till you get inside
David."

David's mother had advised him to say that he had a
lovely home as soon as he arrived but he felt
perhaps that he had peaked a little early.

"Shall I take my shoes off Stephen?" He asked,
looking at the immaculate white Wilton carpet.

"No need for that, no need to stand on ceremony, you just go through."

He walked through the Hall and into the white carpeted living room, leaving black footprints from his walk through the park on the previously immaculate Wilton.

"You can take your shoes off if you want now David. Make yourself at home." Stephen nodded towards the footprints and David started to apologise and take off his shoes and bend down to try and wipe off the marks. It was a complicated manoeuvre and he nearly fell over. It would have been better to try and execute it in three separate stages rather than try to do all three things at once.

"Never mind that David, I'll clean it up when its dried. No good rubbing the dirt in, is there?"

Stephen was all smiles. David tried to smile too but his jaw seemed frozen.

"David! How nice to see you, come on through to the dining room."

"You've got a lovely home Mrs Simpson."

"Thank you David, but call me Sandra, give me your coat love, come on through."

Jenny smiled at him but looked nervous.

"Are you hungry David?"

"Always."

"What are you having to drink David? Beer or wine?"

David seemed unsure but managed to reply, "I don't drink alcohol Stephen, I'll just have water, if that's all right."

"Oh come on Stephen, you can't let a man drink on his own. I'll get you a beer."

David would normally just have insisted that he didn't want a beer, but taking Jenny's advice about thinking before speaking, he thought, and didn't say anything. By the time he'd thought about what to say Stephen had put a beer in front of him.

"No, I really don't drink."

"You don't have to pretend with us David." Stephen waved his hand towards him, in a disarming gesture, with a gracious smile. "Have a drink, relax and enjoy yourself."

"Daddy, David doesn't want it, he really doesn't drink."

"What? Not at all?" Stephen looked at David with suspicion, as if he thought that not wanting a cold lager might be some form of deviant behaviour. But then he shrugged his shoulders and smiled and said, "Well David, if you don't want beer, how about a soft drink, we have coke and juices?"

"Water's just fine." He said, after a short pause.

The dinner went well. David spoke rather hesitatingly at first, giving some time to think before he answered any question posed to him by Stephen. Initially he rather over-egged the process. Thirty seconds of silence can seem quite a long time for someone to answer a question about what subjects they are studying at college. Stephen didn't seem to notice this and other small eccentricities. He treated

David with such respect and showed so much interest in his studies and his family that David began to relax, even to enjoy himself.

"Jenny tells me you are a bit of a genius when it comes to languages David?"

"Well I speak Spanish quite well. We've been on holiday there a few times."

"I went to school with your mother David. Did you know that?"

"Yes, she did mention it. You knew my Dad as well, I think. Is that right?"

"Yes, I knew your father. A lovely man. A very clever man. Very clever."

Jenny and her mother watched the conversation between Stephen and David as the dinner progressed. Jenny with absolute delight. Sandra, with more circumspection. Her mother gave the appearance of being pleased, but behind the smiles and laughter was an undercurrent of concern.

With the parents clearing the dishes in the kitchen, David and Jenny were able to enjoy their own brief conversation.

"You've seen another side to my father now."

"I have Jenny. I must say I'm surprised."

She laughed. "I'm so glad you two got on alright. Mum and me were concerned about getting you two together over dinner but it was the right thing to do. Things will be much easier now. We can be more open about our relationship now that he's got to know you a bit better."

"But not completely open," he whispered.

"Not everyone wants to know the truth about everything David."

"That's something I'm beginning to understand."

"You've done very well this evening, you listened, you showed interest, you were the perfect dinner guest."

"I listened because I was too scared to talk, I wasn't really that interested but just kept nodding and grinning, like an idiot."

"That's what perfect dinner guests do David."

"They don't have opinions, bold insights?"

"They might have but they have the sense to keep quiet about them. They only share them with people who are very close to them."

"Thank you, Doctor Simpson. I think I may be cured."

"I don't want to cure you of your eccentricities David, I just want to help you keep them under control."

"Well I think you're doing a fabulous job."

When Jenny's parents came back into the living room to join them, the happy atmosphere continued without incident. Stephen talked about his work, Sandra talked about ballroom dancing, Jenny and David talked about their applications to University. If Stephen was upset by the fact that they had both applied to Manchester, he kept his feelings to himself.

Eventually David announced that he should go home. He had been agonising for some time about when to announce his departure. He had wanted to leave straight after the coffee. Having got through three courses and coffee without saying anything stupid, he thought it best to quit while he was ahead. However, he wanted to give the appearance of enjoying himself rather than being silently tortured. When Stephen stumbled on his way to his third brandy, he thought this might be a good time to go.

Having said his thanks to Jenny's parents, David kissed Jenny good night at the door and then set off down the drive, to walk home. To his surprise he heard Stephen calling out to him. "Hang on David, I'll walk with you through the park."
David protested but Stephen insisted, saying that the air would do him good.
"I may have had one brandy too many," he said. "A bit of air before I go to bed won't do me any harm." David would have preferred to walk on his own, but after protesting for a short while, he thanked Stephen and the two of them walked towards the park. Stephen couldn't stop talking, mainly about his daughter. Fuelled by alcohol he repeated the same phrases over and over again. "She's very clever David, our Jenny. Very clever. She's always been a clever girl, you know? She's a very pretty girl. Pretty as a picture. Wouldn't you say David? A Beauty. A beauty." This meandering monologue continued

until they reached the park gates. Stephen then stopped, swayed, grabbed David's arm firmly and stared into David's eyes with sudden menace. The bonhomie had disappeared.

"I suppose you think you're very clever David. You might have fooled Jenny and you might have fooled the wife but you don't fool me!" His grip on David's arm tightened and David winced with the discomfort. "I know your sort. I know where you live. You need to mix with your own kind. When you're finished at college you finish with her. You find some other girl to mess with. Do we understand one another?"

David tried to pull his arm free but Stephen's grip was far too strong. Stephen seemed amused by David's pathetic attempt to escape. "You'll go when I let you go," he said, "and you don't tell Jenny about this conversation, right? You just leave her alone after college is over and you don't contact her again. If you do, you'll regret it. You will regret it very badly. Are we clear?"

David nodded, and his arm was released. Stephen glared at him for a moment and then, after one final evil looking smile, he turned and walked away.

Chapter 10.

As the Chief Inspector's car drove towards the top of the quarry, down at the base a crowd was gathering. They were being herded behind a cordon of blue and white tape. There was a journalist from the local newspaper among the crowd who was insistent that he should be able to cross the blue line. The constables on duty were under orders to keep the crowd back.

"They're just ghouls," one of the constables said, quietly to one of his colleagues.

"We should be more careful what we say over the radios. There's always someone listening. Bad news travels fast."

His colleague nodded in agreement and whispered, "I think the Incident Unit Caravan falling into the lake might have created a bit of interest."

David thought that he had overcome his fear of bullies, but Jenny's dad had terrified him. He had no idea what to say to Jenny. Should he tell her what had happened at the park gates? Would she believe him? Her dad had been so friendly, so welcoming over dinner. Even on the walk from the house to the park he seemed friendly, if a little drunk. Jenny had always said that he was a quiet man, a loving father, always kind and gentle. David had never seen that side to his character until the dinner. All that changed at the park gates. He decided not to mention anything to Jenny. The dinner went well. Jenny and her mother were both delighted. It would just spoil everything if he told her what had happened. If he did tell her, she might not believe him. He could scarcely believe it himself and he had lived through it. Even if he could convince her of the truth, she wouldn't want to hear it. He kept the secret hidden, sharing it only with Henry. Henry told him it was the drink that did it. *"Drink can do that to some men. I've seen it a thousand times. Some men just can't hold their booze, they can turn nasty in a second, like turning a switch. I shouldn't worry about it. Just keep away from him when he's drinking."* Having talked it over with Henry it became less of a worry and he told himself to forget all about it and put it down to the alcohol.

Some days later as Jenny and David were eating lunch in the college canteen, Ian Jones came over, "Would you mind if I join you for a while? Just to say hello. Haven't had the chance to speak to you for ages." He was conviviality made flesh.

"Of course not," Jenny said. David masticated.

"I just thought I'd wish you both good luck for tomorrow. I know it's A level results-day tomorrow, isn't it?"

"That's very nice of you Ian," Jenny said. David nodded, it could have been a gesture of agreement or he could just have been swallowing some food.

"You still aiming to do medicine Jenny?"

"Hoping to."

"What do you want to do David?"

"Me?" He hadn't expected Ian to show any interest in what he was aiming to do. "I'll be doing Maths."

"Well good luck. I hope you both get what you want tomorrow. See you. Bye."

"That was lovely of Ian. Wasn't it, David?"

"Was it?"

"Well of course it was, Ian's always very pleasant."

"He's nice to you, not to me. When he sees me, he either ignores me or finds something rude or threatening to say."

"You are always so critical of people. He was pleasant just now and you hardly spoke a word to him."

"That's because, when you're not around he treats me like something he's just stood in. When you are with me, he's like King Charisma."

"He asked me out recently."

"When?"

"A few weeks ago. It was just after you took me on that date, to the sex clinic. I was tempted to say yes."

"Were you really?"

"No, I wasn't *really*." She was laughing at him. "I think it was embarrassing for him, to tell the truth. He asked me in front of everyone, and he seemed so confident that I would say yes. He's quite popular with all the girls. Anyway, I said no. I probably said it a little too quickly."

David shook his head. "Why is it that people who are completely dishonest and synthetic are always popular?"

"Ian isn't dishonest."

"He talks to me like I'm contagious when you're not around, and when you are, he's all over me like a rash."

"He must have caught it from *you*."

"You can't see it, the way he behaves I mean, but it's true."

"You don't have the monopoly on truth David."

"No, I suppose not. But you should see him, when you're not here."

"That might be difficult."

"He's not the only one who's nice to me when you're around and completely the opposite when you're not."

"You're just paranoid."

"I know," he said thoughtfully, "it's because so many people are out to get me."

As soon as David saw Jenny at college the next day, he knew she had failed to get the grades she needed. She was standing in a circle of girls, most of them hugging and jumping up and down like cup winners. She was smiling, but it was with bravery rather than joy. A lot of her friends were delighted with one B or two C grades. She was devastated to receive only one A, when she really needed three. When she caught his eye, she waved and gave him a smile. She was wonderful. It broke his heart to see the disappointment in her eyes and to see her congratulating her friends when all she really wanted to do was cry out in frustration and disappointment. He walked towards her and she broke away from the group. He took her hand and he hugged her and they walked towards the exit gate.

"It's all over David," she said, allowing her tears to flow at last. "I'll not get in anywhere to do medicine. It's all I ever wanted to do."

"You can retake them."

"No, I can't. I didn't even get close. Why I ever thought I could do well enough to get into Medical School I'll never know. I was just fooling myself. I'm really sorry David. You know I won't be going to Manchester now?"

"Don't worry Jenny. We'll work something out."

She shook her head. "I'm just not up to it. I couldn't have worked any harder. If I'd done less work it might have been worth retaking them but I couldn't face going through all that again. I know it would be a waste of time."

She wiped her eyes and looked at him with an attempt at a smile. "Do I even have to ask you how you did?"

"I got A stars," he said.

"In all four?"

"Yes. I'm sorry."

His apology made her laugh. "Only David Watson

could apologise for getting four A stars in probably the most difficult A levels it's possible to take."

"I'm really sorry."

"Don't be stupid David."

"What are you going to do Jenny, if you don't go to Med School?"

"I have no idea."

"You know Jenny, whatever you do, wherever you go, I want to come with you."

"Don't be silly David. You're going to Manchester to become the greatest Maths Professor that ever lived."

"I'm not that bothered about Maths now."

"Don't say that. You were quite happy to do Maths when I was doing Medicine in Manchester."

"I don't really want to go to Manchester."

"Don't let my failure spoil your success. I'll get over it and I'll find something else to do. You need to go to Manchester and get your degree."

David's mother was overjoyed at David's exam success and was a little frustrated that he seemed so indifferent to all the congratulations that came his way. When she showed him the photograph in the local paper, of him with the other A star pupils, he was positively rude to her.

"Is that Maria stood next to you?" Irene asked. "The one you went to that club with? Is she still gay?"

"Please don't order another photograph mum. I couldn't bear it."

"Don't talk soft David. I've already ordered one. I'll

get it framed and put it up in the hallway with the O level one." His mother soon realised the reason for her son's low spirits. She encouraged him and cajoled him to stop worrying about the future and concentrate on the present.

"One day you'll realise that this was the best time of your life."

Over the following weeks, Jenny and David's relationship continued under the dark cloud of uncertainty. But it was, perhaps, the threat of separation that made their love making more intense and more pleasurable than ever. Through the summer and into Autumn they didn't feel the need to discuss what might happen, they simply made the most of the time they had with each other. The time soon came however when decisions about the future had to be made. It was David who finally broached the subject of their imminent separation. They were sitting in the conservatory at Jenny's house, looking out over the garden. Jenny looked at David with concern in her eyes. Neither of them had looked forward to this conversation. Both of them knew it was inevitable.

"I've given a lot of thought to this," David said slowly. "I haven't just thought of it on impulse. I discussed it with my mother and a friend of mine and I hope you won't get upset about anything I tell you. I never want to do anything to hurt you Jenny. I know you won't be coming to Manchester. I know I said that I would come with you, wherever you went and I know you've got a place at Newcastle. I would like to give up my place at Manchester and come with you. That's what I'd like to do but I've talked it over and thought about it a lot. I've decided not to follow you to Newcastle. I think it's best if I go to Manchester as planned and you do your nursing course in Newcastle." She wiped a tear from her cheek quickly but he noticed and his voice almost choked with emotion. "I do love you Jenny. More than I can say really. Anyway, I've bought you a present. I bought you one before if you remember. I thought I would ask you to marry me. That was my first idea. My mother said that was a bad idea, because you're the only girlfriend I've ever had and she said we're too young to get married. I spoke to a friend of mine, he told me to go ahead and ask you. He said, if you don't ask her now, she'll go and meet someone else up in Newcastle and you'll never get the chance again. He said I'd spend the rest of my life regretting it."

"Who is this friend? Was it Ian?"

"No, not Ian. Definitely not Ian. It doesn't matter who it was. Anyway, I'm not going to ask you to marry me. Because you need to go to college and get your nursing degree. Maybe even switch to medicine if you can. I'm sure you can do that. I'll go to Manchester and do Maths, see how I get on without you, all by myself. In the meantime, I want you to have this, because in three or four years, whenever the time is right, I *will* ask you to marry me. In the meantime, well, we can stay friends, or whatever you want...." He couldn't manage any more words at that point and pushed his gift towards her. She could tell it was a ring before she opened the box.

"It's lovely," she said, crying and laughing at the same time. "It's lovely David. It's really beautiful. Thank you."

"You're not to wear it until I ask you, it's sort of a deposit. You don't have to commit yourself now, but keep the ring safe, you might need it one day."

"But can't I wear it just the once? Maybe at the Leaver's Ball? That would be lovely."

"No I think it's better to keep it secret, especially from your parents."

"Well I'll put it on a chain and wear it at the Leavers Ball. I have a long silver chain. Nobody will see it but we'll both know it's there. I will keep it safe. I promise."

David left her, after he gave her the engagement ring, because he thought he might burst into tears and make a fool of himself in her parents' home. She was already in tears and he was aware that her father was working in his office at the back of the house. He didn't want Stephen to walk in on them while they were in a tearful embrace.

"I'll pick you up at seven for the Leaver's Ball on Friday," he said as he stood up to leave. "You're out with the girls tonight, aren't you?"

She nodded. "Thanks David, it's a beautiful present,

even nicer than the one you bought me for my 16th birthday."

David didn't hear from Jenny after the night out. He thought it was unusual not to hear from her and he didn't receive any replies from his messages, but he thought she might be suffering from a hangover. He didn't drink alcohol and Jenny was in the habit of drinking very little when they were together but occasionally, she would drink far too much on a girls' night out. He stopped bothering her with messages and waited for her to contact him. The contact came the following night as he lay in bed. It was late and he was already falling asleep. When the phone vibrated, he ignored it. After a few moments it vibrated again. He glanced at the clock, half past midnight. When it vibrated for the third time he sat up and grabbed the phone to switch it off. Three unread text messages. Not junk mail! Three urgent messages from Jenny. "David can you meet me? Urgent" "David I need to see you" "David we need to meet". He called her but the call went unanswered. It went to her voicemail. The familiar voice made him smile. He didn't leave a message. What could be so urgent? He rang her again with the same result. Call rejected. Then came the fourth and longest message, "David. I'm on my way. Meet me in the park. Don't let me down."

He was dressed and out of the house without waking his mother, or so he thought. He continued to call Jenny but without success. He ran down the steep street and across the road. Along the footpath that ran alongside the railway line towards the park. The park was midway between his house and hers. He had the feeling that this was some kind of joke. Then he had the feeling that it could be something serious. He ran on past the bowling greens and the playground towards the river bridge. Up the steep steps towards the park. The street lights ended and there was no moon. It wasn't the ink black of the countryside but too dark for running. He walked carefully along the path and rang her again. No answer. He texted her and the reply came back. "I'm at the band stand." He could see the vague shape of the bandstand in the distance, but there was no vague shape of Jenny, or anyone else. "Jenny!" he called out, in a cautious whisper. That was when he heard a sudden movement from the bushes beside him. He smiled, half anticipating Jenny to surprise him. Instead he received a massive blow to his head which knocked him to the ground. He fell forward and he heard a loud bang as his head made contact with the concrete path. He was vaguely aware of being kicked as he lay on the ground. He tried to stand but each blow sent him back to the ground. One last attempt to get to his feet was ended by another blow to the head that rendered him unconscious. He woke, he thought instantly, to complete silence. Slowly he crawled onto his knees, not in pain yet, just disorientated, dizzy and nauseous. Slowly he got to his feet. He reached for his phone and tried to focus on the screen. The screen was blurred, the whole shape of the phone was blurred. He covered one eye with his hand, as if that might bring the phone back into focus. He had to ring Jenny. Something had happened to her. She had asked for his help. She had said that she needed him. Urgently. He focused on the phone again but there was blood dripping onto the screen. He wiped it clear and eventually managed to make the call. He held it to his ear. He stood swaying in the cold and dark, half conscious. Then he heard the phone ringing. The sound confused him. The sound wasn't coming from his phone it was coming from the bushes. On the edge of the bushes, beside the path where he was standing, he could see the light of Jenny's telephone and hear her ringtone. He couldn't understand what was happening at first but he eventually retrieved her phone from the ground beneath the bushes. He struggled towards home, down the steep steps towards the river bridge. He sat at the foot of the steps and tried to organise his thoughts. It wasn't Jenny texting him. It was just Jenny's phone. He stood up and then leaned towards the ground and vomited violently into the undergrowth beside the footpath. Breathing heavily and spitting the bitter taste from his mouth he walked across the river bridge.

"Someone took her phone," he muttered. His mind was as blurred as his vision but he had one clear idea in his head.

David had no memory of his journey back to his house, he had no memory of his mother opening the front door to him, or the journey to the hospital. He became aware of what was happening when he arrived at A and E, he could recall the many questions from doctors and nurses, the long wait for 'the registrar on call', the look of fear on his mother's face. He remembered the journey on the trolley to the operating room, the doctor from New Zealand asking him to count to ten. He thought he might have got further than five, but then someone was telling him to wake up, and that it all went well, and that he was fine now. It wasn't until later in the day that he realised what damage had been done to him. His first glance into the mirror was a shock. His face had disappeared altogether in a swollen blue ball of stitches and bruising. There was pain from his right ear and stitches protruding from the base of the ear and his right cheek. His right eye was closed completely and the view from the other eye was limited, like looking through a narrow letter box. His mother heard him swearing at the sight of his face and she burst into tears. He came out of the sluice room and tried to console her but she pulled herself together quickly, realising that it was her job to console him rather than the other way round.

"Who did this to you David? Did you see them?"

"No I didn't see a thing."

"Well what made you go out in the middle of the night like that? Were you meeting someone?"

"I can't remember anything mum," he lied, "I don't know what got into me. I know I went to the park. Maybe I was sleep walking."

She shook her head. "You've never done that since you were small. You don't get dressed to go sleep walking David. You must have gone to meet someone."

"I can't remember," he said, "maybe it'll come back to me."

"The police will want to talk to you. I hope you can remember something, so they can catch whoever did this to you."

They came later in the day and David repeated the same lies he'd told his mother. He needed time to work things out. If he told them about the text messages and the telephone, they might arrest Jenny's Dad. Who else could have taken Jenny's phone? On the other hand, when he told them he hadn't seen his assailant or assailants, nor heard any names or even voices, he was telling the truth. That first blow to the side of his head had been so violent he wasn't really sure if he was fully conscious at all during the attack although he could remember trying to stand up and defend himself. He could remember failing miserably to get to his feet.

He left the hospital the next day with thirty stiches in his face, some in his mouth, cracked ribs and bruises and abrasions to his arms and abdomen. The pain kicked in the day after he left the hospital.

Jenny was keen to visit him but David asked his
mother to tell her to wait. "I don't want her to see
me like this," he told her. He refused to go out. He
said he looked like something from a horror film
which was only a slight exaggeration. Jenny arrived
two days later, still uninvited, refusing to take no for
an answer. She popped her head around his door as
he fed himself on some cold soup through a straw.
"Hey you," she said cheerfully, "what's all this about
not wanting to see me? Something I said?" She had
a smile on her lips but he noticed her eyes dampen
as she saw his face. She couldn't hide the shock of
seeing him. "How are you?"
He didn't answer but the expression, on what was
left of his face, seemed to resent the question.
"Stupid question," she said. "I can see you've had
better days." She leaned towards him as if to give
him a kiss but then paused, as if looking for
somewhere undamaged where a kiss wouldn't give
him more pain. She stepped back without kissing
him and pulled up a chair to sit beside him.
"I've sent you a few messages," she said, "did you
get them?"
"I sent you a few, but you didn't reply to them."
"I lost my phone the night I went out with the girls.
Daddy bought me a new one." She held up the I
phone for him to see.
"That was very good of him."
"He was ever so nice about it. He's been *so* good

184

recently. I thought he'd be mad with me when I told him I'd lost it."

"Where did you lose it?"

"I don't know. I had it when I went out, Wednesday night, the night before you were attacked. I didn't miss it until the next morning. We all had a bit too much to drink."

"He wasn't angry, your Dad, about losing your phone?" David asked.

"No, he went out and spent ages looking for it. Said I might have dropped it on the way home, but he couldn't find it and he bought me a new one."

"Did he look in the park for it?"

She looked surprised. "Why would he look there?"

"I thought that might be on your way home?"

"Don't be silly. We got a taxi."

"Well maybe you left it in the taxi?"

"No, he rang them about it, but they hadn't found it."

"Oh well."

They had a very stilted conversation. His mother brought Jenny some tea. David pretended to be tired, and eventually Jenny left. It hadn't been the most successful visit she had ever made to his bedroom.

He had retrieved her phone from his pocket when he got back from the hospital. He had hidden it at the bottom of the wardrobe. He thought perhaps he should get rid of it. He had lied to his mother and the police. He thought the bang on the head might be his best alibi. If he kept on telling them that he could remember nothing of that night, he could never be accused of lying, whatever happened. There was one more visit from the police and after that they seemed to lose interest. He went back to the hospital to have his stitches removed, the size of his head went back to normal and Jenny told him that the scars on his cheek and around his ear gave made him look 'interesting'.

David soon recovered from the trauma of the attack. His face healed and he learned to live with the scars which were bright red immediately after the stiches were removed but within a few weeks the inflammation had faded. The scars were visible but Jenny didn't seem to mind them and that made David more relaxed about them. His mother was more worried about the attack than he was, she was keen to find out who did it, and why.

"You must have upset someone David? Try and think back. They didn't even steal your phone. Did someone threaten you? You're not involved in drugs, are you?" There was a constant drip feed of questions and suggestions about the motive for the attack and possible culprits. The chief suspect, according to his mother, was Wayne. David assured her that he had had no contact or even conversation with Wayne since he had left Primary School.

Jenny and David's relationship carried on as normal, despite the imminent parting of the ways. Jenny was preparing for her departure to Newcastle and David should have been getting ready for Manchester. The day for departing came, as these days do, however distant they might have seemed on Results Day. David was in his room packing his bags. It was a sad business for him. He had a ticket for the ten o'clock train. Jenny was leaving for Newcastle on the same day but her parents were planning to drive her there in the afternoon. David had to pack two rucksacks, a big one for his back, a small one for his chest, and the large family suitcase on wheels to tow along behind him. His mother had helped him pack the suitcase but he insisted on packing the rucksacks himself. He was getting into a panic because Jenny was due to arrive soon, to see him off at the station. The family suitcase was packed, labelled and parked in the hallway but the two rucksacks were empty. They had been filled, then over-filled and then emptied several times but there were so many books he just had to take, his father's notes and files. Things that he couldn't leave behind, presents that Jenny had given him, all the vital paraphernalia of his life. He looked at Jenny's phone and wondered where to hide it. He knew he had to take it with him, he couldn't risk leaving it behind. Perhaps he would dispose of it when he got to Manchester. He probably should have disposed of it sooner but he liked to look at it, read the text messages he'd sent her over the years, she seemed to have kept them all. The phone was like a secret diary of his relationship with her. There were hundreds of photographs, some of her family, many of him and Jenny laughing, always happy. He thought he might copy some of the pictures before he threw it away. He looked at his favourite picture of her. She was standing in front of a lake in her jeans and green jacket. Her head tilted slightly and smiling at him. Just at him, she wasn't smiling at the view, or the hills in the background or anything else in the world. At that particular moment he had taken the picture, she was smiling only at him. He put the phone down on the bedside cabinet and struggled on with his packing. He was so absorbed in the packing he didn't hear the front door or Jenny downstairs talking to his mother. Then the phone rang. He picked it up, flicked the answer icon and put it to his ear.

"Hello?"

"Who is that?" the voice on the other end of the line was quiet but slightly aggressive.

"Who are you?" he said doubtfully.

"David? Is that you?" The voice was unmistakeable, it was Jenny's father.

"Yes. Stephen? Hello."

" What are you doing answering this phone?"

David glanced down at the bedside table to see his own phone staring at him in silence. He then pulled the phone from his ear to glance at it, as if to confirm his mistake.

"David, talk to me. How did you get hold of Jenny's telephone? It was stolen."

"Well it wasn't me who took it," David said.

Jenny's father laughed at him, but it wasn't a pleasant laugh, it was a sneering snort of disgust.

"Don't lie to me. You've got the phone in your hand. How did you come by it, if you didn't steal it?"

"I found it in the park where *you* dropped it."

"Where I dropped it?"

"I found it in the park, in the bushes, after I was attacked. It was you sent me those text messages and lured me there."

"You're not making any sense lad."

"You never liked me. You never thought I was good enough for Jenny."

"Well so much is true but I've never sent you a message in my life."

"You took Jenny's phone, you sent me text messages, that I thought came from her, to meet her in the park, it was you, not her. It was you that beat me up."

"You'd better be careful about making accusations like that or you'll be in real trouble, so just think very carefully before you say anything else."

"I'm not listening to any more of your threats. It's you who needs to watch out. If I go to the police, it'll be you who's in trouble, not me!" David hadn't realised but he was shouting at the top of his voice. David's mother pushed open the bedroom door and peered in at him. He could see Jenny's face, full of concern, standing behind his mother. "What's going on?"

"It's your Dad on the phone Jenny," he said, pathetically. He held up the phone as if he needed to confirm its existence. They could all hear the sound of Stephen's furious rant, coming from the phone. David hit the red icon, and Stephen was silenced. His mother's voice filled the vacuum. "You need to tell us what's going on David."

"Is that my telephone?" Jenny asked.

"Were you shouting at Jenny's Dad?" Having been struck dumb by the sight and sound of David shouting abuse at Jenny's father, both Irene and Jenny were suddenly both very vocal. David sat down and listened to the onslaught of questions: "Where did he find the phone? Why didn't he tell them he'd found it? When did he find it? Had he recovered from his amnesia? Why had he lied to them? Why was Stephen calling him? What were they arguing about? Did he know who'd attacked him? Why had he lied to the police?"

"The night I got beaten up, I went to the park because I got a text from Jenny asking her to meet me, it said it was urgent."

"I never sent you a text!"

"Please just let me finish," David said, with an awkward hand gesture. The silly hand gesture seemed to work and he went through the story of the attack, how he had been lured there, how he had struggled to his feet, and how he had tried to call Jenny.

"Your phone was in the bushes. Whoever attacked me had dropped the phone he'd used to lure me into the park."

"But who would do such a thing?" Jenny asked.

"It was your Dad Jenny!"

"What?"

"Your Dad. You know he never liked me. He warned me off after that dinner at your house. He told me to stay away from you. He said I hadn't to see you again after I'd finished college."

"That's not true David. He was so nice to you at that dinner, you said so yourself."

"He was nice when you were there but after, when you weren't around, he threatened me. He said I was to keep away from you."

"Why are you telling all these lies David. Daddy has been so good to you, even after the dinner. He couldn't possibly be the one who attacked you. He's not like that. What is wrong with you?"

"There's nothing wrong with me. Why do you think he spent so much time looking for your phone after I was attacked?"

"Because he cares about me, he knew I was upset about losing it."

"No Jenny, he knew if someone found it, they might take it to the police. They'd see the text messages and know he'd tricked me into going into the park."

"Why are you saying all this?" Jenny was in tears now.

"Because it's true Jenny. Why was he calling now? Threatening me again?"

"He's been ringing the number to try and find out who stole it. And why wouldn't he spend time looking for the phone? You said you couldn't remember what happened. All of a sudden you can remember everything. Did you see who attacked you?"

"I didn't see him." David admitted. "He hit me from behind."

"So you didn't see who attacked you, but you know it was my father."

"Yes."

"You always think the worst of people David. You accused Ian of being rude and aggressive towards you, when he's nothing of the sort. And now you accuse my father of beating you up in the middle of the night. It's just madness. You said yourself you didn't see who attacked you. It doesn't make any sense." She snapped the silver chain from her neck and the engagement ring he'd bought went flying across the room. "You can have that back. You're out of your mind. I don't know why I didn't see it before. I never want to see or hear from you again. Go to Manchester and have a nice life. I've had enough of it." Her anger dissolved into misery and she turned away from him, gave a conciliatory gesture to his mother and left the room. She made the most awful wailing sound as she went down the stairs and David's mother chased after her, calling her name and pleading with her to come back. David heard the front door slam and sat in his room, waiting for his mother to return, waiting for a more detailed interrogation.

He had never seen his mother so disappointed in him, she was angry and desolate but she didn't shout at him. He might have felt better if she had, but she didn't. She pleaded with him to tell her the whole story.

"I want you to tell me everything from the very beginning. About what Jenny's Dad said, what happened that night in the park, why you've lied to me and the police. I want to know about that engagement ring, after we talked about you and Jenny getting married, after what I told you about being too young. I said you should wait. What made you go ahead and ask her after we talked about it? You agreed with me David, and then you went and asked her anyway. You tell me why you did that. And don't even think about telling any more lies."

He told her everything and she listened patiently. She made the odd tutting noise, there was the occasional sigh and shake of the head, but she waited until he'd finished before she spoke again.

"I can't believe Stephen Simpson would do a thing like that. He always had a short fuse but to do something like that, it wouldn't be on impulse, it was planned. Premeditated. I never liked him but it's hard to believe he could do a thing like that. Why didn't you talk to me about it? What's

happened to you? I see you're still talking to that dam silly none existent friend of yours. Why talk to him when you could have talked it through with me? Oh David, I don't know what to do with you I really don't." She wiped her eyes which were stained with tears. "Come on, I'll walk with you to the station."
"I don't want to go mum. Not like this. I can go tomorrow."
Mother and son talked for the rest of the morning and David caught a later train than planned.

Chapter 11.

Irene had been putting on a brave face until the car arrived at the top of the quarry. She had kept on saying that David 'wouldn't do anything so stupid' and 'he wouldn't be so cruel' and she managed to keep up this positive façade until she got out of the car, it was then that her knees seem to give way. She stumbled and would have fallen to the ground had the police driver not been there to catch her.
"It might be better if you stay in the car Mrs Watson."
"No, I'm fine," she said in a voice that was as tremulous as her knees.
"I'll walk ahead," said the negotiator. "Why don't you stay with the Inspector?"
The chief Inspector took Irene's arm and they walked slowly towards the cliff edge but the negotiator walked quickly ahead. She wanted to assess David's state of mind before his mother got anywhere near him.

David's first term at University was a disaster. He arrived with his two rucksacks and family suitcase on wheels at the student accommodation block and was allocated a room on the eighteenth floor. Unable to find the front entrance, he carried his luggage up the stairs at the rear of the building and arrived at the eighteenth floor almost drowning in perspiration, only to find that his room was right next to the lift. The lift doors opening and closing meant he didn't sleep more than two hours together for the first three weeks and he became exhausted and depressed in equal measure. He contradicted his tutor, unnecessarily loudly, in his first lecture on Linear Algebra and that was the only significant conversation he had with any human being, other than with his mother by telephone, for the first two months. He made no effort to socialise with anyone, didn't attend any parties, didn't join any clubs or societies. He did his work, he made phone calls and sent text messages to Jenny, and never received a single response. There was a brief moment of elation, after one month, when he received a letter from her. He recognised the handwriting on the envelope and opened it with a flourish of excitement but the message was terse and disappointing.

"With reference to the absurd accusation you made about my father. He checked his diary and was driving back from a business meeting in Southampton the night you were attacked." David was known as the 'ghost' on the landing of the eighteenth floor of the student accommodation block and in the Maths department none of the students even seemed to notice his existence. Towards the end of the first term one of the tutors asked him to visit his office and asked 'how he was getting along'. David told him that everything was fine. The tutor wasn't convinced. When he spoke to his mother by telephone, he managed to put on a show, even invented friends he had made, hinted there might be a girlfriend in the offing. Irene wasn't any more convinced than the tutor was that David was anything other than clinically depressed.

When he arrived home for the Christmas holidays, his mother was shocked by how pale and thin he had become. She was also concerned by his languid and listless approach to everything. Even when his brother and sisters came with their partners, he seemed to have no enthusiasm or energy for the Christmas celebrations or anything else. She was sympathetic at first and when that didn't work, she lectured him about his bad attitude but it was like throwing water at a sponge. He seemed to soak up criticism and encouragement with the same apathetic reaction or no reaction at all. He was polite. He read his books. He was absolutely silent most of the time. His brother and sisters only visited briefly for Christmas and he was soon alone with his mother.

"David, did I tell you? I've a friend coming round on Friday, he's going to have tea with us."

David looked up from his book, nodded and then went back to "Curves and Dynamics" without speaking.

"Did you hear me?"

He looked up again. "Yes mum."

"Well why didn't you say so?"

He shrugged, scowled, and looked back at "Curves and Dynamics".

"What's your book about David?"

"It's all about yield curve modelling," he said.

"And that's more interesting than a friend of mine visiting on Friday, is it?"

"What friend?"

"He's called Lionel. I met him at Yoga. He's coming for tea. He wants to meet you."

"Why?"

"Because I've told him all about you. He's got a daughter at University."

"Is she coming?"

His mother grabbed his book and threw it onto the table. "Put that dam thing down when I'm talking to you."

"I was listening."

"You weren't. You never do. You're in a dream most of the time. You don't seem to be interested in anything these days."

"I am interested mum, in your friend. I'm glad you've got friends. I really am."

"What's his name then? Super Brain. Can you remember what he's called?"

"Yoga."

"Lionel! I met him at Yoga!"

"So are you going out with him?"

"What if I was? Would it bother you?"

"No, why should it?"

"Well he's not your dad is he?"

"Are you going to marry him?"

"Don't be ridiculous. He's coming for tea that's all. We've been out a few times. His wife left him a few years ago. He's an accountant."

" That's interesting."

"No it's not but he's a nice chap and we get on alright. I get a bit lonely on my own."

"I know mum. I'm lonely too. I'm useless at making friends on my own. I have tried."

"Have you really? Really tried?"

He said that he had but they both knew that he hadn't.

"You don't have to stay in tonight David. If you want to go out and meet some of your friends from college. You can go out after tea if you like."

"David glanced at "Curves and Dynamics" lying open on the table and wondered if he would be able to concentrate on it while his mother was entertaining a Lionel downstairs. He thought of all the sacrifices his mother had made on his behalf when he and Jenny were 'revising' upstairs.

"I'll go out after tea," he said. "It'll do me good."

Lionel was a pleasant man and he and David had a pleasant chat about Liquidity, double-entry and depreciation curves. The meal progressed well but Irene and Lionel seemed relieved when David announced that he was going out.

He headed into the cold night air. His mother had 'wrapped him up well' in a large sweater and jacket and overcoat, scarf and hat. He moved from one bar to the next, young people's bars, the ones Jenny and he used to frequent. After years of abstinence he had developed a drinking habit in his first term at University. When he eventually found what he was looking for he was feeling pleasantly numbed by the alcohol he had consumed in the bars he had visited. He saw her as soon as he walked into the pub. She was in a large booth, surrounded by laughing friends. He thought she had grown even more beautiful than he remembered. Her auburn hair was longer, her eyes brighter and her laughter even more infectious. He went to the bar for a drink and then found a small table where he could look across at Jenny. Someone asked if they could take the other seats from the table and he nodded his assent. He was now the solitary drinker with a single stool and a single small round table. He thought she might have noticed him, stuck out as he was, sitting alone silent amongst the animated drinkers, all laughing and talking at once. She was too involved with her friends to even glance in his direction. Ian was sitting next to her. They seemed very close, intimate even. She kept on touching his arm, pushing him in a friendly way and laughing, always laughing. He longed to be touched, to see her look at him with a smile, to whisper to him, 'it's alright now David, it's all fine'. He had sat for what seemed a long time when Ian left her side and after taking orders from the group in the booth, he walked towards the bar to buy more drinks. Another boy, that David didn't recognise, came with him to the bar to help with the round. David looked away to avoid eye contact with them but Ian had noticed him.

"Watson! Drinking on your own? Why don't you come and join us? We're over there." He gestured towards the booth and David saw that Jenny had noticed him at last. She didn't smile. She didn't acknowledge him at all. She looked away and feigned a conversation with a girl across the table from her.

"I'm fine Ian. I'm just going."

"Nonsense, you've half a beer left. Go and talk to Jenny. She'll want to see you."

He knew that wasn't true from the way she had looked away from him but when Ian and his friend had bought the drinks, they insisted that he come over to the booth. When he arrived, he saw there was no room for him to sit down. Nobody moved over to make space and Ian and his friend passed the drinks around and then ignored him, as did everyone else in the booth. He stood there and stared at Jenny. She ignored him too. He felt idiotic standing there, the only one standing up, the only one not involved in a conversation and the only one not laughing. If he continued to stand there, he would appear idiotic, if he walked away without speaking, he would look even more foolish. He thought leaving might be the least bad option. He was about to go when Ian, at last, spoke to him.

"Hey David, did you ever find out who beat you up in the park that night?" Ian laughed, and a few of his friends were smiling now, although they didn't appear to know if the situation was funny or just awkward. Most of the conversation in the booth had stopped now and Jenny, at last, looked David in the eye. "David didn't see who attacked him, did you David?"

"No I didn't see who did it, but I know for certain who it was," he said.

Ian was laughing even louder now. "Hey everyone, what you need to know is that David is a genius. Only a genius would know who beat him up, even when he didn't see who did it. Are you going to tell the police? I didn't see who it was what done it, your honour, but here's his name and address." This caused more hilarity around the booth, although most of them had no idea what they were laughing at. Ian was laughing, so perhaps it was funny, so they laughed along with him. Jenny didn't find it at all amusing. She was furious with Ian for bringing up the subject and she was furious with David for claiming that he knew who had attacked him. Jenny stood up and struggled past her friends, and freed herself from the booth. "You need to come with me David," she said, "we need to have a talk." They walked out into the street, both struggling into their overcoats. They headed along the crowded pavements into the cold winter night.

"What do you mean by saying you know who it was that attacked you? What are you trying to do? Are you determined to spread lies about my father? Is that what you want?"

"I haven't told anyone about who did it Jenny, just you and my mum, that's the only time I've mentioned it."

"But just now you said you knew who did it, in front of everyone."

"I shouldn't have done that, I'm sorry, but I never said it was your Dad, and I never will Jenny. You can trust me."

"Trust you? Look at you! You look half mad or drunk, or both probably. I thought you didn't drink?"

"I started when I got to University. I'm good at it."

"So what did you mean when you said you knew for certain who attacked you? How can you be certain when you didn't see anyone?"

"My friend told me. He saw the whole thing."

"Your friend? What friend?"

"It doesn't matter."

"Oh Christ David, not Henry? The imaginary friend?"

"Who told you about Henry?"

"I've known for ages David. I heard your mother telling my mother. "Your mother worries about you talking to yourself all the time."

"There's nothing to worry about. I'm fine."

"She worries because you're always talking, to your

friend, when you're on your own. She can hear you up in your bedroom."

"Well that's something I've always done. It keeps me calm. It's not a problem."

"David. You could be hearing voices. That's not good."

"But I'm not hearing voices, he's real!"

Jenny shook her head in disbelief. "David, you need help. You had an imaginary friend when you were at primary school. I remember, you used to talk to him in class. It was funny then. It used to make me laugh. It's not funny anymore. This friend of yours doesn't exist. It's all in your head. It was okay when you were small. But now? It's not normal and it's not just the voices in your head. You think my Dad's out to get you. You said the same about Ian."

"Well even you can see, he doesn't like me."

"He's had a few drinks and he was making fun of you. That's all. It's banter, he's not really out to get you. You need to get help. Dad doesn't want to beat you up. Ian quite likes you. This friend of yours doesn't exist. If you can hear him talking it's because you're not well."

"You've got to believe me Jenny, don't lose faith in me please. If you don't believe in me, I don't know what I'm going to do. I still love you Jenny. You know that don't you?"

"Go home David. I need to get back to my friends. Go home and don't drink anymore."

"Can I see you Jenny?"

"Just go home David."

"Or just talk on the phone?"

"No. David. Just go home."

He walked away from her and didn't look back. He thought that she had been cruel to him. "I'll not go home. I'll walk. I'll walk all night." he said in a determined voice, almost Churchillian. "I'll never go home. Never!" He walked for about ten minutes, but felt very cold, and suddenly very tired, so he turned into the park gates and headed for home. Next morning, over breakfast, his mother lectured him on the evils of drink. He'd felt depressed but almost sober when he got into bed the previous evening but as soon as he lay down on the bed, the room began to spin. He sat on the edge of the bed and watched the weird motion of his bedroom walls, he closed one eye but it didn't help. He closed both eyes and the motion seemed to get worse. He stood up and grabbed onto the wall and tried to stop it moving but it wouldn't stop. He ran downstairs and into the backyard to the toilet and emptied the contents of his stomach into the bowl. He had thought that being an outside toilet, his mother wouldn't have heard a thing. But the noise of thunder as he descended the stairs, the back-door slamming and the shouts of 'Huey' coming from the privy had brought her out of her deep sleep. She listened to him creeping back up the stairs and back into his bed. He was still alive, so she

decided to wait until morning to advise him against
strong drink.

"You need to pull yourself together David. You're
going from bad to worse." She listed the many faults
he had developed since he had gone to University.
He couldn't disagree with any of it. He knew he'd
made a fool of himself in front of Jenny and he had
embarrassed himself when he got home drunk. His
mother deserved better and he told her so.

"You're right mum. You're right about everything.
I'll fix it. I'll put it right. I'll never drink again. I feel
awful. I'll clean my room. I'll go for a long walk. It'll
do me good."

"Will you be back for your tea?"

"Back about five."

He walked out of town toward Hambledon Hill.
Across the railway footbridge and up the steep
cobbled streets towards the moor. Over the canal
bridge and through a small mining village and
upwards beyond the last traces of housing to the
quarry. He turned over in his mind everything Jenny
and his mother had said to him. He couldn't blame
them for criticising his behaviour. His only friend
was Henry, he had made no effort to make friends
with the living. Henry had helped him in many ways
but he had allowed him to hide away from real life.
He had clung on to Jenny like a parasite using her
friends, her social contacts, he had fed off her
optimism and her positive approach to life. Without
her at University he had been lonely and depressed,

isolating himself from the world, burying himself in his academic work but completely incapable of managing on his own. It hadn't been easy to listen to their criticism, and he didn't agree with everything they said but he knew he had to do something to make things better. He couldn't go on behaving as he had over the last few weeks. He felt ashamed. He followed the track that meandered up the side of the quarry. Half the hill had been blasted away over the years to leave a long scar of a cliff. It was a magnificent empty space, a half-moon shape, hollowed out by years of quarrying. There was a lake at the base of the cliff and some shanty looking buildings with corrugated steel roofs. The buildings were derelict, the quarrying having been wound down years before. He followed the meandering track up the side of the quarry and climbed over the wire fence, ignoring the 'No Trespassing' sign. It was a long steep climb to the edge of the quarry cliff but the view was worth the effort. From the top he could see all the towns from Blackburn in the west to Nelson in the east. So many rows of terraced houses and redundant mill chimneys. Many of the factories and terraced streets were derelict now, lots of the houses boarded up awaiting demolition. He looked down on the canal meandering its way towards Leeds and the railway threading its way along beside the motorway. He sat on the very edge of the cliff. He liked high places. It made him feel powerful. Henry soon joined him.

"How are you feeling now lad? You got a hangover?"

"Not now. I'm fine. I'll never drink again."

"I used to say that, every Sunday morning usually. Me and the wife used to go out to the pub on a Saturday night. We both liked a drink. We'd get home and usually end up arguing about something, we always made up though. Making up's the best part."

"I've ruined everything between me and Jenny. She hates me now."

"No she doesn't. She's upset with you. She's disappointed in you. Your mum feels the same, but they both love you. You know that don't you?"

"I'm not so sure about Jenny."

"She'll come round, you'll see."

"Can I ask you something Henry?"

"Ask away lad."

"Well, during the war, when things got bad, do you think any of the soldiers deliberately hurt themselves, even killed themselves, to escape the suffering?"

"I'm sure some did, but I never saw it happen. What was more likely was men would do really stupid things, and that often got them killed."

"What sort of things?"

"Well, I've never told anyone this, but you remember I told you about that medal I got for rescuing that officer? When I was lying in that shell hole waiting for it to go dark, I could hear him moaning and

calling out. He was making such a noise I was surprised that the Germans didn't finish him off. Then, when it went dark, I thought maybe they were waiting for someone to try and rescue him. I thought they might want to kill two birds with one stone if you like, I remember that crossing my mind. I should have just got back to my own lines and left him. I knew that but I still went looking for him. That's the main reason I wasn't too proud of that medal. It wasn't an act of bravery. It was more an act of cowardice. That's the way I looked at it. I think I'd had enough. I think a part of me wanted to die. I think a lot of men did things like that. They didn't commit suicide as such, they just did really stupid things that got them killed. I remember when we were captured. We all stood there with our hands in the air. One of our officers started waving his revolver around, he was shouting 'Surrender be damned'. He'd no ammunition left, none of us had. But he started walking towards the Germans and they shot him dead. Some said he was brave. I thought he was stupid. Maybe he just wanted to die."

"You didn't die though, you were a hero."

"Yes, some hero."

David sat for a long time. Staring at the view, eating the sandwiches his mother had made for him, and chatting with Henry. It was a pleasant sort of picnic. PC Wayne Thompson approached the edge of the cliff with caution. This was his first real solo mission as a police constable. He had been asked to 'check out the situation' and report back. As he walked towards the figure, sat on the edge of the cliff, he wished he had asked what checking out a situation consisted of. How close did he have to get? Did he have to talk to the boy sitting on the edge, and if so, what should he say? He looked at the boy and thought he looked familiar. He was sitting right at the edge. That wasn't good. He was gesturing with his arms and talking. That wasn't good either. It didn't look right, him talking to himself like that. *"Hey up lad, the girl guides are here." Henry gestured towards Wayne, who was stalking them about five metres along the edge of the cliff face.* David looked round and instantly recognised his nemesis from his school days.

Wayne recognised David too. "David Watson! What you doing?"

"I'm looking at the view Wayne. What are you doing?"

"I'm just checking."

"Checking what?"

Wayne didn't reply. He looked at David for a while, but didn't speak. He had no idea what to do next. He was wondering if he had checked out the situation sufficiently well. Should he ask David more questions? Try to talk him down? He decided that he had done enough to please the Inspector. He knew the identity of the 'jumper' and that should be enough. He moved slowly, backwards, back down the path towards the car.

"That was very odd," David said. "That was Wayne, and he's a policeman. I wonder what he was doing up here?"

"He didn't stay long did he? I think you frightened him David."

"That's funny. Wayne being frightened of me. Makes a change. He made my life a misery for years."

"He's the one that chased you up that tree. I remember asking you whether you slipped out of that tree or whether you just let go. Do you remember?"

"I remember you asking me and like I said at the time, I don't really know. I don't think I meant to harm myself. Maybe it's like you said, maybe I just did something stupid without realising what the consequences might be. It's not the same as trying to harm yourself but it can have the same result."

"You know David, when I went out to find that young officer, it was a couple of days after my mate was killed. Charlie. We were at school together. We'd joined up together in Burnley. We were in Meerut, then in Ypres. We were best mates, two peas in a pod, we looked out for each other. We were carrying supplies up the communication trench when it happened. He had a bullet, went right through his neck. He bled to death. He couldn't speak but I held onto him and told him he'd be

alright. We both knew he wouldn't be. The blood was pouring out of him, and I tried but I couldn't stop it, or even slow it down. It didn't take long. Seemed a long time. Poor Charlie. I don't know why but I always thought that Charlie and me would survive the war. But when he died, I didn't feel as safe anymore. I didn't think I'd get through it. I suppose when you start to think like that, you start to think you might as well get it over with, sooner rather than later. When I went out to find that officer, it wasn't a brave thing to do at all. I didn't care if I died or not, in fact I think I would have preferred a quick bullet. Coward's way out."

"Well I think you were brave."

"There's nothing brave about wanting to die. It's wanting to survive that takes courage."

"Do you think I'm going to take the coward's way out Henry? Is that why you came to find me in the first place?"

"I think it was you that found me in the first place. Anyway, to answer your question, I didn't think it was an accident when you fell out of that tree. You always seem to like high places. Sitting on the edge of this cliff, well that's risky enough. Some might say downright stupid. But I think that you've made a decision now. I think you're going to be alright. I think you'll make your mother proud of you. I think you'll get that girl of yours back too. You're going to get along just fine from now on."

"I'm not brave enough to jump off," he said leaning forward to peer at the rocks below."

"You're not selfish enough to do that. You think too much of your mother to do something like that. And there's nothing brave about jumping. How long would it take to hit the bottom? Ten seconds. Ten seconds, then bang! Nothing, no pain. No pain for you, but a lifetime of pain for your mother and your brother and sisters, and that girl of yours."

"She doesn't care about me."

"Of course she does. You'll see. Everything will be sorted out."

"I'm not so sure."

Henry looked thoughtful. "I never learned much at school," he said, "didn't have an education like you've had. I was never clever in that way. My education was watching men survive the most awful things. I've seen a lot of things no human being should ever see. I've watched men doing things you couldn't even imagine or even want to think about. That's what makes me good at reading people and that's why I know you'll be alright now. You aren't going to hurt yourself. You're not going to let go again."

"I get the feeling you're planning to leave me Henry."

"Yes lad, I am. You don't need me anymore. I think you know it's the right time for me to leave you. You're a clever lad. You'll work it out with that girl of yours. You'll learn how to get along with people. I've

213

already stayed too long. People will think you're balmy, talking to yourself. They'll put you away if I stick around, like my Mary. Poor girl."

"You'll not come back to see me then?"

"No lad. I'd like to but I won't come back. It's for the best. You need to manage on your own from now on."

"You've really helped me Henry. Helped me understand what's important."

"Well that's good to hear."

"Can I ask you something Henry?"

"Anything lad."

"My Dad. Did he commit suicide?"

"Of course not, he loved you far too much to do that." Henry stood up. "It's been an honour and a privilege lad. I'm going now, so see you take care of yourself."

"Thanks Henry. You too."

Henry smiled. "Now lad, I'll show you how the King's favourite regiment march away." Henry walked back from the edge and then stood smartly to attention. "Company in close order, by the left, quick march!" He started to march away looking every inch the soldier. "To the left salute!" His head flashed to the left and he saluted 'up, two three four five, down and away'. He winked at David a final farewell, and was gone.

David had a tear in his eye and a lump in his throat as he stood in a trance watching Henry march away. Out of his life forever. His reverie was broken by a rumbling sound followed by a huge crash coming from further down the quarry. He peered over the edge to see a huge blue caravan floating in the lake. "I think it's time I went home," he said to himself. "I'm going to be late." He reached in his pocket for his phone. "I'll be in trouble now. It's at home. Mum worries if I'm late, especially after Stephen beat me up. She always did worry but I suppose I've given her plenty to worry about. Need to make things better. Need to stop talking to myself too." He hurried down the track as the winter gloom closed in and darkness began to creep into the sky above him and into the valley below.

By the time his mother had arrived at the top of the quarry by the longer of the two routes, David had already started to make his way down by the shorter, more direct route. He was soon spotted by the crowd who were penned in behind the blue tapes. There was a ripple of applause. The Chief Inspector was informed and he was delighted to pass on the good news to Irene.

Finally, at the bottom, David's mother greeted him with a mixture of tears, hugs and abuse when he arrived. Several policemen were talking to him, all asking different questions at the same time. The negotiator was competing with his mother for his attention.

"I'm sorry if I caused all this fuss," he said when he finally had chance to speak. "If I'd known what was going on, I'd have come down earlier. I didn't know anyone was down here until that caravan fell into the lake.",

"You don't need to be ashamed about suicidal feelings David," the negotiator said eagerly. "Being honest about how you feel is a very important first step."

"You can leave us now," Irene said to the negotiator.

"Are you saying you had no intention of jumping?" The Inspector asked.

"No. I even told Wayne, I was just looking at the view."

"Who's Wayne?" several of them said, all at the same time.

"You mean PC Thompson?" asked the Inspector. "He never came near you. I specifically told him to keep out of sight. He went up to check out the report, it was Thompson that identified you. From a distance!"

"Well he spoke to me, and I spoke to him. He was close enough for me to read the number on his shoulder. PC 911."

"What made you remember his number?" The Chief Inspector asked.

"You can't forget a number like that can you? A prime number, the emergency number in the US, and the date of the attacks on the twin towers. Numbers like that tend to stick, don't they?"

The Chief Inspector had heard enough. "You can take Mrs Watson and her son home now," he said to his driver. "You can pick me up here afterwards. I need to discuss a few things with the Inspector." "Well David Watson," his mother said, when they were safely back in their living room." I want you to tell me everything, everything that happened, everything that went on in that head of yours, everyone you spoke to. I want to know exactly what happened from the moment you left this house to the moment you arrived back down that quarry road."

She wanted the truth, so he told her, everything. Everything that was said between himself and Henry. He told her Henry had gone, left him and wouldn't be coming back. She listened in silence. She was horrified at the detail of the conversations her son was having with 'the voices' in his head. She knew she would have to get him some treatment. She had spent years making excuses for him, never telling anyone about his late-night conversations with Henry. Delighted as she was to have him safe and home, she was haunted by the realisation that she would have to get him some help, psychiatric help.

Chapter 12.

The next morning there was a meeting at the Police Headquarters in Fulwood to analyse the debacle at the quarry. It took two hours of meandering discussion for the participants to realise that there was no evidence that David Watson had any intention of committing suicide. However, there was the small matter of a rather expensive Police Incident Caravan floating in small pieces in the lake at the base of the quarry. Over the next two hours the participants persuaded each other that a young life had been saved and that everyone involved had carried out their duties with a high level of professionalism. After a decent lunch the atmosphere in the meeting room became even more self-congratulatory and by five o'clock that afternoon every difficulty had been overcome. A new Incident caravan had been ordered, the negotiator had arranged for a Psychiatric assessment for the 'survivor' and the Inspector had recommended that Wayne's probationary period be confirmed. It was reported however that the Fire Brigade had shown undue tardiness and complacency and had not contributed to the highly successful outcome of the operation.

The same morning Irene ate breakfast in silence. However, David was cheerfully chatting away about the blue caravan in the lake, Wayne in uniform, the fire brigade, all the blue flashing lights and the whole pantomime surrounding his picnic on the top of Hambledon Quarry. He also talked about the future, how he was going to make a success of University, how he was going to do better, be more sociable. The sun would come out and rivers were going to flow with milk and honey. Irene, while delighted that her son was more cheerful than he had been for months, realised that she would have to talk to someone about his mental health. She felt like Judas just thinking about it. She had decided to make the call when he was out of the house but at the same time, she didn't want to let him out of her sight. Her son was safe while he was here with her, in her tiny house. After the previous day's drama, she didn't feel he was safe anywhere else.

It was late that evening when someone knocked on her front door. The noise was so loud it sounded as if someone was trying to break the door down. Irene opened the door ready to scold whoever was there but stopped short when she saw Sandra and Jenny. They'd both been crying. They stood there with red eyes full of fear. Sandra's voice broke as she asked if they could come in.

"Yes, come in, what's happened?" She ushered them into the living room. David was surprised to see Jenny but concerned by the tears and her mother seemed close to collapse. Sandra was telling them what had happened but she was shaking so much and sobbing so hard that Irene and David couldn't follow what she was trying to say.

"Sit down love, take your time. I'll make you some tea. David..."

Jenny remained silent. She seemed calmer than her mother but was clearly distressed. David touched her on the shoulder, after he'd served them both with the tea. She gave him a brave smile, which he found reassuring. When Sandra became calm enough to talk, she told them what had happened.

"It all started this afternoon. Stephen came downstairs with Jenny's engagement ring on a chain. I knew about it but I hadn't told Stephen. He'd been through her things and found the ring and some letters from David. He was furious. He wouldn't listen to anything I said. He said I'd lied to him. He said I was useless, called me some terrible things. He took the ring and the chain into the back garden and threw them into the woods. I went to look for them but I couldn't find them. When I came back, he told me to get out of his sight, which I did. I thought he was going to kill me he looked so angry."

Sandra's cheek was swollen and bruised. David and Irene had noticed as soon as she came into the room but pretended not to have seen. Jenny sat next to her mother on the sofa and clung on to her as she listened. Sandra gave more terrible details of Stephen's behaviour and then broke down again.

There was silence as nobody could find the right words, but then Jenny took up the story.

"When I came home in the evening, I told mum and dad what I'd heard about David, up at the quarry. How the police had been called. I could see that they had been having words. Anyway, when I mentioned about David, my mum started shouting at my Dad. I'd never heard her shout at him like that before. She said it was his fault that me and David had split up. She said she should have told the police what he'd done. I didn't understand what she was talking about. She called him a bully and a coward. That's when he hit her. I'd never seen him like that before. He was like a madman. He shouted at me too. I thought he was going to hit me as well as my mum. He said I was never to go near David again. He told my mum to get out of the house and never come back. He kept shouting the same terrible things over and over again. When mum ran out of the house I ran after her. We didn't know where else to come."

"I'm so sorry," Sandra said, "I shouldn't have lied to Jenny about her Dad being in Southampton. I shouldn't have covered for him. When I heard about David being up on that quarry, I thought he might have killed himself. I should have said something. I realise that now."

"Do you mean to tell me that you knew all the time that it was your husband who attacked David?" Irene asked.

"I wasn't sure Irene, I had my suspicions, but I didn't know, I was frightened."

"Well Sandra, you should have said something." David intervened. "It's easy to talk mum about what you should do. When you're the one being bullied it's not so easy. I know that. Bullies keep at you all the time. It's not as easy to stand up to them as you might think."

"It's my fault too," Jenny said, "I should have noticed; all those times mum walked into doors and the time she was supposed to have fallen down the stairs. I should have known what was really going on. I suppose I didn't want to see it. I didn't want to admit it to myself. I'm so sorry mum and I'm sorry I didn't believe you David. I should have listened to you too."

"Right!" Irene said, "I don't want to hear anymore apologies. David's right. There's only one person needs to apologise. If you take my advice, you'll contact the police in the morning, it's too late now. It's not going to get any better with Jenny away at college it's only going to get worse. If you like you can stay here tonight or as long as you need to, we've plenty of room. David, go and make up the beds in your sisters' room."

David and Jenny went upstairs to sort out the beds, while Irene and Sandra made drinks and fussed around in the kitchen. With things to do and decisions made everyone felt calmer. Having everything sorted out for the night the four of them sat and chatted about other things and better times and even managed some forced laughter. David was delighted that Jenny seemed to have forgiven him and Sandra kept on saying how grateful she was for their help and Irene repeatedly told her to stop worrying about it.

After an hour or so there was a knock at the door. The atmosphere in the room changed instantly. They all sat stock still. Nobody spoke, but they all shared the same thought. There was a second knock at the door, slightly louder this time.

"Right. Stay there and don't make a sound." Irene was on her feet. "If that's Stephen, I'll tell him I haven't seen either of you. He'll not get past me!" She marched out of the living room and down the passage-way to the front door. She had a look of quiet determination on her face but internally she was frightened. She had declared with calm confidence that Stephen wouldn't get past her but she knew, that if he was really determined, there was nothing she could do to stop him. It was with some trepidation that she opened the door. Before it was fully opened, she was relieved to see that it wasn't Stephen. It was a tall thin man, not much older than David, who stood there with a smile on his face. "This is for David," he said." Irene looked him up and down. His clothes were rather odd and his face looked familiar but she couldn't place it. "Do you want to come in?" she asked.

"No Irene, I've got to get going."

He walked away and Irene watched him go without saying a word. Even though she was relieved that it hadn't been Stephen at the door she still felt frightened. In the living room they sat in silence and listened to the sound of the door opening. They could hear a voice but it was a quiet voice, they couldn't hear what was said but they knew it wasn't Stephen. They could hear Irene inviting someone in. It certainly wasn't Stephen. Irene came back into the living room looking perplexed.

"Who was it?"

"I don't know, he looked familiar but I don't know who he was. He was a strange looking character. He wouldn't come in. He brought a parcel. He said it was for David." Irene handed the package to David. Jenny and Sandra looked relieved that Stephen hadn't followed them. The parcel was wrapped with thick brown paper and tied up with string. The wrapping seemed worn and the string discoloured with age. When it was open, the first thing he saw was a small newspaper cutting. David held it up, to show everyone, and Irene told him to read it out.

"Mr and Mrs Bradshaw, 24 James St Padiham, have been officially informed that their son, Private James Alan Bradshaw has been killed in action in the Mediterranean theatre of war. Aged 20, Private Bradshaw joined the Army in 1942 and went overseas with an infantry battalion in September 1942 and served for a period in Persia. As a boy

Private Bradshaw attended Cross Bank School and later was employed at Progress Mills. His father Henry, after serving a number of years in the army, including 1914-18 re-joined in 1939 in answer to Mr Chamberlain's appeal. He was discharged two years later."

"How sad," Jenny said, "is there a date on the article?"

"No," David said, "but it would be September 1943."

"What else is in there?" Irene asked.

David pulled out some letters, tied with a faded ribbon. "They're addressed to Henry," he said, "from Mary." He opened the first one and read it to them.

"It's dated the 18th of December 1914. 'Dear Henry, I think about you all the time and pray that you will keep safe. I still live in hope that the war will be won by Christmas. All my brothers are keen to join the fight and worry that it will all be over before they get the chance. Young Herbert signed the papers to join the army last week but mum said he couldn't go as he's only 15. She wrote a nice letter to the Barracks at Preston saying she didn't want him to go but would let him when he's old enough. She has sent his birth certificate with the letter and hopes they will allow her to keep him at home. Herbert will be disappointed if he isn't allowed to go. I'm doing well at work and am on eight loom at the moment, but hoping to get moved on to twelve soon. Wishing you all my love, my dearest, with hope that we will be together again very soon, yours with love, Mary.'"

"How lovely," said Irene, "can I see the letter?"

David handed the letter over to his mother.

"I wonder if she ever saw him again?" Jenny said.

"They never saw each other again," David told them. "When he was in Ypres, she stopped replying to his letters. His mother wrote to tell him that Mary and her parents had moved away. She was pregnant and they had the baby adopted. He never knew the baby's name, or even whether it was a boy or a girl. Mary was sent to an asylum, the one that used to be at Brockhall. She spent the rest of her life there. He only found out about that after she'd died."

"Mary's surname was Kelly!" Irene said. "That was you grandma's maiden name."

"Look at this!" David said, suddenly excited. He held a small, slim, leather bound box in his hand and when he opened it, they could see a large, round silver medal. "It's the missing medal that Dad always talked about." He held up the Distinguished Conduct Medal. "Awarded to Henry Bradshaw for distinguished conduct in the field."

"That man at the front door?" Irene said slowly.

"It was Henry." David said. "He looked familiar to you because you've seen his photograph, the postcard he sent from Chemnitz, from the prisoner of war camp. It's up in my room."

"But that's not possible. He wasn't a ghost. He was as real as you and me. He even knew my name. I asked him to come in. I don't really know why I said that. He said he couldn't because he had to get going, and he handed me the parcel. That's for David, he said. Then he walked down the street. I watched him. He was dressed a bit funny but he was as real as you and me."

"I told you mum. He wasn't just in my head. He *was* real. This is just his way of saying goodbye." David held up the medal. "This is his way of telling you that I don't belong in a hospital, or an asylum, as he would say. He wanted you to know that there's nothing wrong with me, that I don't hear voices, that I'm not ill. He's gone now and won't come back but he wants you to know that I'll be alright. He wants you to know that I'm not crazy, that from now on, things will get better."

Irene was pale with fright. "I think I'm going mad, never mind you. It's just not possible."

"Well you can see the things he gave you," David said. "They're real enough. Henry was real too. He came and went like a ghost but he was a real friend to me. He was my best friend. Apart from you Jenny."

Jenny and her mother sat in silence, unable to believe what they were hearing. David handed them the contents of the parcel as if to reassure them that the letters and the medal were real. They held them with care and stared at them, slowly absorbing the situation that had just played out before them.

"Have you ever wondered why Henry Bradshaw would want to help you David?" Irene asked.

"I suppose I did when I was younger. As I got older, I just thought of him as a friend."

"I think he could have been more than just your friend David." Irene went into her room and, after a few minutes, returned clutching a large folder full of papers. She picked out several sheets of paper, some brown with age; birth certificates, death certificates, and finally she found what she was looking for. "This is your grandfather's marriage certificate David. Your Dad's father Michael Watson married Elizabeth Kelly on the 15th of March 1947 at Habergham Parish Church. Your Grandmother Watson was adopted as a baby. Look at the column where it shows the name of the Father of the bride."

"It's left blank," David said.

"It's blank because Elizabeth Kelly was illegitimate and nobody knew who the father was."

"You mean her father could have been Henry?"

"And her mother could have been Mary Kelly."

Chapter13.

The fact that Lancashire Constabulary reported the farcical pantomime at Hambledon quarry as a successful rescue of a potential suicide, was to have consequences for David and his mother. The negotiator had filed a report for the Chief Inspector describing David Watson's suicidal tendencies in some detail. He passed it on to the Forensic Psychiatry Department at Preston Royal Hospital. They read the report and wrote a letter to David's GP asking him to assess David's suitability to be sectioned under the Mental Health Act.

The morning after the night before was difficult for Jenny and Sandra who both struggled with the reality of the previous day's events. Sandra had experienced her husband's abuse and tasted his fists many times but she had never walked out on him before. Talk of contacting the police had just been talk the previous night but now, in the morning, it was real and it was terrifying. Jenny felt as if she had woken up from a long sleep of denial. The rose-tinted view of her family life had been shattered with one sickening blow to her mother's face. Jenny had managed to sleep but her mother looked as if she had suffered a long night staring at the ceiling looking for some clues about what to do next. She knew what she should do but worried that she might not have the strength of mind to follow it through. Irene was almost as pensive as her two visitors, trying to rationalise the visit of her husband's grandfather who had been buried in St John's churchyard sometime in 1965. Could it *really* have been a ghost? She wanted to believe it, of course, because it meant her son hadn't been hearing voices or hallucinating. The fact that Jenny's father could have been guilty of such violence meant that David wasn't paranoid. The symptoms of psychosis had fallen away one by one. She felt frightened when she ought to have felt relief. David was almost too cheerful to be tolerated by the three women in his company. Diplomacy was never his strong suit but when he offered to look for a divorce lawyer on the internet, as his three companions stared into their morning coffees, it was not well received. He didn't notice his mother's threatening posture and carried on tapping on his phone for more information. When he announced that there was a refuge in Burnley for victims of domestic abuse, he would have become a victim of domestic abuse himself had Sandra not stopped Irene in her tracks.

"He's only trying to be helpful," Sandra said.

"Helpful? I'll give him helpful. You want to put your brain in gear before you open your mouth again. Jenny and Sandra can stay here as long as they need to. You're the only one'll be going to a refuge if you don't put that phone away."

"I'm just...."

"Trying to be helpful, I know, well don't."

Jenny gave him a smile which made him feel better.

"I like having you both here," he said, "I'm glad you came and I don't want you to leave. I just thought, well, I won't do any more thinking, not out loud anyway."

"Don't worry," Sandra said with a brave smile.

"You're right. We have to make some decisions. We need to get on with it."

"David," said his mother, "come with me down the shops and let these girls have a chat in private. Sandra, take this and make a list of things you need, me and David will pick them up for you."

When David and his mother returned from the shops, they found Lionel on the doorstep. He was dressed in his usual suit and tie, a dark overcoat and scarf.

He was agitated. There was no physical manifestation of his agitation, his face was its normal default-placid. When he spoke however, there was a trace of annoyance in his voice. David didn't notice the slight tremor in his voice but Irene knew what it meant. For Lionel this was the furthest extreme of his emotional spectrum, he wasn't just unhappy, he was angry-borderline furious. He wasn't a man to display his emotions. When he became ecstatic, at the other end of the spectrum, his happiness was imperceptible to people who didn't know him well.

"We were to have lunch. I booked a table for 12. It's nearly half past."

"I'm really sorry Lionel, I forgot. There's a lot going on. Come in," she said as she opened the door.

"There's someone inside but they wouldn't let me in."

"Yes, I'll explain everything. Come on in."

Lionel was the last person that any of them had wanted to see but once he had been appraised of the story, he became the very person they needed to move things forward. He listened, asked questions without being judgemental, made recommendations and, once he was given the go ahead, he acted. Lunch was cancelled. The police were contacted. An email sent to the family lawyer. He advised Sandra to draw money on their joint account and with their agreement he wrote out a plan of action. Sandra was able to follow the plan without constantly agonising over each step and within a matter of days everything was moving forward. Stephen was put under a restraining order pending investigation, the family home was to be sold and husband and wife were heading towards divorce. Lionel, once the annoying little accountant that Irene had put up with, had become the fountain of all wisdom and good sense. He became the go-to person for Irene, Sandra and Jenny. David was less of a fan and referred to him as 'the undertaker', much to the annoyance of his mother.

When the time came for David to go back to Manchester Jenny offered to go with him to the station. She sat on his bed in his room while he packed his bag. She couldn't help but smile when she thought about him standing beside his bed shouting at her father over the telephone a few months before. "You do know," she said, "I thought you were completely mad, when you told me that my Dad had attacked you."

"You thought I was schizophrenic."

"To be fair, you had all the symptoms. Hearing voices, paranoia, hallucinations."

"And all the time I was talking to a ghost."

"Yes. That's not at all weird."

"If my mother hadn't met him you wouldn't have believed me, would you?"

"I wanted to believe you. I really did. I didn't find it easy."

"Do you believe me now?"

She thought for a moment and that moment answered the question for him.

"You're still not sure, are you?"

"What do you mean?"

"You still think I might be crazy."

"I've always known you were crazy. Idiot. You can still love crazy people David."

"I don't want you to think I'm crazy. I want you to trust me. If I see any more ghosts, I will tell you. I won't keep it secret next time, if there is a next time."

"Do you think you will, see more ghosts?"

"I don't think so but they are all around us, just looking out for us, watching us. You just have to look for them and you'll find them."

"I've never seen one."

"Have you ever looked?"

"No, I suppose not. I wouldn't want to see a ghost. I'd be frightened."

"There's nothing to be frightened of."

"Have you seen other ghosts? Apart from Henry?"

"There was a little girl at Primary school who used to talk to me but mum said I shouldn't talk to her and after a while she went away."

"You're doing a wind-up now," she said doubtfully.

"No, I always do what mum tells me."

"Do you miss Henry now that he's gone?"

"Not when you're around Jenny."

"You old smoothie. Come on, hurry up, you're going to miss your train."

"Are you sure you're doing the right thing," he asked, "staying here with your mum rather than going back to nursing school?"

"The college said I can start again next year. They were very understanding when I told them what had happened. My mum needs my help and I want to help her."

"The good thing is you will be closer."

She laughed at him. "What are you trying to say?"

"I'm saying I could come home every weekend. We could hook up."

"Hook up? Is that what they do in Manchester? Hook up?"

"We could get married Jenny. If you like?"

"You said we should wait three years. Remember?"

"I've changed my mind. I'm in love with you."

"I'm sure you are." She smiled at him and touched his cheek with her hand. It sent electricity through him.

"I don't want to leave you Jenny."

"We're too young to get married. We both agreed and you need to show me you can manage on your own, without Henry, without me. I couldn't marry someone who was incapable of managing life on their own any more than I could marry someone who was hearing voices every night. You go to Manchester and make a success of yourself. Show me you can make friends and manage on your own. You need to find out if you really love me or whether you're just too scared to live without me. We'll always be good friends David but don't ask me to marry you until you've learned to make a life for yourself without relying on anyone else to do it for you."

"Have you been rehearsing that?" he asked but then he noticed she had tears in her eyes. He thought that his heart would break and he had an ache in his chest and in his throat. Suddenly he couldn't speak so he stood up and took her hand and they left the house for the station.

"Mum says you can stay with her if you like, rather than rent a place."

"No, we need to move out. Your mum needs to build a life for herself too. She might want to move in with Lionel."

David didn't answer. He didn't like Lionel but he knew he disliked him for no good reason. He knew that Jenny thought he should look for the good in people rather than being negative all the time. He struggled to see good in people and when he criticised them, he thought he was being honest rather than negative. However, he wanted Jenny's approval so he said nothing.

"You don't like him, do you?"

"I love him, but in a very special way."

"Well, he'll look after your mum."

"My mother can look after herself."

When David entered the bar and lounge at the University Accommodation Campus his confidence evaporated. He walked past group after group of animated students all talking at once, laughing, arm waving, discussing and arguing. All of them so preoccupied with each other he knew he wouldn't be welcomed into their circle. He recalled his hairbrained comments when he had first started college and how he had made some poor Tamsin cry because he'd asked her what subjects she was doing. He would have to be more circumspect on this occasion. He was determined to make an effort to be sociable, to make friends, to prove that he could manage on his own. David did several tours of the lounge looking for a vacant seat where he thought he might feel welcome but without success. He might have felt embarrassed about wandering around like a lost soul if he felt that anyone had noticed his existence but nobody seemed to be aware of his presence. He went to the bar and ordered a drink. He tried to make conversation with the girl who served him but she replied to his searching questions with monosyllables. He thought she was a moron and she thought the same about him. David resumed his peregrination, this time with drink in hand, and was determined to find a place to settle. He spotted a table with four seats where only a boy and a girl sat. They were not speaking, there was no laughter, no animated gestures. This was his kind of table. "Do you mind if I sit here?" he said, half sitting half standing. They looked at him in silence and he hovered half up and half down, in a position that couldn't be maintained for more than a few seconds. He received no reply so sat down next to the girl. She was pretty and blonde. The boy looked at him with something approaching disgust but offered no greeting. David smiled. Jenny had told him he didn't smile often enough so he had been practising in the mirror, trying to make a clear distinction between a friendly smile and a threatening growl. He gave the warm smile his best shot but the boy opposite still didn't seem pleased.

237

His attention turned to the girl who was sat beside him.

"Did you have a good Christmas?" he asked, smiling again.

She glanced in his direction but said nothing.

"Get lots of presents, did you?"

Still no response. This wasn't going well.

"Any surprises? He asked.

"I'm pregnant," she said suddenly and a tear rolled down her cheek, her Manchester accent somewhat masked by the quiver in her voice.

"Oh!" David said, wondering whether congratulations might be in order.

"Why don't you fuck off?" said the boy, suddenly angry. David knew he was being spoken to rather than the girl.

"Don't talk to him like that!" the girl said.

"I'm sorry," David said, "I didn't mean to intrude. I'll find somewhere else to sit."

"Don't go," the girl said, "there's no need to take any notice of *him*." She nodded towards the boy. The boy was tall and overweight. He wore spectacles and had curly hair. When he spoke, it was with a southern accent; more fack than fuck, more owf than off.

David searched his brain cells for something suitable to say, a billion neurons burst into life and released chemicals into a trillion synapses that allowed neurons more numerous than the stars in the galaxy to communicate with one another. All this frenzied biochemical activity produced a question that David regretted the instant he uttered it. "Is he the father?"

"Yes," said the girl "hard to believe it isn't it? You wouldn't think he had it in him." David had the good sense not to answer.

"I've had enough," said the boy. "I've told you what to do. You need to get rid of it and the sooner the better. And you," he looked down at David, "you can go and fack yourself." That was the boy's parting shot. He put one finger to his spectacles, pushed them closer to his fat face and stood up and left.

There was a momentary silence but David was determined to be positive. "Your boyfriend seems like a nice sort of chap," he said.

The girl let out a screech, a see saw donkey-like braying laugh that David thought might be wailing sorrow. Her head moved down towards chest, her shoulders started heaving up and down but it was the hee-hawing sound that turned the heads from the surrounding tables. He looked at her and it *was* laughter rather than tears. It wasn't obvious. He was pleased she was laughing but hoped she would stop because he hated the bewildered attention of the neighbouring tables. He knew some of them would think she was crying and that he had caused her to be upset.

"Can you stop laughing?" he said at last.

This question seemed to stimulate more loud joy from the girl but eventually she calmed down and looked at him. "I'm Rebecca," she said, "and I think you're hilarious."

"You're not the first to think that," he said. "My name's David. David Watson. I'm studying Maths. What subjects are you doing?"

She laughed again and David wished she would stop.

"Why ask about my subjects?" she said." You just found out my boyfriend wants me to abort his child and, like, you ask me about my subjects?"

"I was trying to take an interest. I've been told I don't take an interest normally and I'm trying to improve. Do you want to have an abortion?"

She shook her head in disbelief. "So, I've just done a pregnancy test this morning?"

David knew this wasn't a question. His social skills were coming along in leaps and bounds. "When was your last period?" he asked.

"Oh man, what a question. When was my last period? Christ!" She didn't seem annoyed more amused or bewildered or somewhere between the two.

"I only asked because I think you could have a pharmaceutical abortion within 10 weeks whereas after 10 weeks you have to have surgery. You could always have the baby. I think that could be a good option. If my girlfriend got pregnant, I wouldn't want her to have an abortion. Not that I have any ethical objections. I think it's up to the woman. They're the ones taking all the risks of pregnancy. Pregnancy is a massive strain on the cardiovascular system apparently. A hundred years ago a lot of women died during childbirth. It's safer now of course."

"Wow!"

David gave her a quizzical look. He wanted to know what 'wow' meant but his instinct told him not to ask.

"I mean like you appear out of nowhere, my slob of a boyfriend tells you to fuck off, you ignore it and tell me he seems like a nice bloke and then start giving me medical advice. Are you a medic?"

"No I'm doing Maths, like I said but I researched contraception and pregnancy and abortion before I visited the family planning clinic with my girlfriend. Well, I took her to the wrong clinic at first but that's another story. She wasn't pleased. She said I should have been more organised and she had a point I suppose."

"Which clinic did you take her to?"

"The sexual health clinic, it was an easy mistake to make."

"A sexual health clinic?"

"Is that a question?" he asked her.

"Of course, it's a question. What else would it be?"

"It's where you go if you've got chlamydia, syphilis, that sort of thing."

"And you took your girlfriend, by mistake? Is she still

your girlfriend?"

David pondered the question. He didn't really know the answer. "It's a long story," he said.

"Well man I've got to hear it yea? Stay there don't move. What are you drinking?"

"Water."

She laughed, not at all loud this time and went to the bar for drinks.

David had made his first friend at University. Rebecca found him amusing. Her habit of laughing like a squeaky see-saw drove him crazy and she was a smoker but apart from the smell of cigarette ash and the loud braying noises she was quite good company and she was a friend. She was a friend that he had found all on his own. He had found her in unusual circumstances but he had found her.

Chapter 14.

Back in Padiham, Lionel was driving Irene back to her house from the restaurant where they had enjoyed the postponed lunch. They had stopped at the Pelican crossing and Lionel was talking. He was doing a post-lunch analysis of the quality of food and service they had received at the White Bull Inn. "The waitress was well trained but her apron wasn't clean. I thought my starter was a little on the small side but the main course was excellent." He continued at some length but Irene wasn't listening. She liked Lionel and was grateful for his attentions but she knew she could never love him and she thought that if he didn't stop talking about the lunch, she might scream. His biggest strength was his biggest weakness - the strength being his ability to analyse the fine detail of any situation and the weakness was to talk about it at great length. "Did you notice what percentage service charge they suggested?" He asked her as he started to pull away from the crossing.
"Oh my God look!" Irene shouted. "Stop the car Lionel, pull over."
"I can't stop here, there's yellow lines."
"Just stop as soon as you can."
Lionel continued to drive for some considerable distance to find what he called a 'proper parking place', much to Irene's annoyance. She wanted to

243

shout at him to stop immediately but she knew he wouldn't take it well so she fumed in silence.

"There's a car park near the old post office," he said.

"It was Henry," she said, "at the pelican crossing, he walked straight in front of us."

Lionel pulled a face. Irene had told him about Henry and the parcel with the medal and the letters from Mary Kelly. He didn't believe in ghosts.

"I know you don't believe any of it but if you park the car we'll go after him and ask him. Seeing is believing."

Lionel parked the car and reluctantly followed Irene back towards the town. She wanted to run but Lionel thought it was undignified so they walked along as fast as Irene could persuade him to go. As Irene lead the way back into the town centre Lionel twittered on by her side; "I understand why you want to believe in this ghost friend of your son's, I really do. It's perfectly understandable. However, I still think David needs psychiatric assessment. Mental illness is nothing to be ashamed of and it's eminently treatable. There could be a perfectly logical explanation for all of this. I mean to say, is it really possible that someone who fought in the First World War and died in the 1960's has just walked across a pelican crossing?"

"I saw him," Irene said, irritated.

"You saw someone. You said yourself that this ghost looked like flesh and blood when he came to your door that night. You might find Irene, that the reason he looked like flesh and blood was that he was just that; flesh and blood. Not some spectre from a hundred years ago. I mean to say, if he was a ghost and he told your son he was leaving and not coming back what is he doing wandering around the town now and using a pelican crossing? I mean to say, why would a ghost use a pelican crossing?"

"Stop saying 'I mean to say' for God's sake if you want to say something just say it and have done with it." They had got back to the main road now and Irene was looking to her left and right to see if she could spot Henry.

"Well really Irene, there's no need to be abrupt. I am only trying to help."

Irene had a sudden desire to tell Lionel that he was a supercilious little shit but she ignored the anger that was simmering inside her and focused on looking for Henry. "Come on let's look in the park, he was heading that way." Lionel pulled another face but followed her towards the park. As soon as they entered the park, she saw him walking towards the War Memorial. "That's him! Come on Lionel." She ran after him and called out his name but he carried on walking. Irene was in touching distance of him when he turned round. He looked straight into her eyes and her blood ran cold. He gave her a slight smile and had a tranquil knowing look on his face that made her suddenly frightened but calm, both at the same time. He seemed other worldly. He didn't speak and neither did Irene. It was Lionel who broke the silence as he arrived slightly breathless. "So, this is Henry," he said with something approaching sarcasm in his tone. Irene gave him a look of disgust. 'Henry' didn't respond to Lionel. He was dressed in the same, rather old fashioned, clothes that Irene had seen when he delivered the parcel.

"You brought the parcel to our house the other night?" Irene said at last.

"Yea, were it alright? I thought you'd want it." His other worldliness disappeared as soon as he spoke to her.

"Are you, Henry?" she asked.

"Henry? No, I'm Alan."

Irene was shocked but when she spoke, she sounded annoyed. "But you brought the parcel and it had the missing medal."

"Me Mam hid 'em. She hid a lot a things. When 'ouse were cleared they turned up." He spoke with a thick accent. Not at all ghost-like.

"So," Lionel put in, "you're not Henry, and you didn't fight in the First World War?"

Alan shook his head. "No, like I said. I'm Alan." He looked embarrassed suddenly. "Look, if you don't want the medal and the letters don't worry. It's just that there were no one to pass them onto in

the family."
*Irene was distraught. Lionel was right. Ghosts
don't walk across pelican crossings. Why would
they? They can walk through walls. They can just
appear like Henry did in David's bedroom every
night. But this was no ghost and neither was
Henry. The awful truth was that David had been
hearing voices after all.*
*"I'm sorry, I'll ave to get goin now." He smiled.
"Nice to have met you." He walked away.*
*Lionel had a smug expression on his face but was
diplomatic enough not to say a word to Irene. He
gave her time to absorb the truth about Henry.*

David had mixed results from his efforts to socialise
with his fellow students on the 18th floor. There
were several cliques, none of which he seemed to fit
into. He didn't drink and that seemed to ostracise
him from about half of them and he didn't smoke
which seemed to isolate him from the rest. It wasn't
only tobacco they were smoking. He knew they all
thought he was a geek but he enjoyed being a geek
and he found the endless drug induced laughter
rather tedious and boring. He made an effort to get
along with all of them but became close to none of
them. Rebecca kept in touch with him by text and
What's App, she sent him about a dozen messages
each day, none of them were particularly significant
but he replied to them all because the messages

from her was the extent of his social life. He bumped into her a few times and they met up for coffee during the day but he was reluctant to meet her in the evening as that would seem like a date and she already had a partner. He still thought of Jenny as his partner but he suspected that she didn't feel the same way as he did. She kept in touch by phone and text but she wasn't keen for him to visit her and she had refused several invitations to come to Manchester. He felt as if she were testing him, testing his ability to make a life for himself but he would much rather have made a life for himself with her rather than without her. He felt as if he were in limbo. It wasn't clear to him what she wanted from him.

One weekend he invited Rebecca to go for a walk with him. He thought a walk wasn't really a date and if her boyfriend wanted to come along that would be okay. He called her and said they could catch a bus and walk, up in the Peak District. She asked him what the Peak District was like and when he described the moorland wilderness, she said it sounded cold, boring and pointless. He suggested walking along the canal to the Wharfe and because canal paths are flat and have pubs along the route, she thought that was a better idea. When he mentioned the boyfriend, she laughed and said he was no longer her boyfriend. David met her in the bar and she wanted a drink but he persuaded her to set off, telling her that the Wharfe was a nicer place to stop for a drink than the University Bar. They walked towards Deansgate, towards the Hilton Hotel and the Wharfe.

"Have you seen the Science Museum Rebecca?"

"Hey, I'm a Manchester girl, remember?"

"Of course you are."

"Yea but I've never seen the Science Museum. Where is it?"

"It's just up the road on the left. We'll walk past it."

"Can't wait. Just so long as we don't go in. I'm not a museum type of girl."

The pavement was busy with weekend shoppers. David and Rebecca made an odd sort of couple; the geek and the laid-back hippy. He with his jacket and jeans, she with a poncho and a long bag with beads trailing almost to the floor. A headband holding her long blonde hair from her face. She walked without smiling, as if walking was an unnecessary inconvenience rather than a pleasure.

"Are you still pregnant?" He had wanted to introduce the topic more subtly but couldn't think how.

"From Science museum to are you pregnant, without passing GO. Man, you have a real way with words. "

"Are you?"

"Yea. Sure am."

She didn't seem worried at all, unless it was bravado. He thought she seemed very confident and relaxed for someone in her situation. She had been in tears when he'd first met her, perhaps it was the argument with her boyfriend that had brought the tears rather than the pregnancy. "Do you know what you're going to do?"

"No. There's no rush. I'm only seven weeks. I've done several tests now but they all give the same result. I like thought I might get a negative. I'm not sure how accurate they are but I've been sick in the mornings so I'm pretty certain. Still, I can feel my breasts getting bigger so it's not all bad news is it?"

"Your breasts are getting bigger already?"

"Just a little bit, I could do with a bit more up top. You men get off on that. Yea?"

"You seem quite relaxed about it all."

"No point worrying is there? But I think I'll be really terrified if I have to like, give birth."

" I think giving birth is usually the end result. Did you want to get pregnant?"

"What do you think?"

"I don't know, that's why I asked."

 She laughed. She seemed to find him funny. He didn't really understand why. Most people found him annoying.

"No, it wasn't planned. Poor little thing. How big do you think it is after seven weeks?"

"I've no idea. I can google it if you like?"

"Yea why not?"

They turned off Deansgate and walked towards the Science Museum and the Wharfe. It was a grey sort of day but dry. As good as it gets in Manchester in late January.

"About half an inch it says, about the size of a blueberry."

"Is that all? Christ. It's not exactly got a personality yet has it?"

"It's interesting you refer to the foetus as it." David said, heading off on one of his tangents, "I mean it has a gender the moment its conceived but you wouldn't call it he or she until its born. Once you'd found out the gender with ultrasound you might call it, he or she I suppose. Do you think we call the foetus it, so that aborting it doesn't seem so bad?"

"Whoa. Man, you should be doing Philosophy instead of me."

"I didn't know you were a Philosopher."

"Well you never asked. You should take more of an interest instead of giving out medical advice."

"I am interested," he said.

"Yea, calm down. I'm joking."

They walked onto the Wharfe.

"This is the Rochdale Canal," he said.

"Yea and that's the Wharfe Pub over there. You can buy me a drink to celebrate."

"What is there to celebrate?"

"You asking me out. I thought you'd never get round to it. I've been dropping hints for weeks."

"I haven't asked you out, we're just going for a walk."

She laughed at him. "Don't worry David. I won't ask

you to become the father of the child. Not after the first date. I'm not that sort of girl."

"Stop saying it's a date. Mitch might get jealous."

"I don't care if he does."

"What's he like? Mitch I mean?"

"He's all talk. He's like this big wheel in the Philosophy Department. Everyone says he's going to get a first. I think it's gone to his head. He thinks he's goddam Wittgenstein or something. I thought he was so cool when I first met him. I like hero worshipped him or something. He was so nice when I first met him, so smart yet not at all cocky, like he is now. He was so considerate and caring until I got pregnant. When I told him it was like turning a switch. All he wanted was for me to get rid of it."

"How long were you together?"

"About half an hour? Just long enough to make a baby."

"You're joking?"

"Yea I'm joking. Two years now."

"Do you love him?"

"Not any more. Come on, enough of this heart to heart. Get me a beer."

They sat inside looking out at the canal basin. Trains rattled over the bridge high above the water. Nothing seemed to be moving on the canal itself but there were lots of people milling about and enjoying the weekend. Rebecca talked about her parents and asked David about his family and where he was brought up. Rebecca's father had left and she didn't know where he lived. Her mother had moved in with another man. She had three older sisters. David told her about his brother and sisters. She laughed when he told her that he was an accident just like 'it'. She told him her Dad was a dreamer and an artist although he never made any money at his art but worked behind a bar and it was her mother who had kept the family going and her dad who caused his wife more grief than all the four children. She was brought up on the Witherhouse estate which sounded like a rough sort of place to grow up. Not that he knew anything about Witherhouse but she told him about drug gangs and it all sounded rather grim and frightening. Padiham seemed quite a cosy place to live by comparison. Half way through her lager she pulled a face and looked at him accusingly. "What the hell is this stuff you bought me?"

"It's Heineken."

"It tastes funny. I think I'll take it back."

"It's fine."

"You taste it then. Tell me what you think."

"There's no need. It probably tastes funny because it's zero alcohol."

She looked at him as if he'd said something obscene. "What the hell?"

"Ethanol is a poison. You've built up immunity but the blueberry hasn't. Imagine if you were the size of a blueberry and you drank a pint of lager. You'd be ill."

Rebecca was incredulous. "Who said anything about ethanol. It's lager."

"Alcohol is basically Ethanol. It's ethanol that makes you drunk. It's a poison."

She shook her head in disbelief, "You're such a geek."

"That's true Rebecca. I'm sorry about that but there's nothing I can do about it. I'm not going to act like something I'm not. I was born a geek. I like being a geek and I think I might always be a geek."

"Well I must say it's great that you're happy in your own skin. Good for you. I hate it when kids try and be something they're not, just to fit in."

"Let's drink to geeks then," David said raising his glass of orange juice to Rebecca's Zero Heineken. When they got back to campus Rebecca invited him back to her room for coffee. As they went up in the lift, she touched his leg and smiled. He didn't respond and thought it might have been accidental. He followed her along the narrow corridor and into her room. It was identical to his own; small, one shelf, a single bed and a table and chair. Utilitarian. Compact. A door leading to a bathroom. A large window overlooking the quadrangle. She hung up her poncho and scarf and started to make the coffee.

"What made you want to study Philosophy?" he sat on the bed.

"You want to talk about Philosophy?"

"Why not?"

"I thought we could make out."

"Make out?"

"You didn't come all this way for coffee?"

She seemed to be laughing at him. She was a pretty girl, not as slim as Jenny, more curves. She was a sensual woman rather than a pretty girl. She abandoned the coffee cups and walked across the narrow room and leaned down towards him and kissed him. He was sitting on her bed and she tried to push him back and she wanted to lie on top of him. He resisted and she kissed him again. He didn't respond like he would have done with Jenny. He was aroused by the situation but not by Rebecca. She stood up and pulled off her sweater, she was smiling and undoing the buttons on her blouse.

"I'm sorry Rebecca," he said. "I don't want to."

She ignored him and removed her blouse and her bra and stood before him bare breasted. He stood up from the bed and took her in his arms and hugged her to him. "Listen Rebecca," he said quietly, "I mean it. I don't want to make out as you call it. I like you as a friend but I've already got a girl. I'm sorry."

She didn't respond for a moment but as he held her, he realised that she had started to cry. She held on to him in a tight embrace but he could feel her rocking as the sobs overtook her. "I'm such a fool," she said. She spoke in staccato bursts, tears flowing down her face onto his cheek. "I don't know why I behave like this. I know you've got a girlfriend back home. I hate myself. I don't know what's wrong with me."

"There's nothing wrong with you," David said, "you're frightened and you want to be loved. We all want to be loved. I'm not sure if we'd had sex, you'd feel loved, you might feel used. It's normal to be confused and frightened when you're pregnant. You act like you aren't worried but I know that's not true. There's nothing wrong with you. You're a lovely girl. You're just a bit confused at the moment, that's all. Confused and frightened." He stroked her hair as she sobbed even louder. She held onto him for a long time but when she pulled away, she looked embarrassed and hurt. "I'm sorry," she said, "I shouldn't have done that." She dressed very quickly and looked away from him. She couldn't look him in the face, she was humiliated.

"Maybe I should apologise," David said, "I know I'm a geek. Only a geek would say 'I don't want to' like that. It was a bit pathetic. I'm not cool like your other friends."

She started to fuss with the coffee things and she put the kettle on to boil again. David sat back on the bed and let her get on with making the drinks. She wiped her eyes several times with a towel from the bathroom and at last brought over the two drinks. She sat down in the chair by the desk and they were both silent.

He tasted the coffee and pulled a face and made a 'uugghhhh' noise.

"You don't like it?" she asked.

"It's awful."

"I'm sorry, I always buy the cheapest."

"Well never mind," he said with a smile, "at least I got to see your breasts."

She managed a smile. "They're not too bad, are they?"

"They're magnificent."

"They'll get even better if you wait a few weeks."

"I'll look forward to it." He smiled. He tried to laugh but couldn't quite manage it.

"Can we still be friends David? I could do with a friend right now."

"You're the best friend I have," he said.

"Apart from that girl of yours."

"Yes apart from her." She sipped her coffee. David put his cup down. It really was disgusting. "I've only ever had one girlfriend Rebecca. I suppose I'm a bit old fashioned. A geek, like you said. I don't think real life has to be like those films on the television where people have sex ten minutes after they've met for the first time. Am I the only one who thinks like that? Do we have to behave like they do in the films or is it alright to make your own mind up? To do what you're comfortable with. To take your time and get to know someone first."

"You don't have to apologise," she said.

"I'm not apologising. I'm just thinking aloud really."

"I like having sex," she said. "It calms me down. Although to tell the truth I usually get pissed first.

That may be the first time I've tried to have sex with a boy while I was sober. All that zero lager I drank."
"I think that's a compliment," he said.
"I suppose it is," she said.

Chapter 15.

When a letter came from the GP surgery addressed to David at 29 Altham Street, he asked his mother to open it and read it to him rather than go to the bother of posting it. When she read it out, he wished he had opted for it to be posted. It was a letter asking David to visit the GP for an assessment relating to the incident at the quarry. David told her he would sort it out but she could tell from his tone of voice that he would do nothing of the sort. David had clearly made his mind up to ignore the letter.

After meeting Alan in the park Lionel was very restrained with Irene but if smugness could kill you, he wouldn't have lasted a week. As the week went by his self-control failed him and he started to lecture Irene on her folly. "Ghosts don't use pelican crossings." He must have repeated that about thirty times. It was his favourite line. "You have to admit Irene, you were wrong. It's not a ghost David was talking to all these years it's some kind of psychotic behaviour. I know you hate the thought of him being sectioned but it may be the safest option if he won't admit to himself that he needs treatment. You may have ignored the problem for far too long. I mean to say, you must admit that man we met was as real as you and me. And he explained about the medal, though I must admit I

don't understand why he didn't want to keep it himself. You know, I can always talk to David."
"No Lionel. Don't you dare."
"I'm trying to help Irene. You can't ignore it any longer."

It was late one evening when David wandered into the bar and saw Rebecca waving to him and inviting him to join her and her friends from the Philosophy Department. It was only when it was too late to avoid the invitation that he noticed Rebecca's boyfriend Mitch. He received a warm smile from Rebecca who introduced him to those of the group who could be bothered to make eye contact. She even introduced him to Mitch who gave him a condescending glare. He felt trapped. Rebecca had introduced him to the group but the introduction had met with grunts and nods and several of them hadn't even bothered to look up from their phones. In the Maths department he didn't stand out too much; smart-casual geek was de rigueur. Not so in the Philosophy Department. Most of them seemed to be wearing street-people chic. He sat for a while listening but couldn't find anything of interest or any way to contribute to the chatter. He didn't find them particularly interesting. They were all drinking beer and discussing whether or not they existed and sending each other texts, all at the same time. It occurred to him that socialising wasn't as difficult as he had once imagined but it was certainly more boring. He drifted off into his own private oblivion. He thought about home and wondered how Jenny and his mother were doing. He thought about Henry and pictured him marching away. He meandered slowly through all the happy memories and skated quickly over the mean and lonely periods of his life. It seemed to him that he had felt more lonely sitting in big laughing groups of people than at any other time.

"What do you think?"

It dawned on him that the group had fallen silent.

"I asked you. What do you think?"

It was Mitch, asking him a question. He remembered his experience on the sports field at the age of eleven and the memory made him smile. This innocent gesture seemed to annoy Mitch.

"Well?"

"I'm really sorry, "David said, "I was miles away. I wasn't listening to you and I have no idea what you asked me."

Mitch wasn't pleased, and judging by how attentive the rest of the philosophers were, he wasn't used to being ignored. Rebecca had told him that Mitch was something of a celebrity in the Philosophy Department, a sort of Existential high priest. "We were discussing certainty and knowledge and whether you can know something without being certain and if you can be certain about something without knowing it. Rebecca thinks it's possible to be certain but I said you can't be certain about anything. It's logically impossible to have certainty without knowing the future. As we can't know the future it follows, ipso facto, that nothing is certain." This revelation was followed by a deathly silence. David looked at Mitch, then he glanced at the group. They seemed enthralled by the big man's insights. David thought he had never heard so much tripe in his life.

"So, what do *you* think?" Mitch asked again.

"You seem very certain that nothing is certain."

"I am!"

"But you can't be. Can you?"

"Why not?"

"Isn't it obvious? First you say nothing can be known for certain and then you say that you're certain of it. You're talking crap."

There was something of a sharp intake of breath from the Philosophers.

"David's a mathematician," Rebecca said, trying to diffuse the tension.

"Ah well that explains a lot," Mitch said in a very superior tone of voice. "Only a mathematician would come up with such a superficial remark."

David looked at Mitch with something approaching pity.

"He's such a geek Rebecca. Is that why you're fucking him?"

Rebecca's face flushed with embarrassment.

"I knew it." Mitch said, "you're such a slut. You'll fuck anything. Even a geek like him."

David had had enough of Mitch. His pity moved to anger via contempt. He reminded him too much of Wayne. He no longer felt intimidated by morons just because they might be physically stronger. "I'm glad I'm a geek and not a moron like you," he said calmly. "You should take the advice of your big hero Wittgenstein; "Woven man nicht sprechen kann, daruber muβ man schweigen," he spoke in his fiercest German accent. He did, however, regret spitting into the big man's face when he pronounced schweigen. He would normally have apologised for that but he was not in the mood to back down.

Mitch wiped his face. "What the fuck?" he asked. They were both standing now, it was handbags at dawn. Mitch had to look down to stare into David's eyes. David had to hold his head back to meet his gaze. The brute was at least a foot taller than David. "Woven man nicht sprechen kann, daruber muβ man schweigen. It's the last line of the Tractatus, by Wittgentstein. He's a Philosopher. 'What we cannot speak about we must pass over in silence.' I think it was his way of saying if there's something you don't understand you should just shut the fuck up." This was fighting talk from David. He was flushed with testosterone, it was pouring out of his ears. He was ready for the fight, in the University bar. The only sober human being for a square mile squaring up to someone twice his size and weight. Someone who was really pissed off with him because he had been spending time with his pregnant girlfriend. Mitch looked like he was about to kill David but Rebecca took David's arm and pulled him away. David was reluctant to go but Rebecca was stronger than he was.

"You're such a jerk Mitch," she said and marched away with David.

David apologised to Rebecca when they were outside. "I shouldn't have done that," he said, "I shouldn't have been so aggressive."

"I thought you had every right to get salty with him. He deserved everything he got."

"I know that but I still think I shouldn't have been aggressive."

"Why not?" Rebecca looked surprised.

"Because I'm useless at fighting or anything physical and he looks big enough to kill me without getting out of breath."

"Don't be such a wimp David. I thought you were heroic." She leaned towards him and kissed him. "I know," she said, "you don't want to. You needn't worry David. I'm not such a slut as Mitch seems to think." Rebecca was being brave but he could see in her face that she was shaken by Mitch's behaviour. He felt sorry for her and felt he should give her a hug or hold her hand but he was reluctant to show her any physical affection. He wanted to but was concerned where it might lead. He suspected that Mitch and Rebecca might get back together despite the harsh words and the threats about abortion. He thought the reason Mitch wanted to provoke David was because he was jealous, which meant he still cared for her. In the meantime, Rebecca had persistently refused to talk to her mother about her situation and David felt that he was the only one she had confided in. He couldn't understand why she had chosen him as her confidant but was flattered by her confidence in him. He felt it was a responsibility he must take seriously and not trifle with. He thought Jenny might be proud of him finding a friend like Rebecca. It was as if he was taking part in the real world instead of dreaming in abstractions. He was still in contact with Jenny but only by phone and more frequently now just by text. It seemed to him that as he was becoming more confident, she was moving in the opposite direction. She had always been so optimistic and so full of life but since her parents had separated, she seemed more unsure of herself. Her messages were full of small worries and concerns. Her brave ambitions had given way to self-doubt and fear. The realisation that her Dad was a bully, the separation, leaving her lovely home for a rental, all that had shaken her confidence more than he first realised. He looked forward to seeing her at the end of term. Maybe things would get better when he saw her over the Easter holiday.

"Are you going home for Easter Rebecca?"

"No. I'll stay here."

"You can come home with me if you like. Meet my mother."
"And Jenny?"
"Yes, if you like."
"I'd love that David. Thank you."
He hadn't thought about the implications of his impulsive invitation before he spoke. As soon as she accepted the invitation with such enthusiasm the possible consequences started to flood into his mind. He never used to offer frivolous invitations that he thought nobody in their right mind would accept but he was learning to be more sociable and that's what sociable people do.

Chapter 16.

Irene didn't want to discuss David's situation with Lionel but she discussed it with Sandra. "You promise you won't share this with anyone Sandra?"

"What's the matter Irene? You look like you've been crying."

"It's David. It's a long story but I think he was hearing voices after all." Sandra listened to her story about meeting 'Henry' in the park. "It wasn't Henry like David said it was. It was some bloke called Alan. He did dress a bit odd but that doesn't make him a ghost. He said the medal and the letters turned up when his mother died. Lionel was with me he saw the whole thing. I felt such a fool. I've been fooling myself for years."

"Well who was this Alan and who was his mother?"

"I didn't ask. The point is there never was a ghost. They were just noises in his head and now he's living on the 18th floor in that University accommodation block. I'm frightened Sandra. The doctor wanted to have him assessed but he refused to go."

"Well make him go Irene. He'll go if you tell him he has to."

"He's not a child Sandra."

"Of course he is. He's still your child. You still have

to look out for him. Jenny's the same. She might look like a woman but she still acts like a child. I wish she'd gone to college like I told her. She's working in that office in Burnley and I know she hates it. She says she's happy but I know she's not."

"Tell her to come and see us. David's coming home on Friday. He's bringing a friend with him too."

"That's nice Irene. You'll be glad to have him back for a week or two. Who's this friend he's bringing?"

"I know nothing about him. You know David. He just rang up the other day and said 'Is it okay if I bring a mate?'. I'm just glad he has some mates. He tells me all sorts of stories on the telephone about his friends but half the time I think he makes them up, just so I don't worry about him. I always worried about him when he was younger. Your Jenny was the only friend he had."

"What's going on between them Irene? I keep asking Jenny but I never get a straight answer."

"I've no idea what's going on. I know David invited her to visit him but she said she was too busy. That's what David said anyway."

"I know I promised to keep it secret, what you told me about David, but if he and Jenny are going to be together..."

"No you can tell Jenny. She needs to know. I still think he's going to be okay but you're right, you should tell her."

David and Rebecca caught the afternoon train from Manchester Victoria, it was crowded but they were lucky enough to find a seat. Rebecca's high-pitched screeching laugh seemed to have reappeared and she couldn't stop talking. David could tell she was nervous about meeting his mother. She was intrigued that he had read Wittgenstein. "The Tractatus is incredibly difficult to understand. What made you read it?"

"It's not difficult, it's impossible. I only understood the first line in the book and the last line. I couldn't understand any of the stuff in between. I enjoy languages though and it has the German on one side and English on the other. I enjoyed looking at the translation and the first line intrigued me. 'The world is all that is the case'. I thought it meant that anything that wasn't in the world can't be true."

"Like what?"

"Like geometrical shapes I used to have this thing about triangles when I was little. It seemed to me that people thought they existed but of course they only exist as mathematical ideas, not as real objects in the world. Newton's laws suffer from the same mistake, just because you can divide a number an infinite number of times that doesn't prove that infinity exists in the world. I mean it might exist but that's no proof that it does. Just because we construct the concept of straight lines doesn't mean they actually exist. I think that's what your Wittgenstein was trying to say."

"I've no idea what he was trying to say," Rebecca said, "and I've been studying him for three years. I know he says that the way we think is limited by the vagueness of language. I suppose that's why you enjoy mathematics it's so different from language, it's so precise.

"It's no more exact than language. We understand the variables in maths, plus, minus, equals, because we translate them into language. That's what causes the confusion."

"You really are clever David," she followed the compliment with a bout of her horrendous laughter. Most people on the carriage turned their heads towards them. David took a book out of his bag and pretended to read but he couldn't persuade her to stop talking and laughing until they were well north of Bury. He hoped she might calm down a bit when they got home and that the hyena laugh would disappear again.

When David arrived, he found his mother sitting in their tiny living room. It was fortunate that she was seated because she became light headed at the sight of David arriving with a pregnant Rebecca in tow. Irene wasn't a faint-hearted woman but the sudden appearance of what looked like the mother of her grandchild was too much and too sudden. David was all smiles. Rebecca was all concern. Irene was, for once in her life, completely speechless.

"What's wrong?" David asked. "You don't look well."

"Why didn't you tell me David?"

"Tell you what?"

She gestured at Rebecca, in particular at her bulging tummy, then she regained control of herself and stood up to greet her guest. "You're very welcome love, come and sit down. She walked past David to give Rebecca a hug. She took a step back to look at her and smiled. "Are you keeping well? You're looking well. Is he looking after you? David! Why didn't you say something?"

Rebecca laughed. "He didn't tell you did he Mrs Watson?"

"It's Irene love. No, he didn't. It's just typical of him."

"We're only friends," David said.

"I can see that," Irene said, giving him a viscous look and then turning back to Rebecca with a brave attempt at a smile.

"Mrs Watson. He should have told you. We are only friends." She patted her tummy. "This is my boyfriend's baby. Not David's."

Irene looked at her son for some confirmation. He nodded. "It's true mum, Rebecca's just a friend."

Irene sat down again and shook her head. "Well why the hell didn't you say so on the phone?" She was angry but she couldn't help smiling and she didn't want to create a scene in front of her guest. "This is typical of him," she said to Rebecca. "He always does things back to front. Sit yourself down love. You're very welcome. None of my children are normal but this one's much less normal than the other three."

Irene made a fuss of Rebecca, asked her how she was feeling, whether she'd felt the baby moving, asked her if she was eating properly, how many weeks she was. David stood and listened and was completely ignored. When Rebecca was upstairs unpacking her bag, Irene gave David her full attention. She spoke to him in the kitchen, in an angry whisper. "Did you think that was funny or what? 'I'm bringing a mate home, is that okay?' I nearly had a heart attack when you walked in with her and her 22 weeks gone. I thought I was going to be a grandmother again." David mouthed a reply but Irene was in full flow. "Where's her boyfriend? What kind of boyfriend is it that lets his girlfriend go home with somebody else? Are they still seeing each other or what?"

"It's complicated."

"You're dam right it's complicated. What will the neighbours think?"

"What?"

"What? What? What do you think? They'll think you're the father that's what they'll think and why shouldn't they? This is the first girl you've ever brought home."

"What about Jenny?" David protested.

"That reminds me, she's coming round to see you later."

"Oh good!"

"And I've booked you an appointment to see the doctor at half past four."

"What for?"

"You know what for. For that assessment they've been asking for."

"There's nothing wrong with me. You know that."

"Yes well you're going at half past four and then we'll know once and for all."

"What's that supposed to mean?"

Rebecca's arrival back into the living room stopped their discussion short. "Are you sure it's alright me staying here Mrs Watson? Irene, I mean."

"You're very welcome love. Don't you worry. I'm just telling David he's going to the doctors this afternoon and he says he doesn't want to go. Nothing for you to worry about."

"Is he not feeling well?"

"He's fine. He won't be well if he doesn't do as he's told and get up to that surgery."

Rebecca gave one of her peculiar high-pitched squeaky laughs and that brought all further discussion to a halt.

After David had left for the surgery Jenny arrived to see him. Jenny and Rebecca sat across from each other in the small living room. Jenny, normally so confident and self-assured was ill at ease. Rebecca had been put at her ease by Irene's warm welcome and seemed quite calm. Irene had explained the unusual bond of friendship between David and Rebecca on the short walk from the front door to the living room. The look on Jenny's face suggested that she was not wholly convinced.

"David's told me all about you," Rebecca said. There was no nervous laughter now.

Jenny didn't reply so Irene filled the silence with more information about Rebecca's situation.

Rebecca was only two years older than Jenny but she looked much older. Jenny had a much slimmer figure than Rebecca, even before the pregnancy. Rebecca looked like a woman whereas Jenny looked more like a girl. Jenny thought that Rebecca was the more voluptuous of the two and Rebecca thought that Jenny was by far the prettiest. Irene wondered how on earth she had been left alone to face the first meeting of David's girlfriend and his new friend who just happened to be a girl and pregnant.

"So, your parents must be pleased?" Jenny said, she had adopted the tenuous inquiring tone for questions and statements alike.

"They don't know," Rebecca said, calmly.

"Why ever not?" Irene asked.

"Well. I've lost touch with them really. We never got on that well anyway. Me and mum never saw eye to eye, she lives in Manchester but I never see her. I always got on with my Dad but he left a few years ago. He was okay but like, a bit of a dreamer. He always wanted to be a poet but he never really wanted a job and I don't know where he is now. I know where my mum is but she wouldn't be pleased if I told her about this." She glanced down and patted her belly.

"That's very sad," Jenny said, "not to visit your mum I mean."

Rebecca looked surprised. "You weren't brought up on the Witherhouse Estate," she said.

Jenny and Irene had no idea where the Witherhouse estate was or why that was a reason not to visit.

David's examination at the GP surgery was quite routine. The doctor knew him well and was surprised by the request to check him for mental health problems. He gave him a physical examination and checked for any signs of drug abuse or self-harming. He asked him how he was going on at the University and David told him that he was getting on well in his second term after struggling in the first term up to Christmas. He also told him about his new friend Rebecca. "Her boyfriend got her pregnant and he wants her to have an abortion. I can't decide if abortion is really ethical doctor. I'm not sure all methods of contraception are ethical either. If they prevent ovulation, I think that's okay but once the egg has been fertilised, I'm not sure it's right to stop the development of the foetus. Do you have an opinion yourself?"

Dr Ferguson smiled, "I do have an opinion David but it wouldn't be right to share it with a patient."

"It's something that isn't really discussed is it? I mean everyone assumes that all the birth pills do the same thing but they don't do they? Then the coil, that doesn't stop the sperm fertilising the ovum does it? I think the ethical implications of each form of contraception are quite different but everyone seems to think that contraception is either right or wrong but they don't look at the detail, do they?"

"I think you might be too rational for your own good David. Tell me about this incident up at the quarry. What were you doing up there?"

"I was just looking at the view and someone saw me and phoned the police. Then a policeman came and said hello, an old school friend, well not really a friend but that's another story. He came up and asked me what I was doing and I told him I was fine but he must have thought I was going to jump off the top. They thought I was going to kill myself but I wasn't. I was just eating my sandwiches and looking at the view. I think the police may have over reacted. They wrecked their caravan."

"Yes, so I heard."

"I think they thought I was mad for sitting on the edge like that but I don't think I was quite as mad as whoever tried to drag that caravan up that track."

"David, do you think you have ever had any suicidal thoughts?"

"Oh yes, I should think most people have. They say that's why people are scared of heights, isn't it? It's not the heights that they're scared of, it's the thought that they might want to throw themselves off that frightens them. I read that somewhere, I can't remember where. It said that most people have a small urge to escape from the stresses of life and have a latent desire to end it all and that's why so many people are frightened of high places. I'm actually not scared of heights at all because I know I'd never try and kill myself. I couldn't do that to my mother, or my brother and sisters. It would be cowardly to kill yourself. Don't you think?"

"You may be right David." The doctor smiled and shook his head slightly. He thought that whoever had made the request for this assessment was far more in need of psychiatric care than David was. "Would you say you are a happy person David?"

"No, I suppose I'm not. I mean most people I know seem to think that being happy consists of drinking alcohol in large groups and laughing their heads off at nothing in particular. A lot of the students, smoke dope and walk around in a happy sort of anaesthetic trance. I don't drink and I don't smoke dope and I don't like sitting in the bar laughing my head off at nothing. If that's being happy then I'm not. I like talking to Rebecca. I love talking to Jenny. I have a couple of friends in the Maths Department and we talk about Maths, obviously. Reading makes me happy but it doesn't make me laugh my head off. Apart from when I read 'Catcher in the Rye'."

The Doctor smiled again and managed to restrain his own laughter. "What about this friend of yours?

Henry?"

"I suppose my mother told you about him? Are you supposed to discuss my case with her, even if she is my mother?"

"Well David, we've known each other a long time and you're right, now that you're an adult I can't share information about you with Irene. However, she told me about Henry long before you became an adult. I also think you should take this request from the Lancashire Constabulary seriously. I asked you to come in for this assessment weeks ago. They seem to think that you could harm yourself. That's why they asked me to assess you for referral under the Mental Health Act."

"I'm not going to harm myself."

"I don't believe you are and that's what I'm going to put in my report but if you continue to talk about hearing voices and seeing ghosts you stand a good chance of being referred for psychiatric assessment. I don't think that would be helpful."

"I don't want that," David said. "I don't think there's anything wrong with me."

"I don't think there's anything wrong with you either David but you need to put all this talk of ghosts and voices behind you. Don't talk about it to anyone and just carry on as you are and I'm sure you'll be fine."

"Thanks Doctor."

"It's been a pleasure David."

Jenny and Rebecca were encouraged to go for a walk to let Irene get on with making the dinner. It was a sunny afternoon and although Rebecca was no fan of exercise, she agreed to join Jenny for a stroll. They walked along the railway path and past the bowling greens and towards the park. Rebecca talked about David in glowing terms. "He visits the language department to practise his languages, they say he speaks better than most of the students, Spanish and German in particular. They think he's a genius in the Maths department and he's only in his second term. I'm final year Philosophy and he seems to know more about my subject than I do. He's a bit special. But I suppose you already know that Jenny?"

"He's special alright."

"You've nothing to fear from me Jen. He's mad about you."

Jenny seemed doubtful.

"We really are just friends, me and David, nothing's happened between us you know."

"You sound to me like you might be in love with him?"

"Oh I am. He's been so kind and he's cute, though he doesn't seem to realise it. Problem is Jenny, he's only got eyes for you."

Jenny walked on in silence and Rebecca struggled up the steep steps that lead to Memorial Park.

"I'm going to have to sit down Jenny. I'm all out of breath."

They continued up the hill until they found a bench to sit on. They were able to look down the hill towards the river and the woods and the rows of terraced houses beyond the railway.

"So, what did David tell you about us?" Jenny asked at length.

"Oh, he told me about your visit to the Sex clinic and how angry you were. About hiding in the wardrobe, he's such a geek and then he comes up with a story like that."

"Did he tell you about my dad and what happened?"

"Sure, he said your mum and dad had split."

"He shouldn't have told you about that."

"I'm sorry Jenny. He talks about you a lot. You were all he talked about when I first met him, before we got onto Philosophy and whether I should keep the baby. He also likes to talk about Ethics. It's one of his specialities."

"Did he tell you about Henry and the incident at the quarry and the missing medal and the letters?"

"Henry, yes he talked a lot about Henry, not the other stuff though."

"I think you should know about the other stuff Rebecca. I think it's important you know. If you can keep it to yourself? There's no need to share it with anyone else. The thing is, I think David might be unwell, that's why he's at the doctors right now."

Rebecca listened with concern as Jenny related the whole story of the suspected suicide attempt at the quarry, the police statement that he might be a danger to himself and the possibility of his being sectioned. She explained how they had all been convinced that Henry was a ghost and not a voice inside David's head. She told her that Irene had met this so-called ghost in town with Lionel and that it wasn't Henry at all who had visited the house with the parcel. She told her how worried Irene was about her son. "I do love him Rebecca, I think I always have since I was a child, but I worry about him. He isn't like everyone else. His mind works at a hundred miles an hour. He's brilliant, he really is but they say genius is close to madness, don't they? I'm not saying he's mad but he's convinced himself that there are ghosts everywhere I think he really might be hearing voices and suffering delusions and he just needs to admit it and get some treatment. The problem is he not only convinced himself about Henry, he convinced us as well. I hope you don't mind me sharing all this?"

Rebecca shook her head. She didn't say anything but she was visibly saddened by what Jenny had told her.

David felt relieved after his meeting with his doctor. He had ignored the letters inviting him to visit the surgery and for counselling, but those letters had played on his mind. Now he had faced up to the problem it seemed to him that the problem had finally been resolved. His mother would stop nagging him about it and the Lancashire

Constabulary would just have to admit that they destroyed their precious caravan for no reason. He was looking forward to meeting Jenny again and the fact that he had brought a friend home would, he thought, prove to her that he could manage quite well on his own. As he walked towards home, he felt that things had turned out just fine, he felt very happy. Life was good. It was at the War Memorial that his mood changed. He knew there was something strange about the figure standing beside the granite plinth looking down the long list of over 300 names.

"Are you looking for any name in particular?" David asked him.

"I was looking at the names of the Kings Royal Rifles, there's five from that regiment. Two of them were Dad's friends."

"Henry?"

"Aye, my dad, Henry."

"You must be James?"

"Aye well, I was always known as Alan but christened James Alan."

"Your names on the other side," David said, *"The only one from the Oxford and Bucks."*

"Aye, that's right. The only one."

"Me too," David said, *"I think I'm the only one. The only one that sees ghosts."*

"No, you're not the only one. Many people can see us. Some more clearly than others. Most people can't see us at all, some get a feeling that they

might be able to see us, some see a small detail or hear a noise but can't see us like you can. If it's a problem for you, I won't bother you again. You know that don't you?"

"That's what Henry always said. I've a lot of things I want to ask you but I'm worried what people might think if they see me – talking to myself. I read about your war record in the Oxford and Bucks war diaries. I knew you were in the 7th Battalion and in B Company because of that letter you wrote to your brother. It was quite a coincidence you bumping him to him like that in North Africa. What are the odds?"

Alan nodded.

"It was quite voyage you had; Cape town, Mombasa and then India and then six months in Iraq and then 3,000 miles overland to Tunisia. They took you a long way round to get to Italy."

"I'm not sure they knew what to do with us. We thought we might be going to Burma when we landed in Bombay. Then we thought we would join the fight in North Africa and we ended up in Iraq. We nearly missed the fight in Tunisia. "

"You weren't the last British Battalion to visit Iraq."

"No. We seem to keep going back to the same places over and over again. My Dad was in India. When I joined up that was the last place, I imagined I'd be going to."

David walked down through the park and he and Alan stayed silent as they walked past a group of mothers sat on a bench watching their children on the swings.

"What was it you wanted to ask me?" Alan said, when they had left the mothers and children behind them.

"I just wondered why I can see you, and I could see your father but not my own father, why can't I see him? Why doesn't he come to see us?"

"He does come lad. He's always with you and your mum."

"I don't understand."

"My mum saw me briefly and I was with her a lot through her life but she never saw me again. It would have been too upsetting for her if she had, she had to look after my brother and sister, and my dad. Same with your mother, she needs to move on, maybe find another partner. She couldn't do that if she saw your Dad was around."

"But he is around us? Watching us?"

Alan nodded.

"So there are lots of ghosts? Are there any ghosts around us now?"

"There's ghosts everywhere, especially around war memorials, you just need to look for them and if you really want to see them, you will see them."

"I'm not sure I want to see any more ghosts." David wasn't frightened of seeing more ghosts but he was frightened of the consequences. He wasn't frightened of Alan and he'd never feared Henry but he knew what would happen if he was to be seen *talking to 'voices in his head'. It also occurred to him that he might really be schizophrenic after all, despite what the doctor had just told him.*

"Look lad, I've got some letters here and some diaries. My mam hid them up chimney in James Street. Number 24. In back bedroom. I brought them for you. There's a lot of information here about my father and Mary. My mam shouldn't have hid them. She kept them from Dad. I don't know why she did that. Don't you want them?"

"No." David shook his head. "I don't want them. I'm sorry Alan. I want to look forward, I don't want to spend any more time looking back."

Alan smiled. "Probably for the best. You're a brave lad David."

"You think so?"

"Aye. I do."

"What have I done compared to you and Henry. I haven't fixed bayonets and charged machine guns like you did in Tunisia. I haven't made a beach landing like you did in Salerno. I haven't faced gas attacks like your Dad did in Belgium. I got bullied at school and got beaten up once. It's not the same thing is it?"

"It's not the same thing, but we did what everyone else did. We didn't know what it was going to turn out like and when it did, it was too late to turn back. You went your own way, made your own decisions, you didn't worry about fitting in with everyone else. That takes courage."

"I don't feel brave. I get scared a lot."
"We all do. It's normal. You get scared but you carry on. That's what bravery is. Only crazy people don't get scared."
"I'm not crazy then?"
"No, you're not crazy. Not crazy enough if you ask me." He turned, as if to walk away, but stopped and turned back one last time. "If you change your mind about them diaries and letters. They're still there. In back bedroom. Number 24." With that he left. David felt sad, his happy mood had disappeared like a ghost.

He had shaken off any feelings of sadness by the time he got home because he'd got a message from Rebecca that Jenny was waiting to see him. When he arrived home the atmosphere wasn't quite the happy, prodigal returns, feeling that he might have expected. Jenny gave him a dutiful peck on the cheek rather than the warm passionate embrace he craved. His mother was strangely quiet and Rebecca was the only one who looked pleased to see him.

"I've got the all clear from the doctor," he said, "nothing to worry about. He's going to recommend no further treatment." His happy announcement fell to earth like a feather. It provoked no reaction. "I've just had a check-up to see if I'm mad," he said to Rebecca, "and I'm not. It's official." He waited for his mother and Jenny to celebrate the good news but there wasn't the slightest ripple of a response from either of them. "Aren't you pleased?" he asked.

"I'm just going upstairs to sort out a few things," Rebecca said, and disappeared.

David waited for his mother to speak. He could see she was getting ready to talk to him. Her face was full of concern and foreboding, as if she was about to break bad news.

"Just say it mum. Whatever it is."

"I should go," Jenny said.

"Please stay." David's voice was shaking. This was not the reception he had been dreaming about, all through the University term. He had longed to see Jenny again and it seemed as if she couldn't wait to get away the moment he arrived.

"Yes stay," Irene said. "You need to hear what I'm going to say."

There was an awful silence while Irene struggled with how to tell her son that she thought he was ill, despite what the doctor had told him.

"I saw Henry," she said, "what I thought was Henry, but it wasn't him at all. Lionel was driving and I saw this chap walk across the road and it was the same man who brought the parcel that night. I ran after him and caught up with him. It wasn't Henry at all and he's no ghost either David. The medal and the letters, they were found when they cleared the house after his mum died. So, you haven't been talking to a ghost at all. All these years I've been listening to you upstairs talking to Henry. You were talking to yourself David." David had never seen his mother cry before but he could see tears rolling down her face now as she spoke to him. "I don't know what you told that doctor but I know you're not well, not if you're hearing voices and seeing things that aren't there. It's been staring me in the face for years son, I didn't want to believe it, I still don't want to, but you need to get help."

"Mum don't." His mother was sobbing now and David struggled to control his own tears. He looked at Jenny. She looked broken hearted and looked at him with more pity than love. "Jenny you don't think I'm mad, do you?"

"Nobody thinks you're mad David, you just need help."

"But the medal and the letters, that proves Henry was real."

"It wasn't Henry who came to the door David," his mother said, recovering her composure, "he was called Alan."

"Alan! Alan James Braithwaite," David said, excited all of a sudden. "Henry's son. I've just seen him at the War Memorial." As soon as he said it, he realised it was the worst possible thing he could have said but it was too late now. His claim that he had just met another dead soldier at the war memorial hung in the air like a dark cloud. "I told him I didn't want to see any more ghosts. He won't bother me again. I'm all finished with ghosts!" Irene's tears and Jenny's sadness vanished. Now

288

they just felt pity. David could see the regret in their faces.

"You've got to believe me," He was pleading with them but it just made matters worse. "He wanted me to take some diaries and more letters but I refused. I think he wanted me to finish Dad's book but I told him I didn't want them. I've finished talking to ghosts. You've got to believe me."

"David stop now, please love," his mother said. "Don't say anymore."

"But it's true. Jenny, you believe me, don't you?" She clearly didn't. "Where are these diaries and letters David?" she asked.

David knew if he told them they were hidden up the chimney in the back bedroom of 24 James Street they would contact the emergency services immediately and have him taken away. It seemed the more he said the worse it got. It had always been like that. If he said any more, he would just convince them that he was sick. Maybe they were right. He didn't feel that he was crazy but if he was, he would be the last one to know. "I won't harm myself, if that's what you think and I won't harm anyone else. I'm not having any treatment. You can't force me to have treatment. The doctor says I'm okay. You can't section me against my will, unless I do something dangerous."

"Nobody wants you sectioned David. That's not fair."

"Well that's not how it looks to me. I'll go back to Manchester. I've a lot to do. I'm working on something important. I'll come and see you soon or you can visit me if you want. You know where I am. If you visit me, you'll see I'm okay."

"David, you're not going anywhere. You'll stay here for Easter. We both love you, don't we Jenny?"

Jenny nodded but didn't say anything. She seemed to be in shock. She had never seen harsh words between David and his mother before. When things had calmed down David agreed to stay for the rest of the holiday rather than go off in a huff. He might have grown into a very confident and self-sufficient young man but he didn't have the strength of will to disobey his mother. Few men had the strength to contradict Irene. Nothing more was said about it over the Easter holiday. Irene was more subdued than normal and David remained sullen and disappointed with his mother and Jenny. He felt that things would never be the same again. His mother had always had faith in him, always told him not to worry about what people had said about him but it seemed now that she had joined forces with his detractors. Jenny too, seemed to have fallen out of love with him. She was polite and she tried to be cheerful but she had never needed to try before because her love for him had been obvious. He still loved her, still wanted to tell her that he loved her but he thought it was fruitless to repeat what he had told her so many times before. If she didn't trust him, didn't believe in him there seemed no point in trying to persuade her otherwise. Rebecca tried to raise their spirits. She constantly told them what a happy place their home was, how comfortable and peaceful it was compared with her experience of home life. "You both seem so happy and you can talk to each other. There was nothing but trouble in our house. I suppose that's why I never want to go back there. I want to have a home like this. When my baby's born Irene, can I visit you again some time?"

"You can come any time you like love. You'll always be welcome."

David and Rebecca set off for Manchester a week later and Rebecca wanted to know all about the ghosts and the letters and diaries. She was fascinated by his stories of Henry and the latest visitation from Henry's son. She listened to him all the way home on the train. He told her everything. He told her about Henry and the missing medal. He told her about Alan and why Henry's wife had hidden Mary's diaries. He even told her where they were hidden, which was something he was too worried to share with his mother and Jenny. Rebecca seemed to think that there was nothing worrying or unusual about David's ability to communicate with the spirit world. She accepted it without question, as she accepted all his other extraordinary abilities.

Chapter 17.

It was only three weeks after Easter that Rebecca made a return visit to Padiham, this time all alone. She had asked Jenny to meet her at the station and Jenny had reluctantly agreed. There was something about Rebecca that Jenny disliked. It was nothing tangible, just a feeling. She thought it might have been jealousy of her relationship with David although it had been made clear to her several times that there was nothing to be jealous about. There was a hard edge to Rebecca that Jenny didn't like. A feeling that grew when Rebecca had told her that she had no contact with either of her parents, even though her mother lived in Manchester. The way she seemed so unconcerned about the fact that her boyfriend had abandoned her when she discovered she was pregnant. Whatever her reservations, she was waiting for the train when it arrived from Manchester Victoria. Rebecca seemed delighted to see her and gave her a warm hug which took Jenny by surprise.
"I half expected you to bring David with you," she said.
"He doesn't know I'm here." Rebecca seemed to have lost the nervous laugh which was some relief to Jenny.

"Can you tell me what's going on? Are you visiting Irene?"

"She doesn't know I'm here either."

Jenny grimaced at this, she thought it deceitful of her to meet Rebecca without telling Irene or David.

"I know it's all a bit cloak and dagger Jenny but if I told you what I was up to, well, I don't think you would have believed me."

They walked on in silence Jenny following Rebecca towards James Street.

"You know that Irene lives in the next street?" she said as they came close.

"We can visit Irene if you like but we must go to 24 James Street first."

Jenny smiled but she wasn't happy. When they arrived Rebecca immediately knocked on the door and they waited. Jenny becoming more uncomfortable by the minute. When the door opened, they faced a man their own age, he was a rough looking character; thin with grubby looking clothes, an ear ring and tattoos on his neck and his arms. "You Rebecca?" he said.

"Sright. And this is Jenny."

"Dale," he said and offered his hand. Rebecca shook it enthusiastically and Jenny followed suit, more reluctantly. Dale seemed to eye them both with rather too much interest, especially in Jenny. "Come in. I've got the stuff you wanted."

Jenny instantly thought he might be a drug dealer and she struggled to hide her disdain and anxiety."

Dale stood to one side to let them in. "Chill out love, you're safe enough with us you know." He directed this and a creepy looking smile towards Jenny but it only made her feel worse. When they got into the living room it was tiny, similar to Irene's living room in size but different in every other respect. Whereas Irene's living room was homely, neat and tidy, all cleanliness and orderliness – Dale's was spartan, cold, dirty and had a stale odour to it. There were clothes scattered about and a few children's toys. There was a huge portrait of Dale and what was probably his wife on one wall; they were smiling with drinks in their hands but they were both wearing dark sunglasses which made it an odd sort of portrait. There was an enormous flat screen TV above the fireplace and a large mirror on the back wall opposite. The mirror had an explosion of cracks with a circular piece of glass missing at the centre. It was the most bizarre looking living room that Jenny had ever seen. Rebecca didn't seem to notice anything amiss, she seemed relaxed with the situation, it was as if Dale was a friend of hers the way she interacted with him. "You got the stuff without much trouble?"

"Yea it were just stuffed up there wrapped in some canvas. I chucked the canvas out cos it were filthy like. I put the stuff in this bag." He held out two Tesco plastic bags.

"Sit down if you like girls."

"We're find Dale, we can't stop long." Jenny stayed silent while Rebecca chatted with Dale who was still staring at Jenny with some sort of grubby interest.

"Hey. How'd yer know it was up there? It must 'ave been up there for years?"

"Well," Rebecca said conspiratorially, "What if I told you that a ghost told me that his mother hid it up there a hundred years ago?"

Dale laughed. "Yea right. How'd yer know it was up there?"

"Tell the truth, I wasn't sure Dale, but my grandma told me it might be. She was born here and she told me a story about a soldier in the First World War who wrote letters to his lover and kept a diary and his wife hid the letters and the diary up the chimney in the back bedroom."

Dale looked at the bags with sudden interest.

"They might be worth a bit then?"

"Thirty quid we agreed Dale. Whether there was anything up there or not!" Rebecca's tone changed from benevolent friendly to cold malevolence in an instant.

"Yea right. Deal's a deal." Dale looked unsure of himself.

Rebecca handed him the money and took the plastic bags from him.

"Right well, any time ladies, if there's anything else I can do for you, you know how to find me." He looked delighted with the thirty pounds.

"No trouble Dale, thanks again. We'll see ourselves out." *Dale stood there looking gormless and clutching his thirty pounds.*
Jenny was relieved to get out into the fresh air.
"What's going on Rebecca?"
"David told me about these letters and diaries. He said they were hidden up the chimney in number 24 James Street." *Jenny waited for her to explain further.* *"He told me what happened on his way back from the doctors. He said you and Irene wouldn't believe him if he told you. He didn't want me to tell you either but I know you love him Jenny and I think I know what's stopping you telling him that you love him. I don't think he's ill. I think he really did see Henry's son that day. I know it's hard to believe that he can see the spirit world but it's hard to believe that he can speak four languages fluently and that he can read Wittgenstein and quote him word for word. He seems to have a photographic memory. He can do lots of things the rest of us can't do. If there really was a ghost and if these letters and diaries are a hundred years old it proves David isn't crazy after all. He's half convinced himself that he's been seeing things that aren't there. When you show him these, if they are letters from Mary Kelly to his Great Grandad"* *she held up the bags.* *"he'll feel better about himself."*
Jenny shook her head in disbelief.
"Just listen Jenny, Hear me out. It was Alan, Henry's son that told him where these diaries and

letters were. Alan offered to give them to David but David wouldn't take them. He said he'd had enough of ghosts. He said he wasn't sure anymore if he was seeing ghosts or just going crazy. I found out who lived in number 24 and I contacted him and asked him to check up the chimney in the bedrooms. I told him if he didn't find anything, I'd still pay him but that I wanted to look up the chimney myself. I told him there might be some old letters up there, just sentimental value. He seemed like he was a bit short of money and he agreed. You can have these and show them to Irene if you like. You look at them and decide what to do."

Jenny took one of the bags and looked inside. "You really think that David was right all along?"

"It's up to you Jenny. You are the one he's in love with. It's not important to David what other people think of him, but he really cares what you and his mother think."

"It's just so incredible", Jenny said, "I don't know what to say."

"You could say thanks and I'll buy you a coffee? We can sit down for a while and you can have a look at these letters and diaries. There's a Costa down the road."

"I know," Jenny said, "that's where I first kissed David."

"In Costa?"

"Yes. We got a round of applause."

David had agreed to meet Rebecca at Christie's
Bistro on Oxford Road. She had told him it was her
birthday and that she wanted to treat him to a
special lunch as a thank you for her trip to Padiham
at Easter. He argued bitterly that he was too busy,
he didn't like the food and that it was far too
expensive for two poor students. Her counter
argument was that it would only take one hour, he
had never been to the place before and that she
was paying. She promised that there would only be
two of them and that persuaded him.
"I'll meet you there. Twelve-thirty. Don't be late."
He was never late. Once he had agreed to meet
someone he always arrived early. It was a habit he
had inherited from his mother. It was an impressive
restaurant in a nineteenth century library hall, filled
with statues and bookshelves, with leather bound
books. The ceiling was high and vaulted and some of
the windows were stained glass. There were leather
sofas to sit in and large oil paintings on the wall. It
looked expensive and he was impressed that
Rebecca had offered to pay. He was greeted by a
beautiful young waitress who seemed inordinately
delighted to see him. It was clearly synthetic but he
enjoyed it all the same. "Rebecca hasn't arrived yet
sir," she said. "would you like to wait at the bar or
should I show you to your table?" He chose the
table and he followed her through the building to a
secluded corner at the far end of the hall. She asked
him if he would like to see the menu and if he would

like a drink. He would normally have said no but she was so pretty and so charming and so pleased to see him that he ordered a sparkling water and agreed to look at the menu. The beautiful waitress wasn't his waitress at all and it was someone with pink hair that came back and served him with his bottled water. He tried not to look too disappointed. The place was filling up while he sipped his drink and waited for Rebecca. He got a text from her to say she was running late and to ask him where he was. He sent one back to say that he was already in the restaurant. No reply came back from her which was unusual. He was sending her another message when the pink-haired waitress walked towards him. He hadn't noticed who was walking behind her. He looked up from his phone and expected to see Rebecca but it was Jenny. He stood up quickly and sent his chair flying to the wooden floor. The sound echoed around the high walls and the ceiling and his table was suddenly the centre of attention.

"Jenny," he said. It wasn't the most imaginative greeting. She said nothing at all but smiled, rather nervously, and sat down facing him across the small table. The waitress had righted his fallen chair, which was just as well because he sat down immediately and narrowly avoided joining the chair on the floor. Jenny laughed. "You haven't changed David." She looked radiant in a green dress, his favourite colour for her. When he thought of Jenny, alone in his room, she was always wearing something green.

"Rebecca arranged all this," she said. "She's been really kind."

"Well it's great to see you. I thought you were never going to come to see me."

"But you're glad I did?"

"Of course. You know I am. You know what I think about you Jenny. I've told you often enough. That'll never change, whatever happens." The waitress reappeared with another menu and Jenny ordered a drink.

"Your mum sends her love. She says you've been neglecting her recently. Not phoning her as often as you used to. She misses you."

"I've been busy." She looked doubtful. "No really Jenny. I'm working on a project as well as working through the course. I'm really enjoying it."

"That's good to hear. Rebecca says you're doing really well. She says you're a genius."

"She exaggerates sometimes."

"I was suspicious of her when I first met her. There was something about her that I didn't like, frightened me almost, but I've completely changed my mind now. I think she's a very genuine person."

"She's been a good friend."

"She loves you David."

"That's ridiculous."

"No it's not."

"Did she tell you that?"

"She didn't have to."

The waitress reappeared and they looked at the menu for the first time. The waitress stood waiting but Jenny asked her to give them a few minutes and she went away again.

"What made you change your mind? About Rebecca?"

Jenny leaned down towards her bag and took out a large envelope and handed it across the table.

David took the envelope and looked inside. He pulled out the contents and his eyes widened with delight. "The diaries. Mary Kelly's diaries. And letters. Letters from Henry!"

"David you're shouting."

"Sorry," he said, "where did you find them?"

"Rebecca tracked them down. They were hidden up a chimney in James Street."

"The back bedroom! That's where Alan's mum hid them. Henry's wife. She was jealous of Mary. How did Rebecca know?"

"She said you told her, on the train home, you told her about the conversation you had with Henry's son. You told her the whole story."

"I would have told you and mum but you thought I'd gone mad."

"We did, sort of, but we don't anymore. I showed these to Irene and there's no way anyone could have known about them being there. She said you could always do lots of things that her other children could never do. I know how special you are David but I don't think there's anything wrong with you. Being different isn't a crime."

"I'm so glad Jenny. I don't talk to ghosts anymore you know."

"You're shouting again David."

"I can't stop doing that, when I get excited, enthusiastic even. I don't realise I'm doing it. They've told me about it in the department. Some of them call me Eureka."

"I'm sorry I doubted you David. Irene's sorry too. She told me to tell you."

"I don't blame you, or mum, I was beginning to doubt myself. There's no need for you to feel sorry about anything you said. I know you were trying to help. I shouldn't have been such a sulk over the past few weeks. My mum deserves better after all she's done for me."

"I hope this makes things better between us David. I've missed you."

"I've missed you too."

The waitress came back for a third time and they ordered some food. David looked at the letters and read some extracts from the Diaries. They soon fell back into easy conversation that they had always enjoyed. Jenny told him about her tedious job in the office and David feigned interest. David told her about his project and Jenny pretended to understand. They chatted and laughed constantly through the lunch but avoided the one subject that weighed heavily on their minds. David eventually asked if she might stay over but Jenny said she had a ticket for the evening train. Jenny asked if he had any plans to meet up with Rebecca that afternoon and he said he hadn't.

After lunch they walked into town and David took her to the Science Museum. It was one of his favourite haunts and she enjoyed listening to him describing his favourite exhibits. As they left the Science Museum David took her hand and she didn't resist. Jenny persuaded him to go back to Deansgate where she dragged him into a boutique where she bought him a shirt. He thanked her and kissed her and took her hand again. It was time to walk to the station so they headed down the long shopping street towards Victoria. It was Jenny who eventually broached the subject that they had, so far, avoided. "David, do you want us to be together again, like we used to be?"

"Yes Jenny, I thought I'd told you that's what I wanted"

"So, I could maybe find a job in Manchester? What do you think?"

"Well there is a problem with that."

Jenny was suddenly downcast. "Is the problem Rebecca?"

"Not Rebecca. America. It's America that's the problem. I won't be in Manchester much longer. This project I'm working on, the department want me to go to M.I.T., in Boston."

"For how long?" Jenny was delighted for him and worried at the same time.

"Well, I'm not sure. It hasn't been finalised yet but at least a year."

"A year?"

"I should find out for definite this week. I'm definitely going but I'm just waiting to hear about the funding."

"I always knew you were clever David but to send you to America, in your first year?"

"I won't be going alone. There'll be a group of us."

"Probably some of them will be gorgeous female PHD's?"

"They're all gorgeous female PHD's"

"Well, that's settled then." Jenny let go of his hand and fussed in her bag for her ticket. They were close to the station now.

"What time's your train?"

"I've half an hour yet."

They walked into the station and both of them smiled as they saw the Costa Café on the concourse. They headed towards it without a word.

"I'm buying," David said. "Your usual?"

"Please."

Jenny found a seat and David bought the coffees and brought them over to the table.

"Jenny stop stirring your coffee and listen." She looked up from her cappuccino. "You could come with me, to America."

"That's nice of you to say David but I don't think it's really possible is it? The University wouldn't want me there."

"Well there are a few problems to overcome but there is an obvious solution."

"There's my mum to think about," Jenny said, "then there's the small problem of money. But it's a lovely thought."

"The visa is the real problem," David said, "but there is a way round that."

"I hadn't even thought about visas."

"You could get a visitor's visa but I think that only lasts for three months. I've got a visa because I'll be employed by M.I.T. but if we got married you would get a visa for the whole year."

Jenny stared at him in disbelief.

"I've asked you often enough Jenny. You must know by now that I'll never stop loving you. I know my mum said we're too young but she got married young and that worked out, well until dad died but you know what I mean. We've known each other long enough. You know I'm a bit odd but at least now you know I'm not crazy."

Jenny still gave no answer.

"You said you wanted to see if I could manage to live on my own and I can. I'm not going to ask again. It's humiliating, me keep asking and getting turned down."

"Will you come and see me next weekend?" she asked. She looked tearful and David feared that she would reject him again.

"Don't turn me down again Jenny. Look at M.I.T. on the internet. Cambridge Massachusetts, you'll love it there. You could do some courses. Boston's lovely too. It's probably the most European city in the whole of the US. Much nicer than Padiham."

She was laughing now but she was getting ready to leave for the train. "Will you come next weekend?" she asked again.

"Of course, I will. I'll get the train on Friday. I'll call mum and tell her."

"Are you bringing Rebecca this time?"

"No. I'll be all alone."

"Poor you."

They walked out of the café towards the platform. The train was already in and it was time to say goodbye. He hugged her and kissed her on the cheek. She responded with a more passionate embrace and kissed him on the mouth. She started to cry and pulled away from him and boarded the train. He wasn't sure what that meant.

Chapter 18.

*It was Wednesday afternoon when David went in
search of Rebecca's boyfriend Mitch. He wandered
into the Philosophy Department and asked the
Professor's secretary where he might find him. She
was suspicious of his interest at first but when he
mentioned that he was a friend of Rebecca's her
suspicion melted away. "You must be the
mathematician? Rebecca's told me all about you.
She said you have an interest in Philosophy?"
"Pure Maths and Philosophy sort of merge into one
another, don't they?"
"I'm just the secretary."
"Most important person in the whole department."
"That's true. It's a pity more people around here
don't realise it. Now, Brian Mitchell, where should
he be right now?" She tapped at her keyboard and
stared into the computer screen. If you sit in the
lobby on the corridor upstairs, he should be coming
out of room L4 in a few minutes. He's with his tutor
but he shouldn't be too long."
David thanked her and made his way up to L4.
There was an alcove and David sat and waited.
When Mitch appeared from his tutorial, he caught
David's eye and didn't seem pleased. He turned as
if to walk away from him but David called after
him and walked beside him down the corridor.*

*"What do you want?" Mitch said in an angry
whisper.*

"I just want two minutes."

"I've nothing to say to you."

"Well just listen then. It's about Rebecca."

"I know you've been seein'her."

*"We've been friends, nothing more." Mitch
shrugged his disbelief. "I'm not here to argue with
you. If you don't believe me there's nothing I can
do about that but I'll say what I've come to say and
then it's up to you what you do about it."*

*Mitch shrugged again and as they came to the end
of the corridor, they descended the staircase and
David waited until they reached the next corridor
where he had met the secretary. "Rebecca's baby is
due in August. She hasn't told her mother about
the pregnancy yet and I've tried to persuade her to
visit her and tell her but she won't go. She asked
me to go to the hospital with her when the baby's
born and I agreed to do it but as it turns out I'll be
out of the country in August. I haven't told her I
was going to speak to you about it but I wanted
you to know that despite her sham bravado I think
she's terrified of giving birth to the child all alone. I
just wanted you to know that."*

*"So what do you want me to do about it?" Mitch
was less aggressive now but he still seemed angry
about David's involvement.*

*"Listen, I like Rebecca. I promised to go with her
when the baby is born. I shouldn't have done that*

308

but when I promised I didn't know I'd be away in August. I don't know what I want you to do. It's really none of my business. If you can persuade her to visit her mother, that would be something. If her mother knows about the baby, she might agree to go to the hospital with her. You don't have to go if you don't want to but I can't do much to help her now. It's entirely up to you Mitch."
Mitch pulled a face and grunted. David walked away. He'd had enough of Mitch.

David was thoughtful as he sat on the train on his way home. He had phoned his mother as soon as Jenny's train had left the week before. She was delighted about his visit and seemed pleased about his secondment to M.I.T. He had spoken to Jenny several times during the week and he was invited to her house for dinner. Sandra was cooking a special dinner to celebrate his success at the University. Everyone seemed very excited about him leaving for the States. He knew he would be homesick in Boston because he had missed his home in his first year in Manchester. He had spent the week reading Henry's letters to Mary. They were so unlike the Henry he had known. Full of passionate promises and naïve plans about their future together. He wondered if he ought to write a love letter to Jenny. Perhaps he had been too matter-of-fact, his proposals were perhaps too unemotional. The latest proposal, trotted out on the station platform, sounded more like a visa scam than a proposal of marriage. Perhaps he should have got down on one knee with a rose in his teeth. The train rattled on and he tried to read but he couldn't concentrate.

When he got home his mother made a fuss of him. She offered him cakes and tea and biscuits and said over and over again how glad she was to see him. He enjoyed being home. His University accommodation was just that, accommodation, but this tiny terraced house was home.

"I'll miss you David but you've done really well at that University. Everybody says so. Lionel couldn't believe it. He said they must have a very high opinion of you. You looked so ill at Christmas, I was worried."

"You don't need to worry about me, I'm fine."

"I'll always worry about you. That's what mothers do."

David went to his room to unpack his bag and when he came back down, he showed Irene the letters and the diary.

"Jenny told me what Rebecca did. I'm sorry I didn't believe you David."

"There's no need. It's all good now."

"How is Rebecca? Is she keeping well?"

"Yes, she texted me on the train. Her boyfriend's been in touch. I think they might get back together. He's persuaded her to visit her mother in Witherhouse."

"That is good news. I couldn't believe it when she

said she hadn't told her mum. She'll be delighted
when she finds out about the baby."
"I hope so."
"Anyway, we'll have to get ready soon to go to
Sandra's. Did Jenny tell you that their house has
been sold? Sandra will be able to buy a place of her
own when the money comes through. She says she
wants to move to Clowton. It's nice there. She's
looking forward to making a fresh start when the
divorce is settled."

It was a more relaxed atmosphere in Sandra
and Jenny's house than the previous dinner party
when Stephen had been his host. The rental was
smaller than their executive mansion on Woodlands
but Sandra and Jenny had made it cosy and
welcoming. They had clearly spent a lot of time on
the dinner table which was resplendent with white
table cloth and white candles and the best china
and crystal glasses. Lionel was there but seemed to
want to blend into the background. Sandra and
Jenny were very welcoming although Jenny seemed
slightly on edge for some reason. Sandra was a good
cook and the dinner was magnificent. A different
wine with each course, although David didn't take
any. Three courses, all delicious and beautifully
presented. They talked about old times, swerving
the more stressful times, they laughed and told all
the stories they had heard so many times before
and would never tire of hearing again. Even Lionel
relaxed eventually and Irene seemed to have cured

him of his 'I mean to say' disability. He did say 'well as I don't have to drive' every time he was offered a top up but everyone knew Irene would manage to fix that in time. David avoided any mention of Henry's letters and Mary's diary. He also tried to steer the conversation away from his forthcoming trip to M.I.T. Everyone but David talked louder and louder the more wine they drank. David got louder, without alcohol, because the longer the dinner went on the happier and more enthusiastic, he became. When the dinner was over Sandra and Irene cleared the dishes and insisted that Lionel join them in the kitchen to help. He seemed surprised because he had never been press-ganged into the washing up before. David was delighted to have Jenny to himself but his delight was short lived because she too left for the kitchen. All parties end up in the kitchen and he would have joined them but Jenny had told him to stay where he was. He was very obedient when women told him what to do, a side effect of his upbringing with a very strong-willed single mother. He wasn't abandoned for too long and Jenny reappeared with two glasses of Champagne. "I know you don't drink David but a small sip of Champagne won't kill you. I want to propose a toast. To you, and to wish you a safe trip and every success in America."
"She handed him a glass and they stood and toasted 'success in America'. They both sipped their wine and Jenny stood waiting, expectant.

"Tastes rather nice," he said. "Is it really Champagne?"

"Yes it really is. Drink some more David."

"Well it's very nice Jenny but I'm not sure I want to go back to drinking. You remember what I was like at Christmas? Once I start on something I can't stop. I think I might have a slightly obsessive personality and alcohol is notoriously addictive. It's mainly ethanol you know."

"Just have another sip, it won't do you any harm."

They toasted again. "To you Jenny," he said.

"To both of us."

They drank again. She stared at him again. He looked bemused.

"What?" he asked.

She nodded towards his glass. He looked down and saw what looked like a ring in his champagne glass.

"That looks like your engagement ring Jenny."

"It is my engagement ring David."

"Well how did it end up in there?"

"A ghost?" she asked.

"How am I supposed to get it out?" he said with a pathetic look on his face.

"Idiot." She took the glass from him and drank the wine and tipped the ring into his outstretched hand. He looked at the ring. "You found it? In the woods?"

"Yes, me and mum crawled around for hours but we found it."

"I said I wouldn't ask again but this is definitely the last time." He got down on one knee. "Jenny. I've

loved you all my life and I will always love you. Will you marry me and come to Boston with me and spend the rest of your life with me? Please say yes."
She only hesitated for a second and then smiled. "Yes David. I'll marry you. I love you too and I always have." He stood up and kissed her and she responded with all the passion that had built up inside her over the weeks of separation. As they kissed and embraced each other they began to sense that they were being watched from the kitchen doorway.
"Well?"
"He asked me and I said yes!"
There was a loud cheer from the kitchen and the door opened wide and Irene and Sandra, followed by Lionel clutching the bottle of Champagne, poured into the room.

There were two more parties before David and Jenny flew to Boston. The wedding party was not the fairy tale that Sandra had always dreamed of. They were married in the registry office in Burnley which was decorated like most government buildings with merry grey walls and curtains. Both mothers cried and Jenny's father refused to attend. He did attend the party at the hotel, after the wedding, but he didn't look happy. He left early. Everyone else had a wonderful time, all Irene's children were delighted with their baby brother's wife, a very pregnant Rebecca was accompanied by her very attentive boyfriend Mitch.

At the farewell party, for Jenny and David, in September, Rebecca brought her new baby son Ludwig and asked Irene to be his godmother. Lionel proposed marriage to Irene but had the sense to do it in private and was turned down. On the 1st of October Jenny and David boarded the flight at Manchester and flew direct to Boston.

The End.

Printed in Great Britain
by Amazon